ARCADES, HEARTS, AND OTHER THINGS THAT BREAK

NAT CUDDINGTON

This is a work of fiction. Names, characters, places, and incidents are either products of the author's imagination or used fictitiously.

You can visit Nat's website at **natcuddington.ca**

Find Laura Kulson, the cover artist at
etsy.com/shop/SirenBayStudio

Fonts used as templates and inspiration for the title fonts:

DK Hobgoblin by Hanoded Fonts
Comedy Channel by Woodcutter Manero
Crunchy Time by Daniel Hochard

Other Books By Nat Cuddington

Neighbourly
Turning Thirty
Between Two Worlds

If you would like to be aware of certain story aspects that may be upsetting to some people before reading, please keep the following trigger warnings in mind. If you don't feel the need for warnings, then please skip this page.

This mostly light-hearted story deals with the breakup of a long-term relationship between parental figures, conversations surrounding missing parents who have passed away (which happens before the story takes place), an on-page car accident, and alcoholism.

ARCADES, HEARTS, AND OTHER THINGS THAT BREAK

For anyone who feels like they don't belong.
Even if it doesn't feel like it, you belong somewhere.
I promise.

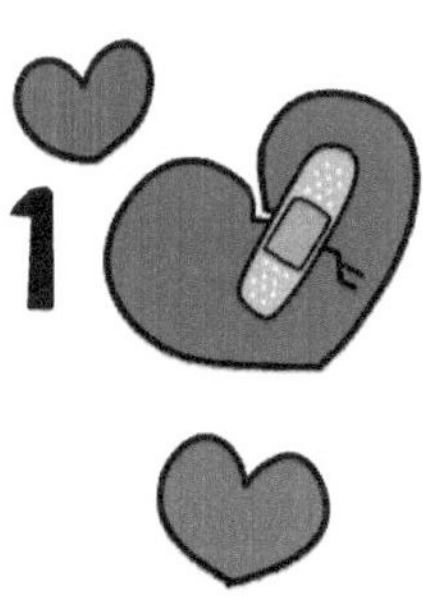

"You can turn right on a red light."

My heart drops into my stomach and I tighten my grip on the steering wheel. I can see out of the corner of my eye that the driving instructor who will decide if I pass this test and get my licence or not, definitely doesn't look impressed. I curse under my breath and double check to make sure the coast is clear. Why do I always have to make a fool of myself when I'm nervous? Why can't I just coast through things that I know I shouldn't worry about? You know, without worrying about them? How long have I even been sitting here? How long has there been no traffic in the direction I'm supposed to go? I have no idea; I've just been watching the light, waiting for it to turn green like a noob.

"Ugh, I'm sorry, I swear I know that." My voice squeaks, making me wince. I even sound nervous, don't I? "I'm just really nervous," I add, not sure if it's a good idea or not. Too late. I already said it.

"It's fine," the instructor says.

I make my turn and hope he can't see my fingers shaking as I drive.

♥ ♥ ♥ ♡ ♡

"Why aren't you smiling?" My Uncle Adam asks as I follow the instructor back inside the Drive Test building.

Normally it would be hard to trick him and keep a straight face, but I still feel like barfing all over the place. Even though I passed, I can still feel my stomach twisting into knots, as if I'm still in the car. I shake my head at him and his shoulders slump, looking so disappointed for me.

"That's okay, sweetie," he says, putting an arm around me. "Most people fail their first time."

"Sadie Zwicker?" the lady behind the counter calls.

I shrug out of Adam's embrace and make my way back to the counter.

"Congratulations," she says with a warm smile.

"Thank you," I reply. At least my voice sounds like it's back to normal. And is that a smile creeping up on my face?

"I just need to get a bit more information from you, dear."

I follow her instructions and before I know it, she's handing me my temporary G2 licence and telling me to expect the official one in the mail. I turn around and am a little shocked to see a line up behind me, and the seats along the wall filled with people. When did it get so busy in here? Where's Uncle Adam? I walk towards the door in a bit of a haze, the rush of everything happening now making me feel overwhelmed. Why do I suddenly feel like I'm going to cry? What's wrong with me? I see Adam just outside the doors, leaning against the brick with his arms crossed over his chest.

"Hey," I say, holding the green slip of paper up.

"You alright?" But then he sees my temporary licence in my hand and grabs it from me, screaming like a teenager. "I can't believe you tricked me!" He wraps his arms around me and spins me around right there on the sidewalk, in everyone's way. Someone clears their throat and he immediately lets me go, pulling me away from the door. "Sorry," he says.

The man who was trying to go in just nods at us and enters. Adam's smile is so big and seeing him this happy for me is already calming me down. I know I was worrying over nothing; even when

I was worrying, I knew that it was nothing to be worried about, but I couldn't help it. I never can.

"You sneak," he says with a smile, shoving me playfully.

"I'm sorry, but I had to."

"Come on. Let's go celebrate."

I follow Uncle Adam to the car and beeline it to the passenger side before he can even assume that I'm driving.

"Really?" he asks with a head tilt.

"Yes, really. You're not supposed to drive after passing a driving test anyway," I say, pushing my glasses up higher on my nose.

He only responds by raising his eyebrows.

"It's true," I say.

"Oh yeah? And why's that?" He unlocks the grey Sportage and opens the driver side door.

I open mine and wait until we're both in the car before I continue. "Something about being excited and overconfident. You don't pay attention properly because your emotions are all over the place. Emma used her driver's ed instructor's car, and he drove her home after."

"Probably because she technically wasn't a student anymore."

"No, he said it was because of the emotions thing."

"Okay." He doesn't think it makes any sense, but the tone of voice he's using tells me he wants me to think he does.

"It's true."

"Okay," he says again.

"So should I go back to school then?" I ask. "I can still make last period."

"No way! You just got your G2 Licence! This is a big deal! You can drive by yourself now! No more needing an experienced driver with you! No more exclusive hours that you have to drive within! No more taking the long way to places because you're not allowed on major highways! Your G2! This is exciting! Don't you remember me saying we were going to celebrate?"

"Well I don't know if I really deserve it, I mean I could have gotten it when I turned seventeen in November."

"So? No one wants to take a driving test in the winter."

"It hardly snowed in November this year."

"It doesn't matter if you took your test late. Who cares? And really, there is no late. Just because you *can* get your G2 when you turn seventeen doesn't mean you have to. Plus you can only get your G2 when you turn seventeen if you've had your G1 for a year already, which doesn't even apply to everyone. I didn't get my licence when I turned sixteen."

"You didn't?"

He shakes his head, and then looks at me as we creep up to a red light. "I was afraid to drive. Your dad used to give me such a hard time about it. Anyway, I didn't write my test until I graduated from high school."

"Really?" Somehow this makes me feel a bit better.

He smiles and nods, scratches his neatly trimmed beard. "You're allowed to be nervous about things, Sadie. And you're allowed to take your driving test later than your friends. If you never wanted to take it, I would be okay with that. You would have to move somewhere that has a better transit system though. I wouldn't keep driving you places after you moved out." He smirks and I stick my tongue out at him.

Adam pulls into a parking spot downtown and already I know that we're going to Carter's, our favourite pizza place. Except that it isn't just our favourite pizza place, it's Mat's and our favourite pizza place. It feels wrong coming here without him. We all discovered it together and hardly ever went without each other. Going just us two feels like we're cheating on him. Even though I know that's ridiculous. But thinking about the fact that it makes me sad that we're here without Mat makes me feel like I'm betraying Adam. I try to shake it off and smile as we cross the street.

The smell of the wood burning stove fills the restaurant and I'm warmed immediately, not that I needed it. There's still snow lining the curbs, but the March air has been nice the last week, something I am actually thankful for when it came to my driving test. As much as I didn't want to admit it while I was booking it, I was afraid we were going to get one of those surprise March snowstorms the day of.

"Hey guys," Isla greets us when we step in. She works almost as often as the owner, but right now it looks like she's the only server in. "Just the two of you today?" I'm not sure if she knows that Mat and Adam broke up, and to me it seems like this is her way of asking if Mat is coming, without asking if Mat is coming.

"Yeah, just us two," Adam says.

"Sit wherever you like."

I look around the empty restaurant and pick a round table in the corner. It's not often that we get to come here at an off-time and have the place to ourselves. The black table has been wiped clean recently and isn't completely dry yet. I wipe the sleeve of my sweater over part of it when I sit down and then smile at Adam.

"What are you getting?" he asks.

"Same thing as always." I smile and tuck my short hair behind my ears.

"Boring." He fakes a yawn, and I gently slap at his shoulder from across the table.

Isla takes our drink and pizza orders and we sit quietly for a few minutes, looking around at the décor in the restaurant. The specials board written in fun, colourful chalk. The black and white photos of our town from the early 1900s with colour 3D buildings from today overlayed. I always liked the atmosphere in this restaurant; the casual and trendy feel has always been something that sort of made me feel at home here. I'm sure the fact that I have always come here with my two uncles who raised me played a big part in that too, so I guess the combination of it all calms me when I'm here.

"I'm really proud of you, you know that?" Adam finally says.

"What? Why?" I pull my gaze from the specials board and look at him to see his brown eyes staring at me. They've got this calm intensity to them, like he's trying not to cry.

"Because you conquered something today. You were afraid to get in a car with a stranger and let him judge you while you drove, and you did it. And now you can drive all on your own! And you can go on the highway!"

"Oh, I don't know about that," I say, waving him off.

"You don't know about what?"

"Driving on the highway. That seems pretty scary." The fact that he mentioned it twice within fifteen minutes makes me feel uneasy again.

"Okay, so after pizza we'll go on the highway."

"Excuse me, no thanks."

"Fine, how about I drive on the highway and I explain what I'm doing?"

"I know what you're doing, I'm just afraid to do it myself," I say.

"You know you have to go on the highway to pass your last driving test, right?"

Isla brings us our pop along with a glass of water each and Adam thanks her.

"I never said I was never going to do it," I say quietly. "Just not… now. Or anytime soon."

Adam laughs and leans back into his chair, the light above us shining over his light brown hair and creamy complexion.

"Whenever you're ready," he says. "Whenever you're ready I can help you."

"I know," I reply. "Thanks."

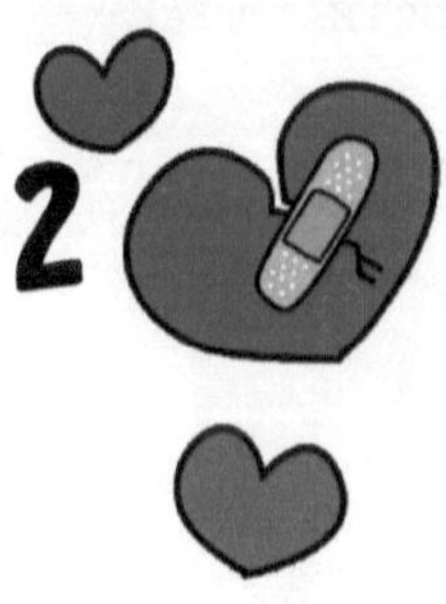

"Are you sure?" Adam asks. "It's so nice out; I don't mind walking to work."

"Yes, I'm sure," I say. "I also don't mind taking the bus."

"Alright, but whenever you want to drive yourself to school just let me know."

"I will."

"Cool. Have a good day." He kisses the top of my head and makes his way to the front door.

I sigh and zip up my backpack, wondering if I'm stupid for wanting to take the bus to school instead of drive myself. But anyway, I can't drive myself to school for the first time without picking up Emma, and there's no time to let her know; she'll already be on the bus at this point. I throw my bag over my shoulder and step out of the apartment, locking the door behind me.

❤❤❤♡♡

Emma waves to me as soon as I get on the bus and I make my way down the cramped aisle to her and sit down next to her on the grey vinyl seat.

"When can we drive your uncle's car to school?" she says to me as she flips her long black hair over her shoulder.

"Oh, it's so nice to see you too, Emma."

"Come on, I know he's dying to let you drive it on your own, I need to live vicariously through you since my parents are evil."

"Shut up, your parents aren't evil," I say.

"Not ever letting me drive their car except to take my little brother to hockey practice is definitely evil."

I shrug and give her a weak smile. She responds by hitting me in the shoulder.

"Hey!" I shout playfully.

"When are you going to drive us to schoooooool?" she whines.

"I dunno. Monday, I guess."

"Really!?" She squees and shoves me, almost making me fall back into the aisle. "We're finally going to be like real teenagers in those teen movies!"

"So, fake teenagers, then," I correct her with a laugh.

"Whatever. You're going to drive us to school!"

We walk the crowded halls together and Emma yells at all the grade nine kids to get out of our way.

"Move!" she yells. "Walk faster! This is a hallway, not a living room! Why aren't you walking!?"

I shake my head at her and shove my way through the throng of teenagers. I make it out the other side without Emma, so I wait for her and laugh when I catch her stumbling out of her left shoe.

"Who stepped on my shoe!?" she calls as she spins around. She slips her foot back in and half hops, half runs towards me.

"You're ridiculous," I say, holding a hand out to her.

She waves me off and rolls her eyes. "I can't believe they still don't know how to walk. It's almost April! They're going to be in grade ten next year and they still just make big piles of stinky children in the middle of the hall."

"No one in this school knows how to walk, Emma. It's not limited to the grade nines."

We make it to our lockers and get out the books we need for our first two classes.

"See you in music," she says, shutting her locker.

"Yeah," I reply, making my way to my first period class.

♥♥♥♡♡

I don't really have any friends in first period, but the girl I sit next to, Summer, is pretty nice. We've worked together on a few projects, and I wouldn't mind working with her on our final one, which I know we're getting assigned today. It's the big one, the big make-a-difference project we were all excited about when we signed up for this class.

Summer smiles at me when I sit down next to her, but the teacher starts talking before I have a chance to even say hi.

"Are you guys excited about your big Challenge and Change project?" Mrs. Henderson asks. No one really says anything, but she doesn't seem to care. "We're going to be doing it in pairs, and I'm going to call out who's going to be working together."

Summer shrugs at me as if to say 'I guess we might not be together', and I shrug back.

I wait patiently as she calls the names, but my heart jumps a little when she says my name right after Teague's. I scan the room to see if he's looking at me, and my stomach tightens when our eyes meet. He nods at me and smirks, and all I can do is nod back. How am I going to save the world if I'm partnered with someone who doesn't even talk to me? He probably thinks that I'm just going to do the project all by myself and slap his name on it.

I realize I've been distracting myself with my thoughts when Teague shoves my desk a little. It startles me and I jump just a little, and then straighten up in my seat.

"Sorry," I say.

He just shrugs and sits down in his chair that he's pulled over, so that we're sitting across from each other.

"So…" he starts, twirling his pen around in his fingers. "What do you want to do?"

"I don't know, I guess we need to brainstorm."

He smirks. "Yeah, that's kind of what I was trying to do. So… what do you wanna do, Zed?"

It catches me off guard when he uses his nickname for me from when we were kids. I didn't think he remembered that.

"I don't know, maybe something to do with kids?" I ask.

He smirks again, this time with only half his mouth. "Okay, good start."

The class around us is getting loud and I feel like I need to lean in closer to really hear him. He's so calm that his voice is almost too quiet. Not in a nervous or shy way, just like, he doesn't care or something.

"So you want to do something to help kids too?" I ask, forcing myself to lean over the desk a little, hoping it doesn't seem obvious or weird. All that's obvious to me is that my face is too close to his, and his glasses look exactly like mine.

"Yeah, sure, sounds great. Do you want to help kids in our town? Like kids who don't have enough money to sign up for soccer, or…?" He trails off like he wants me to finish the thought.

"I don't know, that seems too easy. I mean the class is called Challenge and Change, I feel like it should be…"

"A challenge?" he says for me.

I want to smile, but something about it seems forced. I'm not sure why; it's just weird talking to him when we haven't been friends since we were twelve. He's being nice enough, but I can just imagine him laughing about me to his *cool* friends once class is over. The friends he basically left me for once we were old enough to play on separate boy/girl soccer teams.

"Yeah," I finally say.

"Okay, so how do you want to help kids, then? Maybe you can make a free day camp at your uncle's laser tag place."

"Well we already have day camps bring their kids to us."

"Yeah, but you could make it free," he says.

"I think we need to make a word cloud or something."

Teague smirks at me as I open my notebook, but he helps me brainstorm as I write words down on the paper. I don't feel like we get very far, but at least we're both trying. The bell cuts us off before we come to any kind of conclusion or solid idea, and everyone in class immediately starts packing up their stuff and heading for the door.

"I guess we can continue this on Monday, Zed."

"You don't want to work on it over the weekend?" I force myself to ask.

"I'm working all weekend, sorry." He shrugs and takes his chair back to his desk before grabbing his bag and slinging it over his shoulder. I sigh and force myself not to reply. I want to tell him he can't possibly be working so much that he doesn't have any time to work on a school project that's important to me, and should also be important to him. I want to tell him that I know he works at the post office and I know they close at four on Saturdays and aren't even open on Sundays so he can't possibly be working "all weekend". But instead I just sigh and make my way to music class.

"Ugh, Teague Tremblay?" Emma asks.

I nod, but opt out of answering her with words to suck on my reed.

"Was he horrible?"

I shrug and screw my new reed to my mouthpiece. "Not really. I mean, he totally lied to me when I asked him if we could work on it this weekend. But I guess he wasn't… *horrible.*"

"When's it due?"

"Not til the end of May, but still. It's a big project."

"Of course it is."

"Emma, to your seat please," Mr. Calvin says.

Emma frowns and makes her way over to sit with the rest of the flutes. She puts her instrument together and then looks back at me, giving me a reassuring smile. I smile back and open my music book.

I drop my bag off at home after school and get myself a snack before walking over to Laser Tag. I used to make fun of my uncle for opening a laser tag place and not naming it anything creative. He would always defend himself by saying that he tried to come up with a name, but everything he thought of was cheesy. And the part that I've come to agree with, is that he always said that no one would call it by its name anyway. Even if he thought of a non-cheesy name, everyone would just call it Laser Tag. And with how easily the name always comes off my tongue, I know that he's right.

I try to brainstorm more for the Challenge and Change project throughout my fifteen-minute walk, but come up with nothing. I'm like Adam and his search for a good business name, only worse because if I can't think of anything, I can't do what he did. I have no idea how to help kids in our town in a way that's worth-while for our project. It has to really make a difference.

I make it to work without coming up with anything, so I try to push it to the back of my mind for the weekend. After all, Teague probably already has. There are two birthday parties this evening, one eating and opening presents before laser tag, and the second one afterwards, so they can share the arena and have enough kids to play on teams. Teams are always a lot more fun. I do a double take though, when I see Teague with the first birthday party. His short hair is sticking up at all angles and he's trying to wrangle all the twelve-year-olds and get them to sit at their table so we can bring out the pizza. I put my bag behind the counter and go over to help him.

"Hey," he says, seeming a little unsure of himself.

"Hey," I reply.

We look at each other for about three seconds, and I have no idea what to say to him. He clears his throat and turns away, but then runs his fingers through his thick hair and somehow makes it look neater than it did before. He looks back at me but I don't really know what else to say. Well this is awkward.

"Who's ready for pizza?" I ask, clapping my hands together once.

"Me!" all the kids scream.

"Great. Then you'll all have to pick a seat!"

They stop what they're doing and sit down around the table.

"How did you do that?" Teague asks.

I shrug. "I think it's just because I work here. It's different."

He lets out a deep breath, nods to me, and then takes a seat next to his sister. I wonder where his parents are.

Uncle Adam calls my name and I walk over to the front counter to help him plate the pizza that must have been delivered while I was over with Teague and his sister's party.

"Will you fill the drinks for me?" Adam asks.

"Yeah, sure." I make way into the fridge as Adam reads me what everyone wants, and I pull out the cans, cartons, and bottles, and start pouring them into cups.

"How was your day?" Uncle Adam asks.

"It was fine. Are you leaving soon?"

"Yeah, I'll head home after we get these kids their food. I can walk home and leave you the car if you want."

"No it's fine," I reply. I put lids on all the cups and grab a handful of straws. "I can walk."

Adam shakes his head. "No, I don't want you walking home alone in the dark; I'll come get you if you don't want to drive."

I hold my breath for a few seconds while I put all the straws in the drink cups. I don't know why I'm so afraid to drive alone. It's the same as doing it with Adam in the car, except that he won't be in the car. But I know I can drive. I'm a safe driver, and I think I'm a pretty good driver. But it still scares me for some reason.

"Okay, leave me the car," I finally say.

"Are you sure? I really don't mind coming back to get you."

"It's fine, I'll drive. What's the point in me getting my licence if I'm not going to use it, right?"

"Right." He smiles and starts taking the plates of pizza over to the party table.

Teague doesn't say anything else to me during their party time, except for thank you and stuff like that, but I hang back and stay out of their way anyway. A few people come in to use the arcade, but they have no trouble getting coins from the machine so I just sit behind the counter and wait for the second party to show up.

"Do you have any candles?"

I'm slightly startled and look up from my homework to see Teague standing on the other side of the counter. His dark brown hair is all over the place again, but it actually looks good, like he had done it on purpose. Even though I'm pretty sure he didn't.

"I'm sorry?" I ask.

"I forgot birthday candles. I can run to the store and get some but I thought I'd ask if you had any first. Like an emergency stash, or even packs that you sell."

"Let me check." I put my notebook under the counter and hop off the stool to search through the drawers first. I only find elastics, pens, notepads, and paperclips, so I make my way to the back room where we keep the extra cups and snacks and stuff. I rummage through the drawers in there and find a bunch of loose, half-used birthday candles behind stuff for the popcorn machine.

"Will these do?" I ask, holding them up as I make my way back to the front.

"That's perfect, how many are there? No, you know what? It doesn't even matter. I don't think she's going to count them."

"Okay." I hand him the candles and watch him make his way back to the party table where he bends down to pull the cake out from under his chair. I watch him put the candles on the cake and carefully light them while all the kids laugh and scream over his sister opening her presents. He looks up at them every few seconds, and then goes back to making sure the cake looks good. He starts singing Happy Birthday first and then all the other kids join in. The second birthday party shows up before they're done singing, so I get them to fill out their team names and lead them all into the arena.

♥♥♥♡♡

"Okay," I say once everyone is sitting on the platforms and listening. "We're playing in teams today, one birthday party against the other. The point of the game is to get the most shots on your opponent's base. So red team, you'll want to shoot the glowing circle on top of the blue team's base. And blue team, shoot the circle on top of the red team's base. You can strategize however you like; you can play every person for themselves, or you can set up offence and defence. Each player can only be shot five times before they have to go find a checkpoint and regenerate. There are three of them throughout the arena but it's your job to find them. If you need to regenerate, your gun won't work until you pass a checkpoint. No one's gun works for the first 60 seconds of play, to give everyone time to get away from the door and each other. When there are ten seconds left of the grace period, everyone's vests will make this low chiming sound as a sort of countdown. After the hour is up, the team with the most shots on the other team's base wins. Does anyone have any questions?"

Teague raises his hand and I raise my eyebrows at him.

"Are you playing?" he asks.

"No, I have to work."

"Are they real guns?" a boy from Teague's sister's party asks.

"No," I answer. "They're toys, and they shoot harmless lasers. They only work with the vests that you'll be wearing. So you can get shot in the back, the chest, and the shoulders, but it doesn't hurt or feel like anything."

An angry woman is standing at the counter when I come out of the arena and she starts yelling before I even have a chance to say anything to her.

"Oh, I'm glad to see that someone works here! My son is almost in tears right now because your stupid air hockey machine ate his coins! I refuse to use more coins when I haven't even gotten any use out of these ones!"

"I'm sorry, about that," I start, "I was just getting a laser tag session started. I'll come over and take a look at the air hockey."

"Well maybe if you had more staff I wouldn't have had to wait so long!"

"I was only gone for ten minutes, and I do have the sign out on the counter explaining where I was. You could have come to the arena to talk to me if it was that big of a deal."

"My point is I shouldn't have to! There should be someone at the front desk at all times!"

"The arcade is usually pretty self sufficient," I say. "We'd be paying someone to sit there and look pretty all night if we had more staff. And like I said, you could have come to talk to me at the arena entrance. You didn't have to stand here and wait for me to come out. But I'll come look at the machine."

"Well clearly the arcade isn't *self sufficient*," she says with a tone, "because this thing isn't working and I was waiting for far too long!"

I sigh and let her keep yelling at me while I walk over to the arcade area. It's not a big arcade, and she and her son are currently the only customers, so her shouts break through the silence around us. I sort of wish there was at least one other person in here right now to witness what was going on, like Alex, one of our part-timers. I like working with her on the weekends. Maybe we *should* have more staff for when stuff like this happens. But it's not busy enough during the week to justify having two people in at a time. Plus it's really easy to handle two birthday parties at once the way we set them up, and the arcade is usually only busy on weekends. And busy isn't even the right word considering we only have eight game machines.

I catch her son looking at me as I bend down to find the plug on the table. He doesn't look like he's on the verge of tears at all; he actually looks bored, leaning against the wall behind him with his arms crossed. I unplug the air hockey table, and the lady keeps yelling at me. She just keeps going on and on about how we don't have enough staff and she can't believe she had to wait. I finally tune her out and plug the machine back in. I stand up and wait for it to come back to life, but then I realize that she asked me a question.

"Well?" Her hands are on her hips and her wiry hair is sticking out of her bun.

"I'm sorry, I was focused on fixing your problem here and didn't quite catch what you said."

"I want to talk to your manager!"

"Great. I'm the manager."

"You can't be a manager! You're just a little girl!"

"Um, I am the manager," I say again, "and it doesn't matter how old you think I am."

"Little girls can't be managers!" She steps closer to me and points a finger at my face, so I take a step back. I'm normally pretty good at keeping my cool with rude customers, but this one is starting to make my fingers shake. I feel like I might throw up all over her if she doesn't stop yelling at me.

"I'm not a little girl," I say, hoping she can't hear in my voice how upset I currently am. "And I *am* the manager. My uncle is the owner and I'm the manager. I'm the only one working right now, and I'm doing the best I can. You, on the other hand, are not. You're being very rude to me so I'm going to have to ask you to leave."

"You wouldn't do that!"

"I wouldn't?"

She makes it obvious that she's looking at my nametag, and then she looks back to my face. "Well, *Sadie,* I'm not happy with my experience here. And I will not be a repeat customer!"

"Mom!" her son whines. I turn to look at him and now it does look like he's going to cry. He's probably only about nine years old. "Why can't we come back!?"

"Because this girl is being very rude to us!" she says to him.

I step away from them and put my code into the coin machine so I can get two replacement coins for him.

"Here," I say, walking over to the boy. "Sorry the machine didn't work." I hand him the coins and then I turn to his mom. "You need to leave." Without another word or glance in her direction, I walk over to Teague's party table and start clearing away the plates and cups.

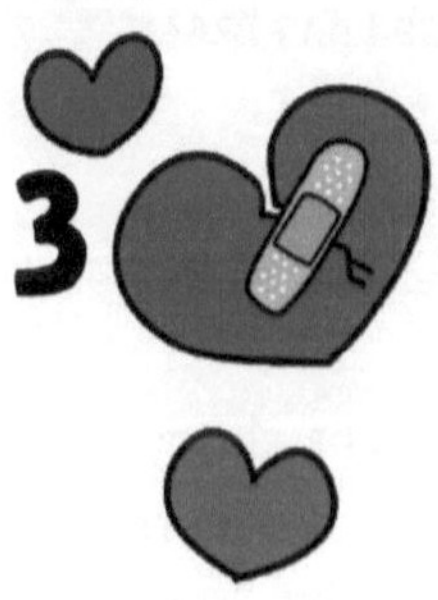

It's ten o'clock at night and I'm standing outside, in front of Laser Tag, staring at my Uncle's Kia Sportage like it's going to shock me if I touch it. I don't know what my problem is. Driving is fine. Driving is easy. Driving in town is easy. I know these roads. I know the car. I've driven it countless times, passed a driving test in it. But I have never driven it alone and that seems to be the problem that keeps coming back to me. If something happens, I'll be alone. But I was alone when that rude customer was all up in my face, and I handled that.

But the rude customer wasn't a car.

I shake my head and my shoulders and unlock the car. Get over yourself, Sadie. I slide into the driver's seat and shut the door behind me. I put the key in the ignition, put it into drive, make sure the headlights are on, and slowly ease on the gas. Okay. I got this. It's a three-minute drive; I can handle it. I've done it countless times with Adam or Mat, or Adam *and* Mat. I've done it with Emma in the back seat, and Adam or Mat in the front, the only difference this time is that I'm all alone. Driving is still the same. It's still the same.

Oh, I'm home.

Okay, so that was easy, then. Maybe I'm worrying for nothing. Oh who am I kidding, I'm always worried for nothing.

I park the car, but I pull into the space instead of backing into it, and make sure it's locked before I head into the apartment building.

"Hey, you did it!" Adam exclaims as soon I step through the door to our apartment.

"Yeah, it was easy," I say.

"Of course it was. You've done it a million times before."

"I know, I don't know what's wrong with me."

"Nothing is wrong with you."

"I know," I say slowly.

He smiles at me. "You don't sound very confident in that answer."

"I kicked a lady out tonight."

"Really?"

I nod at him and take my shoes off before following him into the tiny kitchen.

"Why?" he asks.

"She was all up in my face, calling me a little girl and stuff. Because the air hockey table wasn't working and I was setting up the laser tag."

"Did you have the sign out that said where you were?"

"Of course I did."

"Did you give her new coins?"

"Of course."

"Then you did everything you could. Come on, I made us supper."

He puts on a pair of oven mitts and opens the oven to grab two bowls of French Onion Soup.

"Ooh, yummy," I say as I grab some tea towels for him to set them on top of on the table.

We both sit down at the frosted glass Ikea table, and Adam is the first to take a bite of the soup.

"So I saw Teague there tonight. How's he doing?" he asks.

I shrug and take my own bite of the soup.

"Is he still not talking to you?" he asks.

"It's not that he's not talking to me, we're just not friends."

"Why not?"

"I don't know. We grew apart. We hang out with different people."

Adam nods and takes another spoonful of his soup. "So what kind of people does he hang out with, then?"

"I dunno, the popular people, I guess."

"Wait, you're not popular?"

I tilt my head and narrow my eyes at him. "I basically have one friend."

"So that means you're not popular?"

"Do you even know what popular means?" I laugh.

"I guess not."

"Come on. You went to high school once."

"Yeah. Once."

He smirks at me and we eat in silence for a minute or so.

"So tell me, Sadie," Uncle Adam says, "why do you think you're not popular?"

"I told you, I have one friend. To be popular you need to have many friends."

"I don't think that's right. I think to be popular you need to be liked by the friends you do have."

I smile at him. "Sure. Let's go with that."

♥ ♥ ♥ ♡ ♡

Uncle Adam leaves for work at nine the next morning and I stay in my pyjamas until the last possible minute. He doesn't need my help until the afternoon when it usually gets busy with kids and teenagers, so I veg on the couch until noon. I know I should be doing homework or practicing the saxophone, but I just want to watch TV today. I don't even want to go into work.

I notice when I get outside that he walked to work, probably hoping that I would drive myself. I know I can walk if I want to, but I know he left the car for me on purpose, so I sigh and get my keys out.

Laser Tag is busy, although busy for us is probably nothing compared to arcades in bigger cities. We have two party tables on the left side of the room, but only use them for one party at a time. The cash and snacks counter is along the back wall, with the laser tag behind it, so the building is a lot bigger than it looks until you actually go into the arena and see that there's basically a whole other world inside. The arcade is sort of in front of, sort of to the right of the cash counter, but it only has the air hockey table, *Dance Dance Revolution*, two racing games, a Dinosaur shooting game, a zombie shooting game, Wack-a-Mole, and this weirdly popular, generic clown fish game, that's just called *Clown Fish*. There are kids at every station, a few with friends watching behind them. The noise of the puck on the air hockey table pinging against the sides always seems to be the loudest, and it's the only thing I hear until Uncle Adam waves at me from behind the counter.

"Hey," he says as I walk up to him.

"Hey," I reply.

"Did you take the car?" he asks.

"Yes, I took the car, but I didn't need to. You could have taken it."

"I like walking."

"So do I."

"Excuse me!" a boy about the age of twelve says, walking up to the counter. "The air hockey table stopped working!"

"We might need to get it looked at," I say to Adam as I follow the boy back over to the table. I unplug it and plug it back in, make sure it starts up again, and give him two new coins. "Let me know if it does it again."

♥♥♥♡♡

Adam and I get out of Laser Tag earlier than I did the night before since the two of us are cleaning up together. There were no groups or parties that came in after 4pm either, so it was a quiet night.

Adam starts hooking up his phone to the Bluetooth as soon as we get in the car, but I put my hand over his phone and tsk him.

"No way," I say. "I'm driving so I get to pick the music."

"Come on, it's like a three-minute drive."

"So that means I get to pick one excellent song." I smile at him and pull out my own phone. Once it's connected to the stereo I scroll through my Spotify music until I find my favourite song by my favourite band, *Infinity Pool*. They're loud but not screamy, and I just absolutely melt at the lead singer's voice. Their music is always just so full, if that makes any sense. The music always seems to surround me, and I can feel the emotion in every song, especially the slower ones. The slower ones are always somehow more intense.

"We could have been home by now," Adam says.

"Shush." I hold my hand up and wait for the music to start before I put the car into drive.

Adam throws his head back and does an exaggerated whine. "Always with this song."

"Hey, it's a good song."

"Not when you hear it 90 times a day."

I shake my head at him and manage to hold in a laugh as I turn out of the parking lot and head home.

"So what's your project about?" Adam asks as we get in the elevator.

"Basically making a difference. So far all we got is that we want to help kids."

"And you said that Teague is your partner?"

"Yes," I say.

"Is he coming over this weekend to work on it? I really did like that kid. I'm still sad sometimes that you guys aren't friends anymore."

"No, he lied and said he had to work all weekend."

"How do you know he lied?"

"Because he works at the post office. It's impossible to work all weekend."

"Well don't let him do that too much, alright? It's your project too."

"I know. We just got the assignment yesterday so right now I guess it isn't a big deal."

Uncle Adam unlocks the front door and we both flop down on the couch once we're inside. "What are you up to for the rest of the night?" he asks.

I shrug. "Nothing."

"You want to watch this new show with me? It has magic and stuff in it."

"Yeah, sounds great. Let me get my cozies on first."

And then I proceed to do what I do most Saturday nights. Watch TV in my PJs with my uncle, and eat crunchy peanut butter out of the jar.

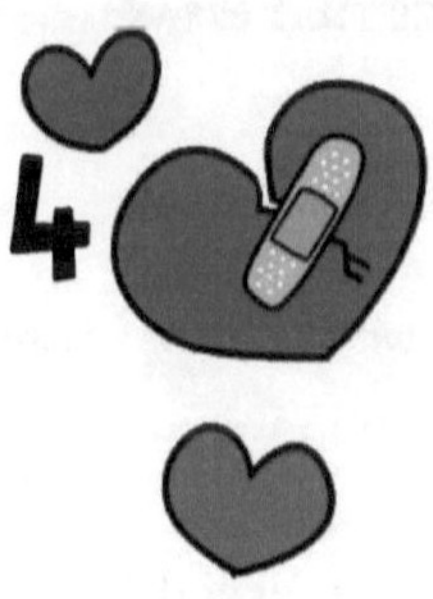

Emma squeals as she gets in the passenger seat.

"Stop making a big deal out of it," I say.

"I can't." She does up her seat belt and squeals one more time. "You're driving us to school!"

"You know, a lot of grade twelves drive themselves to school, Emma."

"I know! And you're one of them! It's so exciting."

"Okay, fine, it's a little exciting."

"Damn right it is!" She shoves me a little and I let myself smile as I back out of her driveway.

"Hey Zed, I came up with an awesome idea over the weekend." Teague is standing in front of my desk and I look up at him from my notebook.

"Yeah?" I reply.

He nods once and smiles before grabbing the chair from his desk and bringing it over to mine like he did on Friday. "Africa," he says as he sits down.

"Africa?"

"Yeah. Kids in Africa love to play soccer!"

"They do?"

"Of course they do. But a lot of them don't have real soccer balls. Instead, they play with like, rice bags and stuff. They barely last three days."

"How do you know this?" I ask.

He shrugs and leans back in his chair.

"Did you do research over the weekend?"

"Maybe," he says.

"Okay. So. Africa."

"Africa," he says with a smile.

"Wait, where in Africa?" I ask. "Africa's a continent."

"I know Africa's a continent."

"So the stuff you researched can't be true for *every* country there."

"It isn't, but it's present in more than one, so I was just generalizing."

"Teague, please go back to your own seat," Mrs. Henderson says.

"I am in my own seat."

"You know what I mean. Sit at your own desk."

He stands up and winks at me before he moves across the room with his chair. That was weird.

♥♥♥♡♡

Teague chases me into the hall after class and grabs onto my bag.

"Zed, wait," he says. I turn around to face him, and he continues. "So do you need to work tonight or anything? We should probably work on our project."

"Oh." Maybe he really did have to work a lot over the weekend. Or maybe he had to take care of his sister and he didn't want anyone to know. "Um, yeah, sure, we can get together. Do you want to go to your place?"

"You don't want to go to yours?"

"Well, my place is kind of small," I say quietly.

"We don't need a lot of room to work on homework, Zwicker."

I want to ask him why he doesn't want to work at his house, but instead I sigh and agree to going to my apartment.

"Do you want me to drive us after school so you don't have to take the bus?" he asks.

"Oh, I actually drove today. I took my uncle's car."

He raises his eyebrows at me. "Oh. Okay, so I'll just meet you there, then."

"Yeah. Do you know where it is?"

"Of course I know where it is," he says with a bit of a confused expression.

"Right. Okay, well I have to take Emma home first, so…"

"So… what does that mean? Do you not want me to come over?"

"Why wouldn't I want you to come over?" I ask.

"I don't know, you just sound incredibly not thrilled to be working on this with me."

"I'm not *not* thrilled, it's just weird, I don't know."

He narrows his eyes at me. "Okay," he says slowly. "So I'll go home first and let you know when I'm on my way. What's your phone number?"

"Um, I'll put it in your phone." He hands me his phone with the contacts page open, so I add my name and number. He smiles and shakes his head when I give it back to him, but I'm too afraid to ask what he thinks is funny.

"I have an amazing idea!" Emma says to me on our way to our lockers at lunch.

"What?" I ask.

"Since you have a car, and since we both have a spare fourth period, I think we should go somewhere for lunch!"

"Oh, that is a good idea. Why did I not think of this myself?"

"I don't know, Sadie. You're just not as smart as me."

"You got me there," I smile. I open my locker and put my binders from the morning away.

"Oh my god and do you realize?" she continues. "During flip weeks, we can just leave school early! We don't have to wait at school for the bus!"

"Yes!" Then I gasp, feeling like something bad just turned on in my head. "Wait. Isn't this week flip week?"

"No. No, we had spare last period last week, definitely."

"Are you sure?" I ask, shutting my locker. "I remember thinking I might be able to make last period after my G2 test last week, but why would that concern me if last period was a spare?"

"Maybe you forgot that it was flip week."

"Maybe we should go by the office on our way out and double check."

"Fine." Emma sighs and links her arm though mine, and together we make our way to the front office to find out if fourth and fifth period are flipped this week or not.

Flip week is just when fourth and fifth period get flipped, which they do because apparently people don't pay attention as much during the last period of the day. It's always annoying because people never remember which week it is, and wind up going to the wrong class. They have a sign in the window of the main office that you can see from the hallway, so that we know what week it is, but half the time the staff forget to change it and so no one ever really knows what classroom you're supposed to be in. I heard that some schools rotate all of their classes on a four-week schedule and I'm just glad that our school doesn't do that because it would be a literal nightmare.

The sign in the office window says Flip Week, and I'm not sure if I'm happy or not. We can't take a long lunch, but we can go home early. Okay, maybe I'm happy. I've never been able to drive myself home early instead of sitting in the library or the caf just waiting for school to be over so I can take the bus.

"No long lunch," I say. "But we can leave before everyone else!" I throw my fist up in the air and Emma does the same.

"Hurrah!"

I don't know why I'm afraid to tell Uncle Adam that Teague is coming over. He used to come over all the time. We used to have sleepovers in the living room after soccer games. Adam and Mat would make us pancakes in the morning and we would eat them at the coffee table while we watched movies. I just feel like Adam's going to make comments or talk about when we used to be friends and it's going to be weird. Or maybe it won't be weird at all. Except that it's weird every time I have to talk to him because we never talk. He doesn't even say hi to me in the halls, so why would working on a project with him not feel weird?

"You can just tell him not to be weird and he won't," Emma says. We're sitting in my living room rewatching episodes of *Neighbourly*.

"I don't think that's a thing."

"Why not?" Emma grabs the throw pillow off the couch and hugs it against her chest.

I shrug. "He's basically my parent, and parents aren't good at being cool."

Emma smiles and tilts her head to the side. "You have met Adam, right? You're not new here?"

"What?"

"Sadie, it's basically impossible for him to be a non-cool parent because he's your uncle! That's the beauty of it. No one ever thinks uncles are lame. And uncles basically have a knack for being cool."

"But I feel like I've just never had the chance to see him be lame because I've never had a boy over before."

"Yeah but Teague isn't your boyfriend."

"But Adam will probably act like he is."

"I promise you he won't. Your uncle is cool."

"I know. I'm just overthinking it."

"I know you are," Emma says. "You overthink everything."

"Um," I say to Adam when he gets home. I've already driven Emma home and come back. All by myself. "Teauge's coming over."

"Really?" he asks. "Are you guys friends again?"

"No, we have to work on our project."

"Is he staying for dinner?"

"I don't know," I say with a shrug. "How was work?"

"Oh, you know, vacuuming that arena is stimulating. Really cool stuff. And working on the books, two thumbs up there."

I smirk at him. "Better than having to deal with stupid customers."

"Except that stupid customers are what gives us a job. But it's fine. It's nice to get all the stuff done while we're closed. It's quiet."

"Yeah," I say.

During the school year, Laser Tag doesn't open until two throughout the week. It used to be open during the day but kids would just skip school to go play games and try to play laser tag, so Adam decided to keep it closed for the most of the day. It was never busy throughout the day anyway; he would randomly get a few older teenagers who weren't in school anymore, or some parents with their toddlers, but some days he wouldn't get anyone until the later afternoon anyway. Keeping it closed until two saves him a lot of money, because he can keep the machines turned off and even keep most of the lights off throughout the building, so he does all the cleaning, ordering, and bookkeeping during that time. He has two staff members who work some evenings and weekends for us so we can have a life too, but mostly it's just me and Uncle Adam who run the show.

Adam orders pizza and we eat it on the couch, the box open in front of us on the coffee table. Netflix opens and Adam starts to scroll through our *continue watching* section, but he pauses on a show we never finished with Mat. I try to not be too noticeable when I look at him, but I notice his jaw clench before he scrolls backwards and picks the show we just started watching on the weekend. I wish I could make him feel better, but I have no idea what to say.

I like the show, but I can't stop looking at my phone to see if maybe I just missed Teague's texts. I feel like a stupid girl with a crush, but I swear I'm not. I swear I'm just anxious about working on our project, and I want to be prepared for when he comes over. I haven't had him over since the summer before grade seven, and I need to work myself up to it. But he still hasn't texted by the time Adam and I are putting the rest of the pizza in the fridge, and he still hasn't texted by the time Adam starts scrolling through Netflix at 7:30. Teague didn't give me his number, so I can't text him myself, but I guess I could find him on Instagram and send him a message request, or a follow request if his account is private. But that seems desperate. A popular boy like him, he would surely get the impression that I have a crush on him or something, and that is definitely not what I want him to think.

So I watch TV with Adam and try not to worry about it.

I take the bus the next morning and to say that Emma is bummed is an understatement. Her voice cracks like she's trying not to cry.

"I thought I had more time to get ready and I almost missed the bus," she whines.

"I told you yesterday that my uncle needed the car today," I say to her.

"Yeah but I forgot. Anyway, how was hanging out with Teague yesterday? Was it weird? Was Adam weird?"

"He never texted me."

"Wasn't it his idea to get together?"

"Yeah," I shrug. "But I'm not surprised. I feel like that's just something he does."

"Was it something he did when you guys were little?"

"No, but he's popular now, and I'm not. So it seems fitting."

"Sadie," Emma says with a bit of a tone.

"What?"

"You're super popular with me."

"Thanks. You are too."

"Even if you can't drive us to school every day."

"Gee, thanks," I laugh.

♥♥♥♡♡

Teague is on the tarmac and I see him as soon as I get off the bus. My heart immediately starts hammering against my ribcage and I feel like I'm going to puke a little. Why am I nervous to pass Teague in front of the school? I'm not nervous when I talk to him in class. Maybe it's because I want to call him out on bailing on me but I don't know if I should. I don't know if I should yell at him for flaking, or if I should act cool, or if I should ask him if everything's okay. I mean, what if he didn't text me because something important happened? What if he had a family emergency?

I nod at him as I pass, but one of his friends, Carter, calls his name and Teague turns the other way almost immediately. I sigh, try to shake out my nerves, and follow Emma into the school.

"Don't worry about it," Emma says in the stairwell.

"Don't worry about what?"

"Teague. He's a jerk."

I shrug. "I guess. But he probably didn't see me."

"Well whatever. If he flakes on you again, I'll help you save the African children."

"Not necessary, but thanks," I chuckle. "And we're not saving them, we're just sending them soccer balls."

♥♥♥♡♡

Teague looks back at me a few times during Challenge and Change but we don't have a chance to work on our projects. For some reason I feel weird about talking to him after class about getting together, so I gather all my stuff before the bell rings, allowing myself to boot it into the hall as soon as I can. I beeline it down the hall and down the stairs to music class, trying not to think about anything except for the fact that we're practicing the *Star Wars* theme song today. Nothing can ruin that for me, I won't let it.

♥♥♥♡♡

Teague finds me in the caf at lunch and it seriously startles me. I look up from my leftover pizza slice and make a face that I really don't think is flattering.

"Hi?" Why did I say it like a question?

"I'm sorry I bailed on you last night. Something came up."

"Oh, okay. Um, it's fine."

I can see Emma out of the corner of my eye and it's so hard to keep a straight face. She's basically freaking out and wants me to be freaking out too.

"So can we get together tonight?" he asks.

"Sorry I have to work."

"Can't your uncle just work?"

"No, he's working during the day today."

He sighs and tilts his head back a little bit. "Fine. Okay." He waves me off and walks back over to the table all his friends are sitting at.

"What. Was. That?" Emma asks with a huge smile plastered all over her face.

"I don't know."

"He actually came over here to apologize to you! Teague. Apologize. To you. In the middle of the caf."

"Okay, make it sound like I'm an alien or something, why don't you," I say, a little hurt.

"No, Sadie, you know what I mean. He's… Teague. He's friends with Carter, and Gavin, and Candace. He's like, school royalty and he just treated you like…"

"Like a regular person?" I finish for her.

"Well, yeah," she says slowly.

"Okay, but he's not school royalty."

"Basically," she shrugs.

"Okay whatever, so he's super popular and everyone wants to be friends with him and all the girls have a crush on him, but that doesn't mean he has to treat unpopular people like they're peasants."

"No, but that's what everyone expects, right? If Candace had to come over and talk to you, do you think she would be as nice to you as Teague just was?"

"Well Candace would just assume that I was having a dream come true getting to talk to her so I feel like she would be overly nice to me. You know, like the way Princesses probably are to little kids at Disney."

Emma lets out a huge laugh and covers her mouth. "My point is maybe he isn't such a jerk after all," she says after she quiets down.

"Why? Because he said sorry for bailing on me and then made me feel bad for having to work?"

"Yeah okay, never mind, that sounds bad."

Hey. It's a text from a number I don't know. The arcade is pretty slow and no one has even come up to the counter to get snacks, so I reply.

Whos this? I type.

Teague

Oh.

Oh? I don't even get a hey back?

Hey back I say.

Sorry about yesterday.

You said that already.

Can we work on our project now?

I told you I'm working.

I stare at my phone to see what his reply is going to be, but it stays silent. Now he's just not going to answer me?

"Even if it's this dead in here?" a guy says.

I look up from my phone and there is Teague standing right in front of the cash counter. I raise my eyebrows at him but can't think of anything to say. I'm afraid it's either going to come out sounding stupid or rude.

"Okay," he says slowly. "How about I just go sit over there and if you get bored behind your cute little snack counter, you can come sit with me."

He makes his way to the party table and I hop off the stool I've been sitting on.

"Excuse me, are you making fun of me?" I ask.

"What? No."

"Why did you call the snack counter cute?"

"Because it is." He pulls a pen out from the kangaroo pocket of his dark blue hoodie and sits down.

"You can't just come to my work. We were supposed to get together yesterday and you flaked on me."

"I know, I told you, something came up. But I want this project to go well, so that's why I'm here now."

"I can't work on a project while I'm at work; I'll get distracted."

"But you can text?" he asks. "Also I'm pretty sure you were doing homework when I was here for my sister's birthday party on Friday."

I put my hands on my hips and hold my breath for a second while I try to think of a response but I've got nothing.

"I'm not here on some popular guy agenda, Sadie." His use of my real name catches me off guard, which is weird, because it caught me off guard when he called me Zed for the first time on Friday.

"I'm not… I didn't think… What's a popular guy agenda?"

"I don't know," he says with a half-smile. "But you act like I have some ulterior motive every time I talk to you. Like I can't just want to talk to you. You're always running off as soon as you can, and answering me in really short sentences, like you're going to get in trouble if you talk to me."

"I'm not…" I sigh and walk over to the table, sit in the seat next to him. "I don't think you have an agenda. But we used to be friends and we're not anymore, so it's weird."

"It's weird?"

"Yeah. Don't you think it's weird?"

He stares at me with tight lips and raised eyebrows. "No," he finally says.

"Well whatever. It's weird to me. We used to be best friends and now you don't even…" I want to say it. I want to say that he never says hi to me at school, but I don't want to sound stupid or desperate. I'm not desperate, it's just a fact. A fact that makes me feel like he doesn't want to be seen with me. Like I'm not good enough. Like maybe he's embarrassed that he used to be friends with me. But if I tell him that, he's going to get a popular boy complex again.

"I don't even what?" he asks.

"Nothing, it's stupid. Don't worry about it."

"Look, Sadie, I'm just trying to do this project. I'm sorry I didn't text you yesterday. Really. I only came here because I thought it would look good."

"You thought stalking me would look good?"

"Okay, whatever," he says, smirking. "I just thought it would show you that I'm serious. That I didn't just bail for a stupid reason yesterday and I actually do want to get together to work on this."

"Okay fine," I say, sitting up straighter. "You can come to my house tomorrow after school. We'll stop for a supper break and then work on it some more, to make up for Monday."

"Great."

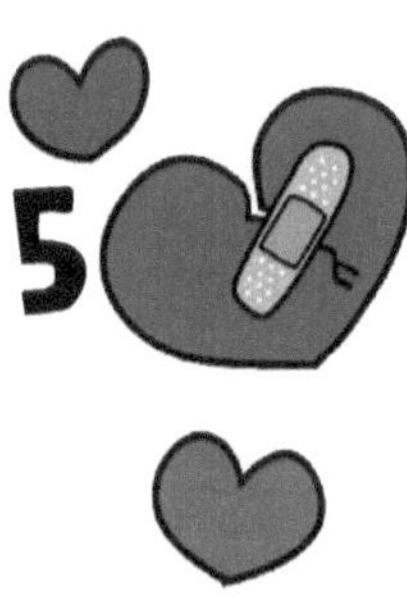

Teague is coming over in less than twenty minutes and I feel like he's going to judge everything about our apartment. Like our framed movie posters on the walls, or our *Star Wars* collection that's so beautifully displayed on the shelves beside the TV. I feel like Teague is a different person than he was when he was twelve. Well I mean, I guess most of us are different from when we were twelve years old, but you know what I mean, right? I mean he thought that I thought he was planning something every time he spoke to me just because he's popular and I'm not.

The knock on the door makes me jump even though I just buzzed him in, and I shake my head to clear it, get up from the couch and open the door.

"Hey," he says. "I almost forgot which apartment was yours."

"Yeah," I say. "Come in." I let him come through the door and then I close it behind him.

"So are your uncles home?"

"Um. No." I don't really want to tell him that Mat and Adam broke up, and I guess it's technically true that neither of them are home. Well, Mat might be home, but he's not at this one, so I'm not lying. But I can lie to Teague if I want to. Why am I rambling to myself?

"Living room?" he asks, already heading to the couch.

"So you're sure we should send soccer balls?" I ask Teague after he explains all the research he did earlier, and after we've done a bit more research together.

"Yeah, they love to play soccer. Or football, they probably call it. Why would we send them something else if it's soccer that they like?"

"No, I just mean this project is supposed to make a difference, so shouldn't we be helping them with access to clean drinking water, or vaccines or something?"

"Zed." He tilts his head to the side as if he's judging me.

"Wh-what?"

"You used to be a kid."

"Yes." I'm not sure where he's going with this.

"So, it would be amazing if people helped you access things you needed, but what kind of a childhood would you have if you didn't also have access to the things you *wanted?* Hurray, you have enough water to drink but can't have fun!"

"Okay," I say slowly. "But you also can't have fun if you're not well enough to do the fun things."

"Point taken. But there are already organizations that help with these things. There are always people helping with things people need, but not as much with the things people want. And that's important too, and does make a difference. Imagine having access to vaccines and then someone else also sends you soccer balls!"

"Yeah, okay, that makes sense." I agree.

"Kids need to be kids," Teague says. "And having fun can help in more ways than people think."

"Yeah. Enrichment is important."

"Of course it is."

"Okay, so what country should we pick?" I ask, scrolling through Google on Adam's laptop.

"Maybe we should pick two countries," Teague says.

"Okay."

"But later. I'm so hungry."

We put our laptops and the printed research that Teague brought over on the coffee table and head into the evening to find somewhere to eat. We walk down the sidewalk with our hands in our pockets not saying anything, each of us looking in different directions. The air is a little chilly, but not too bad. I'm so afraid the whole time that we're walking that we're going to run into one of Teague's friends from school. I live close to downtown though, and I'm pretty sure most of his friends live near the school so unless they were out looking for some good eats too, we probably won't run into them.

"We could just get subs," I say, pointing to the Mr. Sub across the street. Before we get closer to the middle of downtown where there are more things, and by association, more people.

Teague shrugs and we make our way across the road and inside the building.

But when we step through the doors, I want to immediately walk out. Except that I don't want to walk out. I want to run over to the person I see standing in line and hug him and cry, and catch up, and act like nothing has changed. But I can't do that, because the person standing inside the Mr. Sub is not my uncle anymore. I stop in the doorway, and Teague crashes into me.

"What are you doing?" Teague gently pushes me to the side so he can come into the restaurant, and the very thing I was afraid of happening happens. Teague doesn't know that Mat and Adam broke up six weeks ago, and Teague probably hasn't seen Mat in years. Oh no, it's happening. "Hey Mat!" Teague says with a hand in the air.

I want to curl into a ball and die.

"Oh my god, Teague!" Mat says. But then he sees me and pauses.

I don't know what my face is saying. I don't know what my brain is saying. What do I do?

"Sadie, hey," Mat adds in a soft tone.

"Hi," I say quietly. Am I allowed to say hi to him? Am I allowed to be happy to see him?

But then Mat is in front of me and he's hugging me and I'm hugging him back. Oh no, now I'm crying. I don't want to let him go. I hold him tighter and I feel his grip tighten around me too, and for some reason that makes me cry more. I cannot be crying in front of Teague in a Mr. Sub right now. But of course I am. Of-freaking-course I am. Mat finally pulls away but then he gives me another quick hug after he looks at me.

"Are you okay?" he asks.

"Yeah," I say. But then I sniffle, so I guess it's pretty obvious that I'm not okay. Especially because I have no idea why I'm crying. I can't tell if it's because I'm happy to see him, or angry that he's not with Adam anymore, or if it's because I'm confused about whether or not I should still like him, or want to see him.

"How have you been? How's Adam?"

"Um, good. Adam's good. Nothing really exciting. You look good." I look him up and down more carefully, and he's definitely lost weight. He wasn't a really big guy before, but he was definitely starting to get a belly, and already it's noticeably smaller. His jaw is a bit more defined now, too, and his dark, stubbly beard seems more distinguished than it did before.

"Thanks, I've actually been working out."

"That's good. Are you going to the gym?"

"No, I go running in the mornings, and in the evening I do *T25.*"

"*T25*, what's that?"

"It's just a high intensity workout. They're only 25 minutes. It's actually really fun." Mat grew up bilingual, and I always thought that both his English and French accents were perfect, but after not talking to him for over a month, I can hear his French accent when he speaks. It's super mild and I can only hear it on certain words, but it's interesting that when I lived with him I never noticed it and now it's almost all I can focus on.

I want to say something about his accent, ask if he's been speaking more French since breaking up with Adam, but I don't. Instead I just say, "Cool."

I catch a glance at Teague, and I can tell he's trying not to look completely confused, but he totally is.

"Anyway, I have to go," Mat says. He rubs my arm and starts to leave. He says bye one more time as he opens the door, but he's gone pretty quickly. He didn't even get a sub. Obviously he left because of me.

"Hold on," I say to Teague. He nods once and I run outside, trying to catch up with Mat.

"Mat, wait!" I yell.

He stops and turns around.

"You didn't even get a sub."

"Oh yeah," he laughs. "I forgot. Sorry, I'm a little flustered."

"So am I."

"Anyway, I should go. You're clearly on a date or something."

"No, no, no," I say, shaking my head. "We're just working on a school project and we got hungry."

"Oh."

"Yeah. But anyway, you can, um, you can get a sub. You don't have to feel weird about it."

"It's okay."

"It's not weird though. Right?"

"I don't know," he says with a sigh.

"I don't want to just run into you at Mr. Sub," I try. "I want to see you on purpose."

"That would be nice." He smiles, and I notice his cheeks are already a little pink from the cool air.

"Can I text you some time?"

"Of course you can, Sadie. You can text me anytime you want. I'm still your uncle."

When those words come out of his mouth it's like this big weight has been lifted off me. Like something was on my chest and I couldn't breathe, but now I can. Now I can take in a big breath and it feels amazing. This whole encounter I didn't even know what to call him. Even in my head, I didn't know if he was Uncle Mat or just Mat.

I step into him to give him another hug, and this time I can do it without crying.

"It's really good to see you," he says quietly.

"You too. I've really missed you."

♥♥♥♡♡

I step back into the Mr. Sub and Teague smiles at me.

"Don't," I say.

"I wasn't-"

"Don't," I say again.

"I wasn't going to say anything!"

"Yes you were. I said don't."

He sighs and I look up at the menu board, and then realize that my glasses are all smudged from crying. I take them off and wipe them on my shirt, but it doesn't really help.

"Here," Teague says, handing me a proper cloth from his front pocket.

"Thanks," I mumble, taking it from him. It cleans my glasses a lot better and I can see much more clearly when I put them back on my face. I hand it back to him and he takes it with a soft smile.

We don't say anything else while our subs get made, and we don't say anything else while we walk back to my apartment, carrying them in their bags and letting them swing at our sides.

We don't even talk while we eat at the coffee table and I wish I could think of something to say. I can't, and I feel awkward, so I turn on the TV and let my current rewatch of *Brooklyn Nine-Nine* play to make the air seem a little less forced. We both laugh out loud a few times, and when we're done eating, we just keep watching the show. I watch him out of the corner of my eye when he pulls his insulin out of his little zipper pouch that he's had on my coffee table since he came over. He pulls the orange cap off the needle with his teeth and keeps it in his mouth as he draws the insulin and lifts his shirt up to poke himself in his stomach. He never used needles when we were kids, he had this pod thing on his leg, and then he got a pump, so just watching him give himself a needle like it's nothing is a little jarring. He puts the cap back on the needle and places everything back in his pouch and goes back to watching the TV. Not that he wasn't watching it the entire time that he did that; he was definitely still paying attention to the show, like giving himself insulin was more of a reflex, something he did without even thinking about it.

Uncle Adam comes home at 9:30 and puts his keys down on the little table by the door. "Hey," he says. "Get a lot of work done?"

"Oh, um, a little bit. We got distracted."

"I can see that." He smiles and sits down next to me on the couch to watch the show with us. "Do you need a ride home, Teague?" Adam asks after a few minutes.

"No, I took my mom's car. Thanks though." He stands up and grabs his insulin pouch from the coffee table and puts it in his front jeans pocket. "I'll see you at school, Zed." He picks up his laptop and cradles it under his arm.

"Yeah, see ya," I say. I watch him from the couch as he puts his shoes on at the door. He grabs onto the doorknob and smiles at me. I smile back, and he leaves.

I want to tell Adam that I saw Mat at Mr. Sub, but I feel strange about it. I still feel like I'm supposed to be on Adam's side, that I'm not supposed to want to see Mat. That I'm supposed to be mad at him or something. But I'm not mad; I understand why they broke up. I wish it wasn't something that had to come up or be a problem, but it was, and it makes sense. I don't think Adam is mad at him, but I know he misses him. And maybe telling him that I saw him will hurt him. Maybe it won't, but I don't know how to act in these situations. If they were both my dads I feel like it would be different. Or if they had me since I was born instead of since I was four years old.

Thinking about it flashes me back to one of their last fights before they broke up. It was about two months ago, and they didn't know I was home. I was out with Emma and when I came in they were both crying in the living room, but neither of them noticed me walk through the door. It was easy for me to lean to the side and see them from where I was, but harder for them to see me if they weren't paying attention or trying. I didn't want them to know that I saw them crying or fighting so I just went to my room, not wanting to embarrass them. I should have just put my headphones on and blared my favourite *Infinity Pool* album, but I also wanted to know what they were fighting about. They'd been doing it a lot lately but they would always stop every time I walked in the room, pretending like everything was okay. This was my chance to see what was going on.

"I can't, Mat, you have to stop doing this! I'm allowed to not want kids!" Adam yelled.

"And I'm allowed to want them! I don't understand why you don't want a kid!"

"We have Sadie!"

"Sadie was four when we got her!" Mat shouted.

"So?" Adam asked. "What does that matter? Is Sadie not enough?"

"Don't you dare say that to me like I don't love her."

"Then what's the problem?"

"The problem is I still want more! I want a kid I can raise from birth! Someone who will call me dad! Don't you want that?"

"No," Adam had said. "I've never wanted it, I didn't even want Sadie!"

I can't say it didn't hurt hearing that, but I knew what he meant. I didn't want him either. I know he loves me and I knew it then too, but I knew what he meant. He loved me and would do anything for me, which was why he took me in when my parents died, but he didn't want to be my parent. He wanted to be my uncle. He wanted to be the guy who took me out for burgers on the weekends, or to the arcade when my parents went on a date. He wanted to be the guy who came over for Christmas and spoiled me, he didn't want to have to raise me. He didn't want to be my dad. And I didn't want him to be either. I remember hating him when I first moved in with him. I loved him, but I hated him. I made it so difficult for him and Mat for the first year that I lived with him, and not because I didn't want to be in their lives, but because I wanted them to be my parents. I didn't want to live with my uncles, I wanted to live with my mom and dad.

It hurt hearing those words come out of Adam's mouth, but I knew that's not what he meant.

But even though I knew that wasn't what he meant, that was when I decided to put my headphones on and drown out the rest of their fight.

Adam came into my room later that night to find me sleeping with my earbuds in. He gently shook me awake and I pulled them out of my ears.

"When did you get home?" he whispered.

"A little while ago," I said with a shrug.

"Did you hear us fighting?"

"Not really," I had lied.

"Okay. Well I'm sorry about it. We just got pizza, do you want some?"

I looked at my alarm clock to see that it was almost midnight. I looked back to Uncle Adam and shrugged again. "Sure."

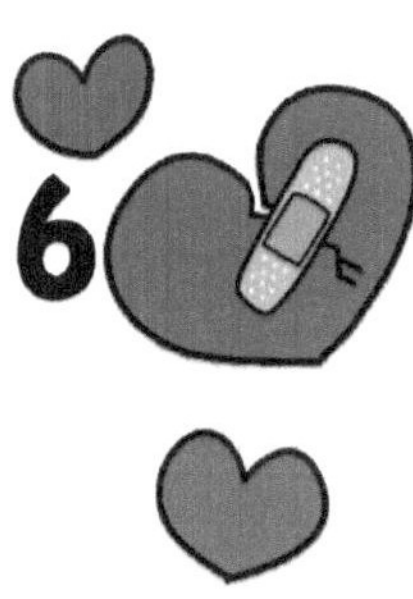

We have a free period during Challenge and Change to work on our projects and we all head down to the library together. I'm not sure why I thought Teague would walk with me, but I'm honestly disappointed when he goes ahead with his friends. I hang back and walk slower than everyone else, feeling weird that even Summer isn't walking with me. Teague glances back at me twice before we get to the main staircase, but I don't acknowledge him. I can't really tell if he's looking for me or if he's just looking behind him for something else and I don't want to make a fool of myself by waving to him in front of everyone and have him not wave back.

Everyone spreads out once we get to the library and Teague and his friends take the lounge chairs in the corner behind a row of bookshelves and in front of two big windows that see into the hall. I follow them over because, hello, we're here to work on our projects, but once I join them, they all stop and look up at me like I'm from another planet.

"What's up?" Candace asks me. I can't tell from her tone of voice if she's being genuine or not.

"Um, Teague is my partner," I say.

"Zed, no one ever works on their projects during free periods," Teauge says.

"Well it's not a free period, it's a library period. So we can work on our projects."

"Mrs. Henderson called it a free period… *Zed,*" Gavin says, putting too much emphasis on Teague's nickname for me.

As if two of his best friends are even in this class with him. I huff and roll my eyes.

"You can hang out with us," Teague adds. "But we sat over here because it's easy not to do work without anyone knowing."

"Whatever." I make my way to the front desk to check out a Chromebook to do the research we didn't end up doing last night after subs. I can hear Candace laugh and make a comment after I leave, but not well enough to know what she says.

I knew Teague was a jerk. Of course he's a jerk. Why wouldn't he be?

I print off a few articles and run into Teague on my way to fetch them from the printer.

"Hey," he says.

"Hi," I reply quietly. I keep walking and he follows me to the printer.

"I'm sorry about my friends."

"Okay." I grab the articles and make my way back to my table in the middle of the library; the only one that doesn't have anyone else sitting at it.

"What did you print?"

"Articles for our project. It's easier for me to go through them if I can lay them out in front of me."

"It's just one day, Zed."

"What's just one day?"

"Today, not working on it. Don't you get excited for periods like this? They're basically asking us not to do work."

"They're trying to make it easier for us to do work, actually. It's so much easier to focus in the library, where everyone's spread out. It's so loud in the classroom when we're all working on our projects."

Teague stares at me for a second, as if he's trying to see my side but doesn't want to. When he doesn't say anything, I continue. "It's also good for people who don't have their own computers at home. Or for people who want more time at home *not* having to do homework." I sit down at the table but Teague stays standing, his knuckles resting on the table in front of him.

"Everyone has their own computer at home."

"I don't," I say sharply.

"What were you on last night?" he asks.

"Adam's computer. Mine died and he can't really afford to buy me a new one right now."

"Why not? Doesn't he like, own Laser Tag?"

"Yes, but he also has a car, and a whole apartment," I leave out the fact that he's now paying for it himself instead of splitting all the expenses with Adam, "and buys groceries and buys me new shoes, and Laser Tag isn't- you know what? I don't need to explain myself to you. I don't have my own laptop, and sometimes Adam is using his."

"Yeah, but you have a phone, right?"

"You want me to do my homework on my phone?"

He's quiet for a minute, and then he slides into the chair next to me. I don't want to look at him so I start going through the articles I printed off.

"Why don't you just get a Chromebook? They're cheap. Plus you work too, can't you buy one yourself?"

"Good ones are expensive, and then you might as well get an actual laptop at that point. Look, it doesn't matter. Adam will let me use his computer if I need to, but I feel bad using it when he might–" I cut myself off, sort of throwing my hands in the air. "No, I said it didn't matter. Because it doesn't. My reasons don't matter, but you're my partner, Teague, and you're not even trying to help."

He looks at me for a good couple of seconds and then nods. "Okay."

"Okay?"

He nods again. "Yeah. You're right. Plus that does make sense what you said, if we get a lot of work done now, there's less for us to do after school."

"Of course it makes sense."

He smiles at me, so I smile back.

"Do we have the same glasses?" I finally ask.

"What? No way. I got these in the men's section."

I smirk at him. "So did I."

"Oh."

"Give me your glasses," I say, taking mine off.

"What's that going to do? I'm sure our prescriptions aren't the same."

"Just take them off, Teague."

He shakes his head and hands me his glasses, and I take mine off too, and set them next to each other on the table, on top of my scattered articles. I bend down in my chair and make my eyes level with the edge of the desk, inspecting them as if it was actually something important. I turn them around at the same time, look at the arms, the nose piece, the inside of the frames. They're definitely the same. I give him his back and he puts them back on.

"We're basically twins," I say.

"No," he says, shaking his head, and I'm immediately nervous about making that joke. He's going to say something about how I'm lame, or how we aren't the same, but he surprises me by saying, "Basically? I'd say it's more accurate than that. You can't get any closer to being twins with someone than having the same glasses."

I'm glad the conversation ended the way it did. I didn't want to have to talk to him about how much money our families made. And I know Adam would give me his computer to use if I needed it, but he needs it for work and I'm not about to kick him off his own computer. Especially when I can go to the town library or rent a chrome book from school, or like Teague said, *use my phone.* I know there's nothing wrong with borrowing a Chromebook from the school, that's why they're there, but I'm afraid someone will see me doing it and make stupid comments. It's almost the end of the year anyway, why would I spend money on a new laptop for less than four months of use? I might as well just keep saving and wait to buy a good one before I go to university next year.

My thumb hovers over Mat's name in my phone, but I'm too afraid to open our conversation and add to it. I want to talk to him, even just say hi, but every time I think about it I think of Uncle Adam. If I had a boyfriend and we broke up and I was sad about it, it would hurt my feelings if Emma hung out with him without me. But what if Emma and my ex-boyfriend were already friends? But Emma would be my friend before she would be friends with my boyfriend, so she should be taking my side, right? And Adam was my uncle before either of us even knew Mat, so I should be taking Adam's side.

But there are no sides in this situation, are there? They broke up because Mat wants more kids and Adam doesn't. Mat needs to find someone who wants the same things as him, and they wouldn't be happy if they stayed together. Only one of them would be getting what they want in life, and the other person would resent the one who did get what they want, and it would be a huge mess. Of course it would. That's why they broke up. It's not like Mat cheated on Adam or tried to hurt him or something. They didn't do terrible things to each other. And Mat is my uncle too; I've known him since I was three, lived with him since he moved in shortly after I did when I was four. I've known him basically my whole life, and just because he's not my uncle's boyfriend anymore shouldn't mean that I don't get to be a part of his life anymore. He broke up with Adam, he didn't break up with me.

I turn my phone off without texting him and fall asleep on the couch.

♥♥♥♡♡

Uncle Adam comes home and I feel him pull my phone from my grasp but I still find it hard to wake up. He brushes my hair out of my face and I open my eyes a little bit.

"Why don't you go to bed?" he whispers.

"I didn't mean to fall asleep," I say.

"That's okay, it's late. Come on, let's get you to bed."

I almost tell Adam that I saw Mat yesterday, but it stays on the back of my tongue. He pulls me off the couch and to my feet, and he walks with me to my room. I pull my jeans off and leave them in the middle of my floor, and climb into bed in my underwear and the same shirt I wore all day. I don't even take my bra off; I'm so tired.

"Is everything okay?" Adam asks, sitting on the end of my bed.

I snuggle into my pillow and pull the blankets up to my chin. "Yeah," I say.

"Okay. It just seems like you have something on your mind."

"No," I lie. "I'm just tired."

"Okay. Well good night."

"Good night."

He stands up and walks across my room, but pauses in the doorway. "I love you, Sadie."

"I love you too, Uncle Adam."

He smiles and shuts the door quietly behind him, but now all of a sudden I'm wide awake. I take my bra off through the sleeve of my shirt and toss it on the floor with my jeans, and go to grab my phone. It looks like Adam put it on my nightstand for me, so I turn the screen on and go back to looking at Mat's name in my contacts. My heart thumps just thinking about texting him so instead I text Emma.

Are you awake? I type.

Barely.

I saw Mat at Mr. Sub yesterday

Really? Was it weird? Why didn't you say anything at school?

I dunno. I reply. **It wasn't weird at the time but I felt weird about it after. I feel like I'm betraying Adam if I talk to him.**

Why?

Because Adam's my real uncle.

Mat is your real uncle too.

I know. But like. He's like the step-dad of the situation. If my parents were alive and my mom and dad broke up, and then my mom got a new boyfriend, but then they broke up, I wouldn't still talk to the exboyfriend.

I guess it depends on how long she was with this fake exboyfriend Emma says.

What do you mean? I ask.

If they were together for a year, maybe you wouldn't talk to him. But if they were together for 13 years I think you would still see him.

I dunno. Maybe.

It doesn't even matter because he's your Uncle Mat. He raised you.

But Adam is my dad's brother.

So?

I sigh and throw my phone into the covers of my bed as I flop back into my pillow.

Are you still there? Emma types.

I stare at my phone half buried in the blankets, thinking about Mat and Adam. Thinking about what would possibly go through

Adam's head if I tell him about Mat. Would he be jealous? Would he feel left out, or feel like I don't love him enough? Maybe he wouldn't care. Why am I so confused about this? Teague's parents split up when we were nine, and he saw both of his parents an equal amount of time, but separate from each other. Why should my situation be any different? It's not different. Is it?

I'm still here I finally say back.

Are you okay?

I don't know why I'm confused.

Parents breaking up is a confusing thing <3 she replies.

But they aren't my parents.

Maybe that's why it's confusing.

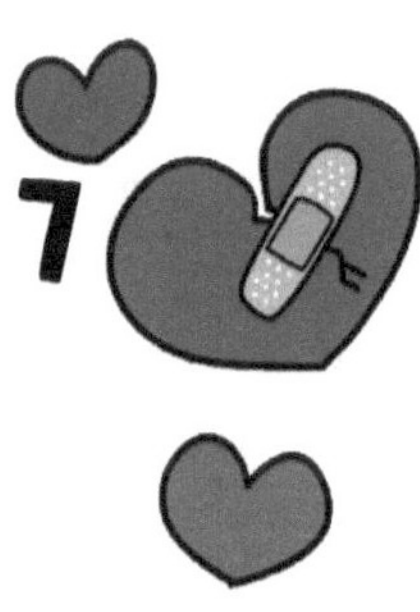

"I can't believe I'm saying this on March 29th, but we got 40cm of snow overnight, and it's still coming down out there! We're expected to get at least another 30 throughout the day, and the drive in to work this morning was treacherous! There's almost zero visibility out there! So I've got some bus cancellations for you guys today." This is an interesting thing to wake up to when my radio alarm goes off. I'm immediately awake and just wishing, hoping that our buses are cancelled. I don't get up and look out the window to see what it looks like, and I don't even wait to hear the radio guy to list off school zones. I reach over to my nightstand and turn off my radio, grab my phone, and open the school bus app and check to see which buses are cancelled. Just this one thing would be excellent. A snow day to give me a long weekend before I will never get another snow day again would be perfect. Please.

And there it is, clear as a sunny summer day on my phone screen. Buses in my school zone are cancelled due to white-out snow conditions. As soon as I see it, I smile, roll over, and go right back to sleep.

This is excellent.

But then I am woken up by a very rude phone notification. I groan and look at the time. Oh, it's almost 10am. I guess the notification wasn't that rude after all.

Is your uncle opening Laser Tag early since it's a snow day? It's Emma.

He doesn't normally. But we can still go over and play if you want.

I will start walking to your place in 10.

Ok see you soon. I plug my phone in so it can charge a little while I get ready.

I put on my *Star Wars* Christmas sweater because when it snows you get to pretend that it's Christmas, and my pom-pom toque with pineapples all over it. I'm super fashionable.

The wind hits me first when I step outside. It's so strong that it's actually hard to breathe. I plant my feet on the ground and my legs far apart until I get used to it, and then I walk up the sidewalk and away from the downtown area to meet Emma. The roads are completely empty and the snow blows across and into the side of my face. I should have worn a scarf. Already the snow is piling up on the sidewalk so I step onto the road where some cars going into work this morning have seemed to flatten it just a little bit. I look behind me once or twice to see my footprints being covered almost immediately. I can hardly see across the road, and I can hardly make out the glow of the traffic lights up ahead. Emma comes into view after about ten minutes, but not until we're about ten or fifteen feet apart.

"This weather is ridiculous!" Emma yells when we meet.

"I know, eh!?" I shout back over the wind. "I can't feel my thighs or my face!"

"I wore leggings under my jeans."

"You're smart," I say.

We turn around in the direction I had been coming from and make our way to the street that Laser Tag is on. My apartment building is only two streets over from Laser Tag, but closer to the downtown core. Laser Tag is up the hill near the strip mall, which normally isn't a terrible walk, but today it seems to take us twice as long.

We're completely covered in snow when we step inside the warm building, and Adam laughs as soon as he sees us.

"Did you two seriously walk here in that?" he asks.

"No, we drove but decided to roll around in the snow first before coming in," I say.

He puts his hands up in mock surrender and then comes around the counter. "You guys want a hot drink?"

"No, we want to play laser tag."

"No way, I just vacuumed in there yesterday. You'll track dirty snow in."

Vacuuming the arena takes forever, and I would normally be sympathetic, but I really want to play. I look down at my boots and then back at him. "It's pretty clean snow," I try. "It's basically just water. And when it melts it will be water."

"You can play in your socks," he says.

"Excellent."

♥♥♥♡♡

We set it up for manhunt, which just counts how many times each person gets shot and I take a red vest while Emma grabs a blue one. We watch our names show up on the TV above the entrance to the arena before we go inside.

"Okay," I say, holding my gun with both my hands. "Same as always. We each go to opposite sides of the arena and can't start making our way back to the middle until our vests are done counting down."

"May the best woman win," Emma says with a smile.

"Oh it'll definitely be me."

"Except that it won't."

I turn the black lights on and shut the arena door behind us and immediately start walking to the right. The colourful splatters all over the carpet shine up at me as I make my way over bridges and around dark columns. I find myself out of breath too quickly so I slow down my pace a little. I make it to the far right wall and sit down, but then my vest starts making its ten, low pitched chimes, counting down to the end of the grace period. I stand up and take a deep breath. I can do this. I can win. I make sure to always hide behind posts or crawl through tunnels, always looking around before I break for another hiding spot. I make it to the fake river in the middle of the arena and crouch behind the railing of the bridge, looking out for her. She always comes here first. Or maybe that was her plan all along, knowing I would look for her here. I spin around, but already know I've been shot. My vest beeps and I swear under my breath as I make a run for the next hiding spot. But she's already following me; I can hear her footsteps on the carpet behind me. I turn around and shoot at her, not even aiming, but I think I get her. Before I get a chance to shoot her again, she turns the other way and sprints behind a big wall. I chase after her but I'm too slow. I have no idea where she went.

I've been walking quietly for about three minutes and I actually start to think we're going to go our entire hour without running into each other again. But then I see a glowing blue patch in the distance bob up and down ever so slightly. It's Emma's vest. I tiptoe towards it ever so carefully and hide behind a big, orange, glowing rock. I peer over the top and watch her as she looks around. She's looking all around except for where I am. I feel myself smile as I prop the gun on the rock, and I stay hidden behind it. I can get her from here, I know I can. She knows she's been shot as soon as it happens, but I duck down quickly, hoping I'm fast enough for her not to know which direction it came from.

Uncle Adam has popcorn ready for us when we come out, and we take it to the arcade where we take turns eating and playing *Clown Fish*. Adam joins us after about fifteen minutes so we make our way to the air hockey table and we take turns playing against Adam. I'm pretty sure he lets Emma win, but he most definitely does not let me win; I win fair and square. I beam at him every time I score a goal, but on our third game, the air stops running and the lights turn off.

"Not again," I whine.

"It might be the end of this one," Adam says, patting the table like it's a dog.

"Can't we just get it fixed?" I ask.

"Yeah, I'll call someone to come look at it before we just get rid of it. I'm not that heartless."

Emma and I both put our hands to our hearts to show our relief and then get more coins with my code so that we can play *Dance Dance Revolution.*

Adam buys us chips and pop for lunch, because he feels bad making any pizza delivery person go out in the weather.

"Other people are probably ordering pizza," I say, opening my bag of ketchup chips.

"Well those people are evil," Adam says. "You walked here, so if you want pizza that badly, you can go walk to get it."

"No way, it'll be cold by the time we bring it back!" Emma whines.

Adam just shrugs. "You could take the car."

"No way. There's no way I'm driving in that. Have you seen outside? We're basically in the North Pole right now," I argue playfully.

"You've driven in snow storms before."

"Yeah, with you or Uncle Mat." Adam nods once and looks away for a second. As soon as I say it I immediately regret it. Calling Mat my uncle just came out; it was just like a habit. I almost always refer to both of them as Uncle when I talk to them. But I still feel weird about it. I want to apologize, but that's just silly. Now I don't know what to say to him. I need to say something.

"Driving by yourself is the same," he says, looking me in the eyes. "It feels like it's different, but I promise you, it's exactly the same."

"It's okay, I'm fine with having chips for lunch."

"Me too," Emma says with a smile.

The snow is still blowing wildly when Adam opens at two, and it doesn't look like anyone is on their way in. We stop playing at about 2:30 and just watch the snow at the main doors and listen to the wind. Adam brings us hot chocolate and we sip it quietly, hearing only the howls outside and our occasional gulps.

The phone rings and all three of us jump in surprise. I laugh at us for being so startled and Adam shakes his head at me as he makes his way to the counter to grab the phone.

"The birthday party tonight just rescheduled for next week," Uncle Adam says when he hangs up.

"Everyone's staying in today," I say, looking out the front door again.

"Maybe I should close up. No sense staying open if no one's coming in. Plus driving in this in the dark will be no fun at all."

"Oh. we live like three minutes away, you big baby," I joke.

"And there's a pizza place right around the corner but you didn't want to drive there."

"Have you seen the weather outside?"

Adam smirks. "Tell you what. You can empty the games and refill the coin machine, and then I'll drive Emma home."

"Well that sounds like work," I say, getting off my chair.

"Who let you play here all day for free?"

"I dunno," I say, taking my chair back to the party table. "Some guy. You should probably find out who it is so you can ban him."

"I'll get right on that."

Once we have Laser Tag all shut down and all the lights are off, we hang up a closed early sign on the door and get bundled back into our winter coats and hats, and brave stepping into the cold. I stick my face into the neck of my jacket as much as I can and follow Adam to the car. I put the seat warmer on as soon as I get in, and feel a little bad that Emma doesn't have one in the back. Adam drives Emma home and she thanks him as she gets out of the car. He tells her to come by any time and then we back out of her driveway and make our way home.

The plow for our building hasn't been by since this morning, and we almost get stuck coming into the parking lot. The car fishtails a little as Adam slowly tries to push through to our parking spot. The plow must have done its rounds before Adam left for work, because there are huge lines of snow on either side of our spot.

"I can shovel that out of the way," I say.

"That's very nice of you. If you're going to shovel, I can go start making us something warm to eat. You can pull into the spot yourself and when you're done, the food will be almost ready."

"Yeah, okay." I smile, and Adam runs into the building. I grab the shovel from the trunk of the car and start on moving the snow out of the way. It takes me a while to chip away at the snow plow pile that goes across either side of the space, and I silently curse Uncle Adam for having a job that doesn't start early enough for him to be gone by the time the plow comes by. But it isn't a whole driveway, so it's not too bad.

Uncle Adam just made Kraft Dinner, but I'm grateful and fill my bowl to the top. I add extra milk into mine because I like it runnier than he does, and then stir the macaroni around with my spoon. I grab a can of Diet Coke from the fridge and sit down on the couch where the new show we're watching is ready to go. We watch a few episodes before Adam takes my bowl and empty can back to the kitchen for me and I contemplate telling him about Mat while he's on the other side of the wall. Maybe it will be easier if he's not looking at me. My throat closes up when I'm about to say something though, so I just keep watching TV and hate myself a little bit instead.

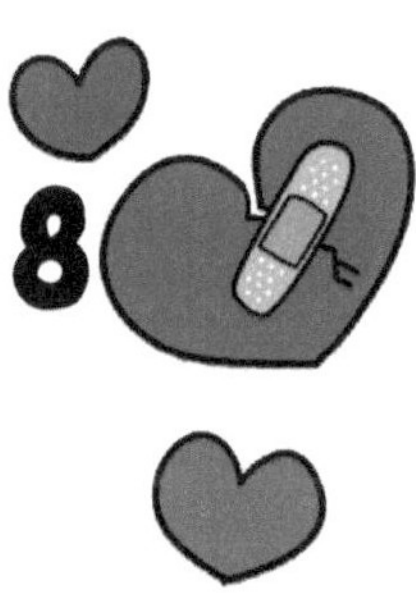

Teague comes over on Saturday afternoon while Adam is at work. The snow and wind has stopped, but it's still cold, so the snowbanks and annoying peaks of snow in the middle of the downtown roads have yet to melt. We work together in the living room at the coffee table with the TV on but we keep getting distracted so we move to the little dining room table instead. We think having a set up closer to a school setting might make it easier for us to work.

"We could have a soccer shoot-out at the school, and you have to pay to enter. And if we get local businesses to donate prizes, people will want to do it," Teague says.

"Will there be a goalie?" I ask.

"I guess there would have to be. I'm sure Gavin would do it; he's our goalie for the school team."

"Of course he is."

"What's that supposed to mean?" Teague asks.

"Nothing, it doesn't mean anything. I just thought maybe we should have a teacher be the goalie? Have them get involved? Maybe your soccer coach? I don't know, it might make people want to participate more, because they can try and beat the teacher or whatever."

"Oh, yeah, okay, that sounds like a good idea."

"Okay so how much should it cost to enter?"

"How come you don't play soccer anymore?" Teague asks.

I shrug. "I don't know. It got too competitive. It wasn't fun anymore."

"You don't think winning is fun?"

I smile at him but shake my head. "Winning is great. But my coach would yell at me if I missed a goal or a good pass or something. And then turns out I was good at midfield, and I hated midfield, but since I was good at it she would always stick me there."

"Why didn't you just pretend to be bad?"

"Are you kidding? If I did that she would have never let me play at all."

"But you would get yelled at if you didn't do what she wanted."

"Right. It was always a mix of emotions. Anyway, I was thirteen. I just wanted to play soccer. I didn't want to take it seriously."

"I guess that makes sense." Teague looks a little startled and pulls his phone out of his pocket. It's vibrating so I guess someone's calling him. He answers and puts the phone to his ear. "Hey… No I can't, I'm working on a school project… No, mom, this is important… Why do you always do this to her? … Ugh, fine I'm coming." He ends his call and stands up. "I'm really sorry," he says to me, "but I have to go. Do you have any plans later? Maybe we can get together after dinner or something."

"Yeah, sure. Adam's working all night so I'm just here by myself."

"Okay cool, I'll text you if I can come back."

He walks himself to the door and I immediately wrap myself in a blanket and curl up on the couch. I'm about to turn on the TV when I think of the fact that Adam won't be home until at least ten tonight. I take out my phone and scroll down my text message conversations until I see Uncle Mat. I open our convo and read my last message to him.

Movie night tonight. Bring movie theatre popcorn with extra butter ☺ that was sent just over six weeks ago, right before they broke up. We did have the movie night, while Adam was at work, and Mat did in fact bring popcorn from the movie theatre.

I stare at my message for too long and my eyes start to go blurry. I shake my head a few times and let out a deep breath. And then I start to type.

Hi. I really thought I would have more in me, but I guess hi is as good as anything.

Hey how's it going? he replies.

I let out a relieved breath and start typing back right away. **Okay I guess. I miss you.**

I miss you too. Do you want to get coffee or something?

Yes please.

Do you want to meet somewhere or can I come pick you up?

You can pick me up I reply. **I'm ready whenever.**

I wait outside the building for Mat to come get me and he pulls right up to the door. I get in and smile.

"Hey," I say.

"Hey. Is everything okay?" he asks as he drives out of the parking lot.

"Yeah," I sigh.

"Doesn't sound okay."

"It's fine," I reply, waving him off.

Even though the Tim Hortons is closer to my place, he drives us to the local coffee shop down near the water. They grind the coffee beans right in house and you can watch them doing it and everything. It smells amazing as soon as we walk in and I'm immediately ten times more comfortable.

I look up at the chalk menu behind the counter to see my options. I don't usually get the same thing when I come here, and after about a minute I decide on a mint hot chocolate. Mat just orders a coffee with milk and together we take our drinks to the lounge chairs by the window.

Mat takes his coat off and drapes it over the chair and I almost gasp at his finished sleeve tattoo. He had been doing multiple sessions to get a sleeve last year, but hadn't gotten the inside of his arm done and he always brushed me off when I asked him about it.

"Your tattoo!" I say excitedly, getting up from my chair and leaning closer to him.

"Oh yeah," he says, looking at it, turning the newly finished part up so I can see it easier. "I got it done last week. It's scabbing a little."

"It looks amazing, though," I say, admiring the dark, photo realistic images covering his light skin. It's mostly done in greys, but there are a few soft colours here and there, mixed into the different parts. I thought it looked cool before, how he had the solar system on one part of his arm and mountains on another, but now there's also an ocean, and it all blends together so seamlessly. And it looks amazing mostly in greyscale, with some blues and purples showing up in the stars, in the ocean, and in the snow on the mountains. It doesn't even end harshly at his wrist and elbow, it fades out in a perfect way.

"Yeah, I'm pretty happy with it," he says, looking at it himself. "Took a while to get it finished, but I finally did."

"Yeah," I say slowly, wondering if he only got it finished to help him with the breakup.

"So you're hanging out with Teague again?" he asks.

I half nod and sit back down in my chair "We got paired together in a school project," I say.

"So you're not friends again?"

"No, not really. He doesn't want to be my friend anyway." I blow on my drink and start to take a sip but decide against it once I put the cup to my lips.

"Why not?"

"I would ruin his reputation."

"His reputation?"

"Yeah," I say, blowing on my drink again and just keeping the cup near my mouth. "He's basically the most popular guy in our grade."

"So?"

"So and I'm not."

"So?"

"Do you not understand high school?" I ask.

"People aren't popular on purpose. And I don't think he cares what people think of him or who he hangs out with."

"Then why has he not hung out with me since we started playing on all boy and all girl soccer teams?"

"Is that why you guys stopped being friends? Because you were on different soccer teams? I knew it had to be something childish."

"Well we *were* children, to be fair. And it's not just because we were on different soccer teams… But he made new friends on that team, and I dunno, I guess he liked them better."

"Well have you tried to be friends with him since then?"

"Yes. He always blew me off. And by the time high school came, we were just with completely different crowds. Two people who ran in different circles and didn't associate with each other."

"Purposely?"

"Sort of, I guess. I tried waving to him a few times in grade nine when I passed him in the halls, but he never waved back."

"Hmm."

"So anyway, now he has to come over so we can work on our project and it's weird."

"Weird how?" he asks.

"Just because we don't talk. And now we have to. And when there's silence between us I don't know what to say. You know he was at Laser Tag last week for his sister's birthday party, but neither of his parents were there. He forgot candles for her cake too, and he was freaking out a little bit."

"Did you talk to him about that?"

"No, I was working. Neither of us has mentioned it since then, though."

"Maybe you should."

"And make it even more awkward between us? No thanks." I finally take a sip of my hot chocolate. It's really creamy and delicious.

"He might benefit from talking to someone about it."

"If I talk to him, it will definitely make things worse. He doesn't want to talk to the girl he used to play soccer with about his troubles at home."

"I'm sure you're more than just the girl he used to play soccer with."

"I don't know. It sure seems like I am."

"Alright, I guess the question I have for you then, is *he* just the boy that *you* used to play soccer with?"

His question catches me off guard and I have to think about it for a few seconds. "I don't know," I finally say. "He used to be."

For a while I always thought that we would be friends again. That he was just excited about having new friends, but that he would realize he could have more than one group of friends. But Gavin and Carter weren't always the nicest boys and seemed to always make faces or comments when I was around. Teague wasn't particularly mean to me, but we were kids, and he probably wanted his new friends to like him. I was hurt the first bunch of times that he blew me off, but a part of me believed it just wouldn't last. We weren't in the same class in grade eight, so I had even less of a reason to run into him so at that point it was easy to just hang out with different people without it seeming like it was on purpose. For a while there, he was definitely more than the boy I used to play soccer with. But I couldn't keep letting him be that boy that I missed being friends with. He had to become just the boy that I used to play soccer with.

Uncle Mat gets us some peanut butter cookies before we finish our drinks and we talk about the snow storm that happened yesterday. I want to tell him that Emma and I hung out at Laser Tag while it was closed and how we ended up closing it early too, but I'm afraid to bring up Adam. Mat hasn't mentioned him since Mr. Sub and I don't want to be the first one to bring him up. I've never had parent figures break up before; I don't know what you're supposed to do or how you're supposed to talk about it.

"Oh, I got my G2," I finally say.

"What? How have we been sitting here for twenty minutes and you're just telling me this now?"

"I don't know, I forgot," I say.

"That's great news! When did you get it?"

"A little over a week ago."

"What!?"

I smile. "Yeah."

"Congrats, that's awesome. I failed my G2 test twice."

"I know," I laugh.

"Did they make you parallel park?"

"Ugh yes, right downtown with people waiting behind me and everything. I thought I was going to barf."

"But you did it!"

"Yes. Yes I did," I beam.

"Hey you can even drive yourself out of town now!" he adds excitedly.

I cringe a little. "Yeah," I say slowly. "I don't know. I can't go on the highway."

"What? Of course you can. You can do almost everything with your G2."

"No, I mean I'm too scared. I feel like I'll be so nervous that I'll crash."

"We can go together sometime if you want."

"Yeah," I say with a bit of a sigh. "Maybe."

"Do you need to be home by a certain time?" He looks at his watch for a second.

"No. Teague might text me if he can come over later to work on our project, but I've got nothing else happening."

"Do you have any plans with Adam for dinner?" He brings him up so casually that it almost feels like they're still together. Maybe Mat isn't as upset about the breakup as Adam is.

"No, he's working tonight."

"Cool. Do you want to go see a movie or something?"

We each get our own popcorn with layered butter and large pops, and make our way into the theatre. The movie is based on a YA book that Mat read a few years ago and I think he's more excited to see it than I am. The main girl in the movie was in some other YA adaptation last year and was pretty good in it, so I'm sure the movie will be fun. I follow Mat up the steps to the seats in the very back of the theatre and we get a spot near the middle, making sure to leave empty spaces between us and the other people already there.

I finish my popcorn before the middle of the movie but manage to go through my drink slowly enough that I don't have to get up to pee before it's over.

It's still light out when we get out of the movie but you can tell the evening is quickly wanting to turn into night. I pull my phone out of my purse and turn it back on, only to get a text from Teague that he sent at 4pm.

Can't come back over, sorry.

No worries I reply.

Tomorrow? he asks.

I work until 8

Ok see you at school then.

"Is that Teague?" Mat asks.

"Yes. He's just telling me he can't come back over."

"Well then my darling, let's go get something to eat."

Even though I just ate a giant bag of popcorn, I'm totally down for something to eat. Especially if it's with Uncle Mat. We almost go to Carter's downtown, but I convince him otherwise, luckily without having to say that I was just there last week. Instead we go to Pete's for wings and poutine, and I only just realize that most of the restaurants in our town are just named after their owners.

There's a band playing in Pete's so we can't talk much, but it's nice to have live music to listen to while we eat. We stay long after we've finished our meals to watch the band until about 8:00.

"Should we go?" Mat finally asks.

I nod, and together we leave the restaurant and walk the dark street towards his car.

"Thank you for today," I say. "I really needed it."

"Of course. Is everything else okay? How's Adam doing?"

I shrug, afraid to say anything.

"That bad, eh?" he asks.

"It's not. It's not terrible. I mean, he's handling it. But he's still really upset about it. He just misses you."

"I miss him too."

"Really?"

He sighs and kicks a chunk of snow in front of him. "Yes, but not… Not like that. I mean, yes, I miss him, I miss him a lot. But I don't want to get back together with him if that's what you're thinking."

"Why not? Don't you love him?"

"Of course I do. A part of me may always love him. It's hard to forget someone you've been with for fourteen years. But we just don't want the same things, Sadie, and that makes it hard."

"I know."

He nudges my shoulder and then pulls me into him for a sort of side hug. He's a lot taller than me so my shoulder fits under his armpit easily.

"But like…" I start to form a question, but it gets caught in my throat.

"But like, what?" Mat asks.

"Why did you wait so long?"

"What do you mean?"

"Well didn't you always know that you wanted kids?"

He sighs and tilts his head from side to side as if he's trying to figure out how to answer me. "I mean, yes? But also no."

"Ah," I say with a smile. "Makes total sense."

He smiles too. "I don't know if I can explain it without giving you the wrong impression."

"You won't."

He sighs again. "I've always wanted kids. And when Adam and I got you…" He pauses and runs his hand over his face. "I didn't really want a kid so soon, that young, you know? But at the same time, I couldn't really bring myself to say no. And after a short time, it felt like you were our kid. And I loved you. I still love you."

I think he's going to say more, but he doesn't.

"You still haven't answered my question," I press.

"The whole time I've known you, I've been Uncle Mat. And for a while, I was okay with just being Uncle Mat. I thought that would always be enough. Because I loved you. But..." He pauses again and swallows. "When Adam took you in, he and I both made sure that you knew we weren't replacing your parents. We knew that being your uncle and being your dad wasn't the same thing, and we wanted you to know that too. So I guess all the reminders that we gave you growing up was also a reminder to me." He stops and looks at me, and I nod, assuring him that he's not hurting my feelings. "A reminder to me that I would never be your dad. And I wanted to be. I so wanted to be your dad, Sadie." I can see tears welling in his eyes and all of a sudden I have to hold them back too. "The first time I mentioned it to him, I brought it up casually. But Adam didn't want kids of his own. And I didn't want to leave him, or you, and I thought to myself... Maybe it's okay if I'm just Uncle Mat. And for a while, for a while it was okay. I was happy. But as I got older, and as you got older, I just kept thinking about how I always thought there would be... Ugh, I can't talk to you about this, Sadie, it sounds terrible. It sounds like you weren't good enough for me, and that's not it at all."

"It's okay," I say, "I understand. I love you and Adam too, and I'm grateful and happy that you raised me, and for the way that you guys raised me. But if I could have my parents back, I would."

He smiles, but it feels sort of sad.

"But I also..." I pause for a second or two. "Wouldn't."

"What do you mean?"

I shrug and look down before I continue. "I mean it's hard to imagine my life without you two. I love both of you so much, and thinking about not being raised by you makes me sad. I'm sorry that you didn't feel like being my uncle was enough. If I had known that, maybe-" but I cut myself off. Because maybe what? Would I have called him Dad just so that he would feel better? Probably not. I had a dad. And even though he's not alive anymore, he's still my dad. As much as Mat and Adam have been my parents this whole time, I don't think I could call either of them Dad. I know there are other people in my situation who would call them Dad, and that's great, but for me, I would feel weird about it. Like I'm erasing him or something.

"It's okay," Uncle Mat says, his tone quiet and soft. "Really."

I swallow and nod. "I just feel bad that it took so long for you to really realize what you wanted."

"I don't," he says confidently.

"You don't?"

"No. If I realized it sooner and left then, we might not have stayed in each other's lives the same way. And that would have been a shame."

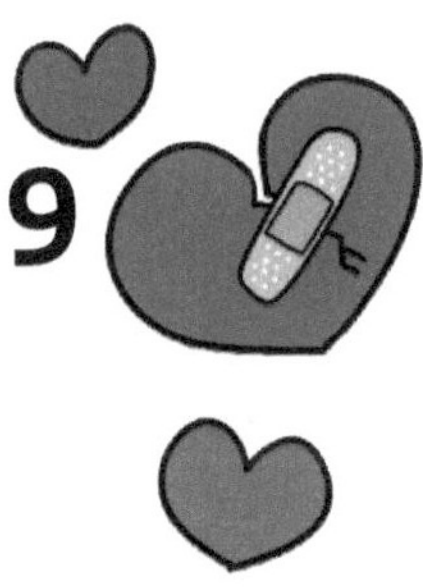

I'm watching a Netflix movie about people in space falling in love when Uncle Adam comes home. He sits next to me on the couch and takes my bag of chips from my lap to have some. I've basically just been eating food all day, so it's good that he has them now.

"How was your day?" he asks.

"Fine."

"Wow. Sounds exciting. Did you and Teague get a lot of work done?"

"No, he left early. Sounded like a family thing."

"Oh. That's disappointing. So what did you end up doing today, then?"

"I watched a movie." It's all I can say. I try to tell him about seeing Mat but I freeze up any time I even think about it. I try to form the words on my tongue but they just stay hidden in the back of my mouth. I can't do it. I just feel like it's going to hurt him so much.

Teague comes over after school on Monday, and again, Adam is working until closing. We figure out costs for our shootout, and other ways to fundraise. If we're going to send a bunch of soccer balls and pumps over to another continent, we definitely need more fundraising than just a shootout. The shootout will be the main event though, and we'll be asking for donations that day as well. Teague already asked his soccer coach if he would be the goalie for the shootout and he was super excited about it, so that's good.

Teague orders some Chinese food for us and has it delivered to the apartment. I try to pay for half of it, but he keeps telling me it's fine and that it's not that much. We didn't order a lot, but I still feel bad just letting him pay.

We eat at the coffee table again and watch *Brooklyn Nine-Nine*. We haven't talked about anything besides our project, but after he checks his blood and then pulls out his insulin, I dare to ask a question.

"I thought you had a pump?"

He stops and looks up at me. "What? Oh. Yeah." He pokes himself with the needle and then recaps it. "I did. I didn't like it."

"Really? But can't you just like, press a button instead of having to give yourself a needle every time you eat?"

"Yeah, but I didn't like always having something attached to me. And the pod was easy to manage when I was a kid but I always hated having this thing sticking off my leg. So I switched to the pump, which was better in some ways, but the tube always got caught on things, and sleeping with it was a pain. It was just a hassle. I find the needles a lot easier, actually."

"Oh. I guess that makes sense."

"Yeah, plus it gave me major calluses on my stomach. I've been on needles since grade ten. Seems kind of backwards, I guess, not too many people use needles anymore, but I like them better."

"Oh."

He smiles with half his mouth. "Yeah."

I want to say something else to him that's not related to school, but I don't know what to say. I don't even know what he likes anymore.

"So did Adam and Mat break up or something?" Teague asks.

"Yeah. Almost two months ago, now."

"Oh, so it's still pretty fresh. Sorry."

"It's okay. I mean it's confusing, but it's okay."

"Why is it confusing?"

Do I really want to talk to Teague about this? Do I want to confide in the popular boy? The popular boy I'm only hanging out with because we got paired together to do a school project? Maybe it's not a good idea. I don't think he would say anything mean, but I'm sure he would tell his friends, and his friends are definitely the kinds of people who love to do something with that kind of information.

"No reason," I say, "it's fine."

Teague still doesn't talk to me outside of class unless it has something to do with the project, and he still doesn't acknowledge me in the halls. I try not to let it bother me, but it does. It bothers me more now than it ever did because now we're actually talking. Now we actually hang out outside of school and have civilized conversations, yet he still doesn't say hi to me unless it's going to be followed up with a "can we work on our project?" or something similar. At least before, we hadn't really spoken since grade seven, so it wasn't a big deal if he didn't say hi to me in the halls. We weren't friends. I guess we're still not friends, but it's like he's pretending he's in two different worlds, and when we're not working on our project, he's in the world where I don't exist.

He comes over about twice a week and we always work on it for a bit before getting food and watching *Brooklyn Nine-Nine*. I work at Laser Tag, and the snow melts, and the weather warms up really quickly. I see Uncle Mat one more time while Uncle Adam is at work, and the entire time I feel like I'm doing something wrong. Not that seeing him feels wrong, it's the fact that I know I'm going to keep it a secret. We talk about the Challenge and Change project, TV shows we're watching, and of course we talk a little about Teague. He doesn't bring Adam up, so I don't either.

♥ ♥ ♥ ♡ ♡

Teague passes by me and Emma while we're at our lockers just before lunch, and I watch him the entire time. He looks at me and then looks ahead again, not even making the slightest move to acknowledge that I'm there. I've finally had enough.

"Seriously, Teague?" I say loud enough for him to hear.

"Sadie, what are you doing?" Emma asks, grabbing onto my arm.

Teague turns around. "Excuse me?" he asks.

"You're too cool to be seen socializing with me, is that it?"

"What?" He narrows his eyes and walks towards me.

"You looked right at me and then kept walking like you didn't even know me."

He half laughs and looks up at the ceiling. Emma is still clutching my arm. When his gaze meets mine again, his expression has completely changed. His face is softer, more innocent looking. But instead of saying anything, he gently pulls Emma's grip from me and then takes my arm and leads me through the crowded hall into the stairwell. He waits until the door slams shut behind us before he lets go of my arm and starts talking.

"You think I'm pretending not to notice you?" he asks.

"That's what it certainly looks like."

"So what is it that you're doing?"

"What do you mean?" I ask.

"I could say the exact same thing about you."

"I'm confused," I say slowly.

Teague laughs again, a soft, low chuckle. "You're confused."

"Yes."

"You're angry because I just looked at you in the hall and didn't nod, or smile at you, or wave, or say hi."

"Right," I say.

"But you just did the exact same thing to me."

"What? No I didn't."

He widens his eyes at me but doesn't say anything.

"I didn't," I say. "I was waiting for you to say something."

"So was I."

"You were waiting for me to say hi to you?"

"Of course. Why wouldn't I be?"

"Because… because we're not friends anymore?"

"Why are you saying that like it's a question?" he asks.

"Because I don't know if you think that we're not friends anymore."

"You're not making any sense, Zed."

"I just want you to say hi to me every once in a while. I don't want to be the girl you only talk to because you have to."

I notice Emma and a few other people pressing their faces up to the glass of the stairwell door, trying to find out what's happening. I try to ignore them and focus on Teague.

"And I don't want to be the guy who always has to say hi first," he says. "You could have said hello to me too, you know. And you didn't. You just glared at me as I walked by."

"I did not *glare*," I say defensively.

"Oh you glared."

"Okay, well I didn't mean to glare at you. I'm sorry about that."

"Thanks," he says. But then he turns around and opens the stairwell door, leaving me alone.

Emma watches Teague walk through the thinning crowd for a few seconds and then comes to see me at the top of the stairs. "What was that about? What did he say?" she asks.

"He said that he was waiting for *me* to say hi to *him*."

Working on our project tonight is tense. Also, Uncle Adam is home so we're in my room, me on my bed with my legs crossed, Teague on my fuzzy beanbag chair in the corner of the room. I made sure that my childhood narwhal stuffy, Whally, was well hidden in my closet before I let him in, but now he's here, and it's weird. I can hear Adam watching TV but I can't tell what's on. Teague taps his pen against his head repeatedly and I look through the notes we've previously taken, but neither of us says anything.

"I'm ordering pizza, do you guys want anything?" Uncle Adam asks, hanging inside the doorway of my room.

"Um, sure. Hawaiian?" I reply. "You still like Hawaiian, Teague?" I ask him, turning to look at him.

"Whatever, I don't care."

"So… yes?" Adam asks. "Large Hawaiian? You want wings or anything?"

"None for me," I say.

Teague just shrugs. Adam tilts his head in confusion before leaving and closing the door halfway.

"What's eating you?" I ask.

He shrugs again.

"Seriously," I say. "You're being ridiculous."

"I'm being ridiculous? Like you weren't being ridiculous in the hall today."

"Is that really what this is about? You're mad at me for calling you out?"

"No, I'm mad at you for being a hypocrite."

"I'm not a hypocrite! So I didn't say hi to you today, but I have said hi to you in the past, and you brushed me off. I'm done trying to say hi first."

"When? When have you said hi first? You literally always look away from me when we pass in the halls at school so I can't even try to say hi to you because you wouldn't even know."

"In grade seven, and in grade eight, and in grade nine. I look away now because I don't know what to do. I don't want to watch you watch me as you pretend I'm not there. I look away because I don't want to have to see you because then I just might say hi, and I know you won't say it back."

He's quiet for a minute and I'm just surprised that I actually told him that. My heart is racing a little and my mouth suddenly feels dry as cotton balls.

"We were just kids," he says quietly.

"What?" I ask.

"When I brushed you off before. We were kids."

Now it's my turn to be quiet, but for different reasons. His excuse isn't good enough.

"I don't really know why I did it," he says. "I was a kid. I was stupid."

"You have to have a reason," I say.

"I don't remember the reason. But today... Today, when I passed you in the hall and you looked right at me but didn't say anything... that hurt. I'm sorry that I did that to you when we were younger."

I nod, but I don't tell him that it's okay, because it's not. Not really. I mean I'm over it I guess, but at the time it was terrible. And I'm sure he knew that when he did that, it hurt my feelings. So it's not okay. So I don't tell him that it is.

We look at each other in silence for a few minutes and for some reason I feel like I'm going to cry so I clear my throat and look away. Always with the looking away, apparently.

"I'm sorry," he says again.

"Thanks," I reply.

"Are you always going to hate me because of how I acted when we were twelve?"

"I don't hate you," I say quietly.

"But you sort of do."

"No, I don't. I just-" But then my voice cracks and I know if I keep talking, I'm actually going to cry. I can't cry in front of him, not again, especially when this time it's clearly because of him and not some outside thing he doesn't understand. He can't know that he's making me cry. But he moves from the beanbag chair and next to me on the bed, and I gasp a little, because now I'm nervous. I don't know why, but I am. I feel my fingers shake and I clench them into a fist so he can't see.

"I was a stupid kid," he says.

I look away more, and he stays where he is, not trying to get me to turn back to him. Which I appreciate.

"And maybe I'm a stupid teenager, too," he adds, "but I hope I'm better than I was. Twelve-year-olds do stupid things when they want to be friends with someone."

"But you already had me as a friend," I sniffle. "Ugh, I don't know why I'm crying about this, this is ridiculous!"

"Do you normally cry about this?"

"No! You are not someone I normally think about, let alone cry over."

"You don't think about me? Geez, Zed, way to make me feel good about myself."

I laugh a little and dare to look at him. "Why would I think about you? We haven't spoken in years."

"I'm just making sure that this isn't a regular occurrence. The last thing I want to do is make someone cry."

"It's just me; I get emotional easily. I'm just… I'm just upset about other things, and-"

"Like your uncles?" he interrupts.

"I don't want to talk about it."

"Why not?"

"Do you want to talk about why you were the one taking care of your sister's birthday party?"

He stops for a second, his eyes wide. He straightens up a little almost immediately, like my question threw him off. "No," he says quietly.

"Then let's work on our project."

"But can't we talk about this more? About me being a jerk five years ago but not being a jerk now?" He forces a smile and I know he's trying to be funny, but I don't laugh.

"You're still a jerk a lot of the time, Teague. Let's just work on our project. We need to make posters for the shootout."

We don't have much time to work on ideas for our posters because the pizza comes and Adam calls us to the living room to eat it. We watch some FBI show that Uncle Adam likes because of a character named Rich Dotcom, but I don't really pay attention to it. I haven't seen it before so I have no idea what's going on or who anyone is. Except for the Rich guy, because Adam loves him and lets us all know when he shows up and tells us how hilarious he is.

♥♥♥♡♡

"Sorry about that," I say to Teague when we go back to my room after eating.

"About what?"

"My uncle being weird."

"I didn't notice any weirdness."

"Okay," I say.

"Seriously." His voice is sterner this time, but I'm not sure why.

I squint my eyes at him, but I'm afraid to say anything else.

"I remember your uncle," he says. "He gets excited about stuff. There's nothing wrong with being enthusiastic about something."

"I know. He was just acting like…"

"Like we're still friends?" he finishes for me.

"Yeah," I say slowly.

"It's fine, Zed." He grabs his pouch from my nightstand and takes his blood meter out, so I go back to trying to design our poster on Teague's laptop.

We end up designing two different posters and a brochure explaining what we're doing and why, and how donating helps. We both hover over the laptop, pointing to the screen and taking over using the trackpad or keyboard. It's not even weird working on this with him; it's only weird when we start talking about personal stuff. But this, doing this soccer ball thing, it's almost natural. It's easy to talk to him and joke with him as we come up with designs and slogans for everything. My eyes start to water from being really tired but I figure it's just from staring so closely at a computer screen in a dimly lit room. But then Uncle Adam pushes the door open and sticks his head in, startling us a little.

"How late were you planning on staying, Teague?" Adam asks.

"Uhh…" We both look at the time in the corner of his laptop and I'm a little shocked to see that it's 11pm. "Oh shoot, I didn't realize it was that late. I should go," Teague says, closing his laptop and jumping off my bed.

"Okay, see you at school," I say, watching him leave.

Once he leaves, Adam sits down on my bed. I know he wants to know if anything is going on with me and Teague but I don't want to say anything without him asking first.

"So?" he asks.

"So… what?"

"Is anything going on with you two?"

"No, I told you we're just working on a project together."

"Okay," he says, getting up, but his tone of voice tells me that he doesn't believe me.

"I'm serious," I say. "He's still… Teague."

"I would hope so."

"You don't know what I mean. You don't go to school with us. You don't see him when he's with his other friends."

"Are his other friends jerks?"

"Yes. They act like they're all better than everyone."

"Does Teague act like that?"

"I dunno. I thought he used to."

"You just thought?"

"I don't know," I say again. "I guess I didn't really know him."

I get out of the shower and towel off my hair as much as I can before putting on my PJs. I like the look of my hair when I've just toweled it off after a shower. I look at it in the mirror and wish I could just freeze it like that. Maybe if I have my showers in the morning I can hairspray it like this. I just think it looks so great over my ears when it's still damp because it's sort of messy but in a good way, and pieces of it separate from the rest of it in cool strands. I run my hands through it and let it fall back in place just below my earlobes, looking at the different layers. When it's dry you can never see all the cool, chunky layers. They just blend together so easily. Maybe next week I'll shower in the morning and try hair spraying it before it dries. I nod to myself in the mirror like I've just come up with some amazing plan, and then put on my PJs.

I head back to my room and I'm suddenly so tired that I have a feeling that I'm going to have a very hard time getting up for school in the morning. But when I go to set my alarm, I notice Teague's insulin pouch still on my nightstand. Oh my god. He needs this, doesn't he? What if he needs it and he doesn't have it? I have to take it to him right away. I grab the pouch and start to head for the hall when I realize he only needs it when he eats. No. Yes. He only takes it when he eats. Right? Yes, that's right. But what if he eats when he gets home and he needs it? What if there are other things in here that he needs? Should I open it and see everything that's in there? No. I should just take it to him. I don't need to look in it; I know it's his and I know he needs it. He wouldn't take it with him everywhere if he didn't need it. Maybe I should text him first.

"Uncle Adam," I call. But I don't wait for him to come to me; I walk into his room right away. "Teague left his insulin and stuff here."

"You should bring it to him."

"But he probably doesn't need it until the morning," I say, which is a ridiculous thing to say and I can't believe that I'm saying it.

"You should probably just take it to him anyway."

"Will you come with me?"

"What? No. Why would I go with you?"

"I don't know… Because it's late?"

"So?" Adam says with a laugh.

"Will you walk me to the car in case I get attacked?"

"Of course."

We walk down the hall to the elevator together and I have Teague's pouch clutched in my right hand. We don't say anything to each other but the entire time I just want to tell Adam about my secret. About Mat. But this is a weird time to tell him, and I don't want to make him upset. If I make him upset then I'll get upset, and oh, who are we kidding, I'll probably be the one to get upset first and in turn make *him* upset. I always get upset first. He walks me through the dark parking lot to the car and even though there are lamps scattered over the tarmac, he uses his phone as a flashlight to light the way better.

"Alright just text me when you're on your way back, okay?" he says to me as I get in the car.

"I will."

"Drive safe."

"I will." I smile at him and he waits in the parking lot until I've pulled out onto the road.

It's weird to drive to Teague's house. Even though it's near the school and I come this way all the time, I never come this way knowing I'm going to Teague's house. I'm not sure that I remember which house is his, and all of a sudden I'm nervous about pulling into the wrong driveway. It's almost midnight; I can't just knock on someone's door hoping that it's Teague's house. I can't knock on the door even if I know for sure that it's his house because everybody inside is probably sleeping. Teague might even be sleeping. I turn onto his street and I feel like I'm inside a postcard. All the houses are similar, all the lawns and driveways are the same, each with a little tree at the edge of the yard by the road. It looks like there are only four models of houses, and each one has a mirror image version. I remember when I thought all the houses on this street looked fancy and expensive, like dream homes. But driving past them all now, they're just regular houses. Two stories, single car garage, brick front.

I come up to the house that I think is his and I slowly pull into the driveway behind a car that I'm almost positive is his mom's.

Now what? I definitely can't knock on his door. I pull my phone out of the cup holder and text him.

You left your insulin at my house I type. But I don't hit enter. My hands are shaking and my heart is beating a thousand times a minute and I can feel it in my throat, like it's trying to work its way up to my mouth. I don't understand how I can get so nervous so quickly about such little things. I'm just bringing Teague something, it's not like I'm asking him out on a date or something. But I feel like I'm putting myself out there, giving him a chance to reject me, even though I'm not even asking for him to accept me. I'm just bringing him something that he needs. So why does my heart feel like it's going to break out of my chest if I don't barf it up first? I let out a deep breath and lean to the side to try and look into the living room windows from behind the steering wheel. I can't see anything. I take in another breath and hold it for three seconds before slowly letting it out. I'm still nervous and I know it's not going to go away until I'm on my way home so I just do it. I hit enter.

That's it. It's done. Message sent.

He replies almost instantly. **Crap. Can you bring it to school tomorrow?**

So he doesn't need it? It's not an emergency? I freaked out and drove over here for no reason? What do I do now? Do I tell him that I'm at his house? Will he think I'm a stalker?

I'm in your driveway I force myself to type. Hitting enter is hard, but I do it.

Oh.

Oh? Really? That's all I get? Oh? But then the front door opens and he walks down the pathway in his socks to the driveway. I quickly look in the rear-view mirror at my hair, and now that it's almost dry it doesn't look as good as it did back at my house. Even though I still think it looks pretty cool, I'm self-conscious of it and

I flatten it down with my hands and tuck it behind my ears. Teague opens the passenger side door and slides into the car, gently shutting the door behind him.

"Hi," he says.

"Hi."

"So you brought me my insulin?"

"Yeah," I say quietly, handing him the pouch.

"Thanks."

"No problem. I thought you would need it." I can hear the unsteadiness in my voice. I can feel it like there's actually something in my throat, constricting my vocal cords and not letting them speak out the way they normally do. I can feel it like someone is sitting on my chest and pointing at me, laughing, daring me to speak anyway.

"Nah, I have a bunch of it in the fridge, it would have been fine," Teague says easily. "But I'm in the middle of this bottle, so it's better. Thanks. I really appreciate it."

"You're welcome." It's quiet for a second and then I ask, "What about your blood meter thing?"

"Oh, I have an extra one I could have used. It's older, but it still works."

"Oh, you're just super prepared, aren't you?"

He tilts his head to the side and half shrugs. "Well, I try to be."

I smile. "Right."

He nods and is about to get out of the car when he notices my BB8 pyjamas. Or maybe he doesn't notice that they're BB8, just that they're pyjamas. "Were you about to go to bed?" he asks.

"Yeah, that's why I found your pouch; it was next to my alarm on my nightstand."

"Aw man, you didn't have to bring it all the way here."

"It's fine, really. I thought you would die or something without it."

"Well I mean, I would, eventually, but I wouldn't die tonight." His grin is contagious and I find myself smiling back at him. "It's pretty bad though, when you forget the thing that keeps you alive, isn't it?"

"I think it's okay."

"Well if you think it's okay, then I feel much better about it." He's still grinning, and also not moving to get out of the car anymore.

You see, this is the part that I feel like most people would start to get nervous. Or maybe not. Maybe I just think about things too much. But now that I've spoken to him a little bit and he's smiled and made me smile, I feel pretty normal again. Except I have this weird emptiness in my hands and in my chest, a lingering feeling I normally get before I feel totally calm again. It's like my body knows that it was just really nervous and it's having a hard time forgetting and moving on.

"Seriously though, thanks for bringing this all the way here for me," he says, holding the pouch up a little bit. "If I didn't have more in the house, it would have sucked not having it."

"Really?" I ask.

He nods. "Yeah. Like, a lot."

"Oh. well, you're welcome," I say again.

"Can you tell me one thing, though?" he asks.

"Um, okay."

"When am I a jerk to you?"

"What?"

"Earlier tonight, you said that I'm still a jerk a lot of the time."

"Oh. Just." Now I'm getting nervous again. I swallow before trying to continue, and already my mouth and throat are dry. "Uh… When you bailed on me. And when you came to say sorry for bailing but then you made it sound like I was working on purpose to get back at you or something, and not because I actually had to work. Like you were trying to turn it around on me and make me feel bad. Those are the recent things, anyway."

"I had a reason for bailing."

"Okay, and that's fair, but you should have told me. I was waiting for you."

"When else have I been a jerk? Besides the ignoring you thing when we were little."

"I don't know, Teague, I don't keep track. But you have this," I pause, trying to come up with the right words, "this look. The way you look at people and the way you talk to them, it's like you know you're popular and you're doing a service to them by talking to them."

"Seriously?"

"When you're with your friends, at least. You haven't seemed like that when it's just you."

"You think my friends are jerks too, eh?"

I raise my eyebrows at him and half nod.

"I think you just don't know them," he says.

"That could very well be. But I don't like how they portray themselves in front of everyone. It's like… like they're trying?"

"Nothing wrong with trying," he says with a bit of a head tilt.

"Yeah, that sounds bad," I say quickly. "I didn't mean it like that. I meant like," I pause, looking for the right explanation. "Like sometimes you guys will do things that are annoying and obnoxious, knowing it's annoying and obnoxious, but if some lesser-known kid in the school did the same thing, you'd make fun of them for it. Or maybe *you* wouldn't, but people would."

"Like what?" Teague asks, scrunching his eyebrows at me.

"Like when you and Gavin came to school with those big clown glasses on last year. If I came to school with clown glasses on, I would get weird looks, and people would laugh or whisper about me. But you guys know you're popular and people will think you're cool no matter what you do. You know you can get away with doing stupid things, so you do stupid things."

He opens his mouth to say something but stops. He smiles a little, shakes his head and then lets out a breath. "You're right."

"I am?"

He just nods.

"But you don't have anything to say about it?" I chuckle a little, trying to keep the mood light.

"I just never really thought about it like that. I don't do stupid things with my friends because we know we can get away with it. We just do stupid things, and I guess we get away with it. But I also think we've all matured a little since the clown glasses incident."

"Yeah," I say. "I just said that because you asked."

"Well please know that if you decide to show up to school wearing clown glasses, I will not make fun of you, and I will yell at anyone else who tries to. And you can tell anyone else at school that the same goes for them."

I don't say anything, I just smile, and he smiles back.

"Anyway," he adds, "I should probably go back inside."

"Yeah, and I should get home."

"Okay." He opens the door and hops out of the car. I smile at him as he shuts the door and I wait for him to get back inside before I back out of the driveway and start making my way home. I realize when I get to the end of his street that I was supposed to text Adam before I left his house so I pull over and bring up my conversation with him on my phone.

Coming back I say. I don't wait for his response; I just put the car back into drive, check my blind spot and pull back onto the road. My nerves go away for good on the drive and I feel calm and relaxed by the time I pull into the parking lot of our apartment building. It's funny that driving alone scared me only just a few weeks ago and now it's helping me to feel like myself again after being anxious. I just need to give things a chance, I guess.

Uncle Adam is waiting for me by our parking spot when I get there, and I wave at him as I pull in. He smiles at me when I get out of the car and we walk together into the building.

"So? Did he need it?" he asks.

"No," I say. "He has some at home. But he was still grateful that I brought it to him."

"That's good." He pulls me into his side and under his arm, and I wrap my left arm around his back.

"Thanks," I say.

"For what?" Adam asks.

"Just for being here."

He squeezes me a little. "Of course."

I pick Emma up for school and she beams at me as she gets in.

"What are you so happy about?" I ask.

"My parents said I could have the car on Saturday and take it to Barrie. Wanna go shopping?"

"Absolutely!" I say.

Our town has a strip mall with a few stores, and a lot of great family owned shops downtown, but it's not really what someone thinks of when they say the word shopping. Our selection is great for when you need something, but not so much when you want to actually go have fun and browse all day. We don't have an actual indoor mall, or a lot of brand named stores. Which is great for the people who own their own businesses, and I'm happy to support them. But sometimes I just want to go on a shopping spree, you know?

"I want to get new summer clothes, but also maybe a prom dress," Emma says.

"*Maybe* a prom dress?" I ask.

"Well I don't know, are you going to prom?"

"I guess. I feel like I might regret it later if I don't."

"But we don't have dates."

"So?" I say. "We can be each other's dates."

She smiles. "Okay!"

"Okay, so we'll get prom dresses!" Now I'm really excited. Going to prom will be fun.

"Maybe we should match somehow," Emma says.

"Like wear the same dresses?" I ask.

"No, but like, have the same accent colours or something. Like if one of us had a yellow dress and the other person had yellow shoes."

"That sounds like fun. We should get each other corsages."

"Oh my god, yes please, yes, let's do that!" She claps her hands and jumps up and down in her seat.

I laugh a little. "So when do you want to pick me up, then? Should we get breakfast on the way? Make a day of it?"

"Breakfast before prom?"

"No silly, before shopping! On Saturday!"

"Oh right." She jokingly hits herself in the forehead. "Duh. Yes, let's get breakfast before we go shopping."

Teague is walking in the opposite direction as Emma and I as we head to our lockers, and my stomach starts to tighten up into knots when I think about saying hi to him. What if he ignores me? I want to say hi to him, but my mouth isn't opening. We've almost passed each other and he's going to get mad at me if I don't say anything. He's with Carter, but not Gavin or Candace, so he must not be heading to first period.

"Hey Zed," he says with a head nod and a smile just as we pass each other. I turn and look back at him for a second as I keep walking, but he's still looking ahead. He said it at the last second, there's no way I could have said hi back and not have it directed at the kid walking behind him.

"Oh my god, Teague just said hi to you," Emma says.

A smile starts to creep up on my face. "Yes he did."

He says hi again when I walk into class and Candace gives him a weird look but he doesn't seem to notice.

"Hi Teague," I reply. I give him a little smile and head to my desk.

"How's your project going?" Summer asks when I sit down next to her.

"Oh it's going okay, I think."

"What are you doing?"

"Sending soccer balls to kids in Mozambique and Niger. What are you doing for yours?" I ask.

"We're making a highway overpass for animals."

"No way, that's so cool. Do you think it would actually work?"

She nods enthusiastically. "They have one outside of Sudbury and animals use it all the time."

"Wow. You guys are definitely going to win."

She smiles at me. "I don't think anyone wins."

"Well you know what I mean. You'll get a good mark for sure."

"It's hard though, these things are expensive. We need to make sure that this is something the city wants to spend money on. And we need to fundraise some of the money to make it more convincing. Plus they're really expensive."

"But it'll definitely make a change. A good one."

"I hope so. If we get the city to build it, it won't be in time for our presentation, but we'll have a lot to talk about and we'll still have a lot to do in order to convince the city to build one."

"Oh I'm sure your presentation will be amazing," I say,

"Thanks. Sending the soccer balls is a good idea, too," Summer adds. "Kids need to be kids."

♥ ♥ ♥ ♡ ♡

Emma picks me up on Saturday morning and I skip down the walkway to her car. She does a little dance in the driver seat when I get in and we turn up the music on the stereo playing our favourite band, *Infinity Pool*. I turn it up even louder when my favourite song comes on and I sing along even though I can't sing to save my life. Emma laughs and joins me, and we serenade each other basically the whole drive. We stop for breakfast at a pancake place near the mall that neither of us has been to before.

I order chocolate chip pancakes and Emma gets a cheese and bacon omelet, and when we're done, we make our way across the street to the mall. We head into the first dress store we see and wander towards the back, where the seasonal dresses are always kept. They have prom dress after prom dress, different styles and colours, and I have no idea which one I want or which one I can justify spending money on. We wander the mall and try on about ten different dresses in each store we visit, and make sure to show each other outside the dressing rooms before trying on the next one. We take a break for lunch and get fries in the food court, and then go back to trying to find our perfect dresses. We're on our way back up the escalators to the first dress store we went into when I see Teague walking by with Candace. I don't know why, but I don't want him to see us. I try to turn towards the dress store as soon as we get to the top because I don't know what to say to him, and us not seeing each other is just easier, but he sees us right away. He raises his eyebrows and walks over to us, Candace slowly following him.

"Hey, Zed, what's up?" he says.

"Um, just dress shopping with Emma," I say, pointing to my friend.

Candace smiles and Teague nods. "Cool," Teague says. "We're looking for a birthday present for Candace's sister."

She gives me a tight, forced smile, and I don't smile back.

"Okay, well, have fun with that," I say, grabbing Emma's arm and turning us away.

"You too," Teague says.

"He's gotten very friendly," Emma says. "I think you're rubbing off on him."

"He's just trying now."

"Trying to do what?"

"I don't know," I say. "Be nice."

"Sadie, I don't think that's a bad thing."

"I know. I just told him that he was a jerk the other day and so now he's all… trying not to be a jerk." I look back to make sure they're not around. "Which okay, I guess is good, but he should just not be a jerk without having to be told."

She shoves me a little. "At least he's not one of those people who say 'I'm not a jerk!' while they continue to do jerky things. I think him trying to be nice is … well, nice."

"Yeah," I say. "It is." It did make me happy when he said hi to me in the hall yesterday at school, and again in class. It's nice to be acknowledged.

We try on some of the same dresses from this morning, the ones we thought we liked the best, and I end up getting a purple strapless dress with a poofy and bunchy just-above-the-knee-length skirt. I feel very cute slash sexy in it, which I wasn't aware was a possible combination but there you have it. Emma's dress is more simple, a soft yellow halter that goes to the floor, with a slit up the side. The colour looks really great against her brown skin, and we decide to get mix matching accessories. Mine yellow and hers purple, to go with each other's dresses. We're going to be adorable. We head to the next store to find our bags and shoes and end up getting everything we need before the mall closes at six.

We sing the whole drive home again and I skip to the building when she drops me off. I skip to the elevator and hum as I wait for it to take me to my floor. Uncle Adam isn't around when I get into the apartment so I head through the little kitchen and around the small dining table to see him sitting on the balcony with a book and a Caesar.

"Hey," I say.

"Hey," he says with a smile. "Did you get a dress?"

"Yes." I sit on the Muskoka chair next to him and grab his Caesar.

"Hey, that's got vodka in it!" he screeches in a bit of a panic.

"I know." I take a sip and hand it back to him. "I just wanted a little bit."

"I'll make you a virgin Caesar if you want," he says, putting his book aside and getting up from his chair.

"Sure. But you're acting like it's not normal for teenagers to drink alcohol."

"You drink alcohol?" He pauses in the doorway and looks at me with wide eyes.

"No," I laugh. "But I could."

"It would be illegal," he says, narrowing his eyes at me.

"But I mean, like, you drank in high school didn't you?"

"No. I was a model student."

I laugh again and follow him into the kitchen. "Sure you were."

He sighs as he pulls the clamato juice out of the fridge. "Please don't drink. Ever. Even when you turn nineteen, please just don't. I'll worry too much about you."

"Why would you worry? I would make sure I'm with people that I trust."

"I know. You're a good kid. And I know you would be careful. But sometimes it's easy to drink too much even if you're being careful." He runs a lemon slice across the rim of a new glass and dunks it in a little plate of rimmer before putting in some ice and the clamato juice. "Just…" He stops and turns to look at me. "Just promise me that if you do drink, even if it's before you're legal age, that you tell me. Tell me if you're going to be drinking and who you're going to be with and where you'll be. I won't be mad at you or punish you. I just want to know that you're safe."

"I promise," I say.

"Good. Now how spicy do you want this?"

Uncle Adam and I sit on the balcony until it's dark and chilly, sipping our caesars and talking. I show him the pictures that Emma and I took of us posing in front of the dressing room mirrors in our dresses, and he 'oohs' and 'aahs' like he's properly impressed. He even takes my phone from me so he can get a better look and says how grown up we both look.

"You're beautiful," he says, 'both of you."

"Aw, thanks," I say quietly.

I tell him about our project, and the songs that we're playing in music, the books we're reading in English. He doesn't say much about himself and I want to ask him about Mat but I'm not sure how. I don't know what to say or how to bring it up. Do I ask him if he misses him? Of course he misses him. I don't need to ask him that. I've noticed him taking longer showers, or staying in his pyjamas on his days off. I've noticed him trying to be himself around me but being slow and sad when he thinks I'm not looking. Even the way he paused when I mentioned him during the snow day at Laser Tag. He wanted to be okay with it, and he wanted it to not bother him, but I could tell that it did.

"Are you doing okay?" I finally ask.

He chews on the leftover ice from his glass. "Yeah, of course. What do you mean?"

"I mean… Mat…"

"Oh. Yeah." He gets up from his chair and takes my glass for me.

"Do you want to talk about it?"

"No, I don't need to talk about it. You shouldn't have to be the person to talk about that with me, Sadie."

"I know, but I can be."

"It's fine. Are you coming in?" He's standing in the opening of the sliding glass door so I nod and get up and follow him inside.

"Do you think you want to date again?" I ask.

"Not right now. Why? Do you want me to date again?"

I shrug. "Not right now."

"Okay. Anyway, I'm heading to bed."

"So early? You don't want to watch a movie or something?"

"No, sorry. Maybe tomorrow."

I watch him drag his feet out of the kitchen and then I follow him as far as my own room. I flop down on my bed and let out a big breath. I should have told him about seeing Mat. I'll tell him. I'll tell him when the time is right. I grab my bags from today's shopping and take everything out so I can look at it and get my mood back up.

♥♥♥♡♡

Teague and I are heading to the front office to announce our soccer shoot-out on the morning announcements.

"Are you nervous?" he asks.

"Not really. I will be once it's our turn to start talking, though."

"Don't be."

"Oh, okay, thanks. I never thought of that."

He shoves me with his shoulder and I exaggerate a stumble, which makes him laugh. "I can do the talking if you want," he says.

"No, I have to do it, too."

"Alright."

We make it to the office, and Tyler, the guy who always does the morning announcements is there to meet us. "I'm so excited for you guys to be my guests!" he says.

"We're just letting people know about a shoot-out," I say.

"Nah, this is like my one-man talk show, but now I've got you guys! It's going to be great!"

We follow him through the office to the back where he's got a microphone and papers set up.

He starts by putting on O Canada and we stand quietly while it plays. As soon as it's over, he says our land acknowledgement and I hear a shuffle around in the office of the admin staff sitting back in their chairs. Then Tyler gets right into the announcements. He talks about sports team scores, the drama class putting on a play soon, and everyone's birthdays.

"And now I've got two very special guests, Teague Tremblay and Sadie Zwicker, here to tell us about some very exciting news!" He motions for us to step up to the mic and he takes a step back from it.

"Hey," Teague says. He stops and looks at me, shrugs, and goes back to the mic. "This is Teague, and I'm here with Sadie."

"Hi," I say into the microphone, my voice already constricting.

He looks at his notes and reads from them. "On April 18th, we will be gathered in the gym during second and third period, that's lunch, in case anyone was confused, for our first ever Soccer Shoot Out Competition!"

"It costs $7 to enter and $5 to get out of class and come watch the action!" I say. I feel like everyone can hear the shakiness in my words.

"All proceeds are going towards sending brand new soccer balls and pumps to children in Mozambique and Niger who love soccer but don't have real balls to play with," Teague continues.

"You can buy tickets or sign up to be in the shoot-out at the front office before first period or during lunch."

"You can also sign up or purchase tickets directly from us," I say.

"We'll be back next week to remind you all of this amazing event! Don't miss it!"

Tyler takes over and thanks us for being his guests and we just smile and head out into the hall as the announcements continue.

"You did great, Zwicker," Teague says.

"Thanks, you did too."

"You didn't sound nervous at all."

"Yes I did," I say.

He shakes his head. "I swear you didn't. You sounded really confident, actually."

"Really? You're not just saying that?"

"I swear. Why, did you get nervous?"

"Super nervous. I thought everyone listening would be able to tell."

"I couldn't," he says. "I know you can't just make yourself not be nervous, but maybe it's helpful to know that people aren't just out there judging you all the time. Even if you could tell that you were nervous, no one would have cared."

"But people do judge, Teague. I remember when I did my first presentation in grade nine, I was shaking so much that one girl at the back of the room could see the paper shake, and she commented on it to her friend loud enough for me to hear."

"Well, then she was being a douchebag. Some people are douchebags. But most people aren't. You're not friends with this girl are you?"

"No," I say slowly. "But you are."

"What? Who was it?"

I cringe a little as I quietly answer him. "Candace…"

He stops walking, so I do too, and then he steps in front of me and puts his hands on my wrists. I look down at them for a second and then look up at him. He's about the same height as me so we're standing eye-to-eye.

"I'm sorry she said that," he says carefully. "I'm not going to make excuses for her, okay? That wasn't a nice thing to do. Sometimes I think maybe I understand where you're coming from when you say that you don't like my friends… and when you didn't used to like me."

"Who says I like you now?" I say, narrowing my eyes at him but also smiling.

"You don't like me?" He lets go of my wrists and mocks being shocked. "How dare you?"

"Pretty easily, actually," I joke.

He smiles, but a teacher comes out of a classroom and spots us in the hall.

"Where are you supposed to be?" he asks us.

"Challenge and Change," I reply.

"And why aren't you there?"

"We were doing the announcements," Teague says, "and we got a little distracted on our way to class."

"It's not that hard to walk down a few hallways. Off you go."

Teague smirks at me and we both keep walking towards class. Without stopping, he takes a small stack of yellow cards out of his pocket and hands them to me. "Here are some guest tickets," he says. Then he grabs some red cards from his other pocket. "And here are some participant tickets."

"Great," I say, taking them from him. My jeans pockets aren't big enough to put them in so I make a note to put them in my backpack when we get to class.

"I'll go to the print shop tonight to get more done."

"I can come with you," I offer.

"Sure, okay. Did you drive here today or take the bus?"

"I took the bus."

"Okay so do you want to just go right after school?"

"Sure."

"I can't ride the bus with you after school today," I tell Emma in Music.

"What? Why not?"

"Teague and I are going to the print shop to get tickets for our soccer thing printed."

"Oh, really?" She wiggles her eyebrows at me.

"Yes really, but it's just homework."

"Sadie, to your seat please," the teacher says with a sigh.

"Sorry." I get up and move to sit with the other saxophones. Emma turns to look at me once I sit down and I stick my tongue out at her, which she returns.

Teague meets me at my locker and I feel all flustered and anxious like I did when I decided to bring him his insulin that he apparently didn't need. He's got his thumbs hooked around his backpack straps and he nods and says hi casually to Emma. She smiles and waves at him and then he looks at me.

"Ready to go?" he asks.

"Yeah. See you tomorrow, Emma."

"Bye," she says.

It feels so weird leaving without her, but I guess we have to do things separately at some point. I wave to her as we head down the hall and away from her, and she waves back.

His mom's car is really clean and smells like cinnamon, probably from the red tree hanging from the rear-view mirror. He looks around before he backs out of his space and I look out the window at all the kids walking through the parking lot. I almost jump out of my shoes when Gavin slams himself into my window. Teague laughs and uses his controls to roll down my window.

"What are you two doing?" Gavin says, hanging inside the car and forcing me to lean away.

"Homework," Teague says.

"What's your problem?" I say to Gavin.

"I don't have a problem." He winks at me and I can feel myself grimacing at him.

"Why did you slam into the car like that?" I ask.

"Because it was funny."

"Sorry dude, we gotta go," Teague says, leaning over the steering wheel a little to see past me.

"Whatever man." Gavin steps back and gives us a stern look as we drive away.

"Gavin's not the kind of guy he makes himself out to be at school," Teague says.

"Sure."

"I'm serious. He's…" he pauses and licks his lips. "He's actually a big softy but I think he just doesn't want people to know that. He plays rugby too, and he wants people to think he's tough."

"People won't think he's tough from playing rugby? It's a pretty contact sport."

"I know, but he doesn't want people to think that he gets emotional about things. So he tries to act like he doesn't care about anything."

"And throws himself at car windows," I say.

"Yeah."

"I don't care," I say. "If he doesn't want people to know that he gets emotional, there are other ways to do it. Being a moron isn't one of them."

"I know. I was just trying to help you understand. He's not a bad guy."

"Okay," I say. "I believe you."

We're quiet the rest of the ride and I'm not sure if it's because I made Teague angry or if it's because we just don't have anything to say right now. He parks in a pull-through spot in the middle of the parking lot and we walk across the tarmac together, still not saying anything. Once we're inside, he smiles at the girl behind the counter and she asks us what we're in for.

"We need more of these tickets printed," he says. "I have the files on a flash drive."

"Perfect."

The girl goes through the order and tells us it can be ready in two hours if we want. When we go over to the cash register to pay, and I grab my wallet but Teague shakes his head.

"I can pay for half," I say.

"No, it's fine."

"But you paid for the first bunch," I say. "Let me at least pay for half."

"It's fine, don't worry about it."

I roll my eyes, but let him pay, and he smiles as he taps his debit card on the machine.

"Let's go get something to eat," he says.

"Um, okay."

He drives us downtown to Pete's without saying anything, but I like Pete's so I follow him inside. I order wings and poutine and he gets a burger and a poutine. I want to talk to him while we wait for our food to come, but all of our conversations so far have either been about our project or him being a jerk. I want to talk about something else, but I don't know how. I end up pulling out my phone, but then realize that's rude and put it away.

"Not as important as you thought?" he asks.

"Hmm?"

"Were you about to reply to a text or something? But then changed your mind?"

"Oh. No, I felt awkward and didn't know what to say, actually. So I was going to go on Instagram."

"Ha. Fabulous." I can't tell if he's being serious or not. "You don't have to feel awkward around me," he says after about a minute of silence.

"I know I don't *have* to."

"But you do?"

I shrug. "Sometimes."

"Do you still think I'm judging you or something?"

"No," I say easily. "I just… Okay, I'm going to be vulnerable for a minute here."

The corner of his mouth curls just a bit. "Okay."

"When we were kids, and you stopped being my friend, I always wished it was a phase. That you found new people to hang out with, and it was fun, and I cramped your style. Because I wasn't new. But I always thought that once they weren't new anymore either, that you would come back. That maybe we would all be friends. Or that you and I would still be friends separately. But that didn't happen. And so I started to hate you. And then when high school started, I thought, 'Perfect! We're all here from different schools and we'll all get new friends and it'll be easier to be his friend again.' But that didn't happen either. I wanted to still be your friend for so long, Teague, but you didn't want to be mine, and now… Now that you're friendly to me and you want me to like you, it just feels like too much too late."

"It's not that I didn't want to be your friend," he says.

"Then what was it?"

He sighs and shakes his head, opens his mouth to say something, but someone comes with our meals.

"Who had the burger?" the server asks.

"I did," Teague replies, holding up his hand.

"Great." He puts the food down in front of us. "Does anyone need any ketchup or extra napkins or anything?"

"I'll have some ketchup, please," Teague says.

The server leaves for three seconds and comes back with a French's ketchup bottle. "Enjoy."

I'm interested in what Teague was going to say until I see him start pouring ketchup all over his poutine. "What are you doing?" I ask.

He stops, holding the bottle nozzle-down over his fries. "Um, eating?"

"No, it looks like you're putting ketchup on your poutine."

"So?"

"So? Why are you ruining it?"

"I'm not ruining it!"

"Yes you are! You aren't supposed to put ketchup on your poutine."

"I can put whatever I want on it," he says as he continues to pour it all over.

"But … But it already has cheese curds and gravy. You don't need ketchup."

"No," he says, setting the bottle down. "But it makes it taste delicious." He pokes it with his fork and takes a big bite, smiling the whole time.

"But it's already delicious," I say.

"Yeah. But I like ketchup and it's also delicious with ketchup."

"But you're… You're-"

"I'm not ruining it," he says. "Have you ever eaten a poutine with ketchup on it?"

"No. It doesn't need it."

"Try it. Try it and tell me it doesn't taste good."

"I don't need to try it."

He stabs more fries with his fork and holds it across the table to me. "Try it."

"No. I like it without ketchup."

"So do I. You're allowed to like things more than one way, Zed."

"I don't need to try it to know that I won't like it as much."

"I think you're being stubborn."

"Ugh," I say, grabbing the fork from him. I put it in my mouth and chew. Dammit. It tastes good. I can still taste the cheese and gravy, and the ketchup doesn't overpower it, it just adds to it. "It's fine," I say, handing the fork back to him.

He laughs and actually throws his head back. "You liked it and you know it."

"Fine," I say. "It was good. It tasted good. But I like it better without it. It's perfect the way it is." I take a big bite of my own, non-ruined poutine, and beam at him. "Mmmm," I add as I chew. "It's *soooo* good."

He takes a bite of his and does the same. "Mmmm, fries, cheese curds, gravy, and *ketchup!* The combination is *so delicious.*"

♥ ♥ ♥ ♡ ♡

Teague drops me off in front of my apartment after we go back to the print shop to pick up the tickets. I'm about to open the car door when he puts his arm out to stop me. I turn and look at him, my hand still on the door handle.

"Wait," he says. He looks at me and I look at him but he doesn't say anything else.

"What?" I ask.

"I'm sorry. I thought that I could say it right now, but I can't. I'm not as strong as you."

"You're not as strong as me?" I ask, confused.

"With being vulnerable. I'm not good at it."

"I don't think people are *good* at being vulnerable, Teague."

"I mean you're good at allowing yourself to show it. You're strong enough to admit things to me that most other seventeen-year-olds would not. The way you sort of spilled your heart back at Pete's, I'm in awe. Seriously. You're a lot more mature than most people our age."

"Okay," I say slowly.

"That's a compliment, Zwicker."

"Thanks," I say. "But you know you can be vulnerable, too. Especially after I've been. I'm not here to judge you."

"I know. But I can't. I thought I could, but I can't."

"Alright. Well, what was it about?"

He sort of shrugs and looks away, puts both his hands back on the steering wheel. "I… I can't. I'm sorry. And please just know that I'm sorry for everything that happened when we were younger."

"Okay."

"I'll see you later."

"Okay," I say again. "See you later."

He gives me a weak smile and I let myself out of the car. I notice he doesn't drive away until I'm inside the building and the door is closed behind me.

By the end of the week, Teague has sold all his tickets to the soccer shoot-out and has to take mine. I've only sold a guest ticket to Emma and a participant ticket to Summer. I sheepishly hand them over but Teague doesn't notice anything and just thanks me as he takes them. I notice people stopping him in the halls, and there always seems to be a group of people, mostly girls, gathered around him in between classes. It's good that his popularity is helping us sell tickets, but it's also annoying. It's not like people don't know who I am to buy tickets from me. Right? People know who I am.

"Do people know me?" I ask Emma at lunch.

"What? I don't know."

"Like, even the grade nines are buying tickets from Teague, but no one is buying them from me."

"That's just because Teague is cute."

"Really? You think Teague is cute?"

"Sure. Don't you?"

I shrug at her and take a bite of my sandwich. "I don't know, I guess he is. I mean he's not terrible to look at. But I've never thought about it before."

"That's because you spend all your time hating him. But now that he's nice to you, you can focus on his cuteness."

"I don't know, I don't really think he's that cute. He's just a regular guy. Plus you used to hate him too."

"I didn't really know him enough to hate him," she says with a shrug. "But you hated him so much so I just let you. But he's always been cute."

I scrunch my face at her a little. "No, I don't think so."

"Well I want to know what he's like without his other popular friends around."

"He's nice," is all I say.

We have our spare during last period this week, but Uncle Adam needed the car to get stuff for Laser Tag so Emma and I are stuck at school waiting for the bus. We head to the library so we can hang out in the lounge chairs and talk, but there's some author presentation happening for one of the grade nine English classes. We turn around to head to the caf when someone taps me on the shoulder. I spin around to see a girl from our music class who plays the clarinet.

"Hey Alisha," I say.

"Hey. Do you have tickets for that soccer thing?" she asks.

"I do!" I start to take my bag off when I realize I gave them all to Teague. "Oh no, sorry, Teague has them all. I'm pretty sure they still have some in the office, though."

"Okay, thanks. Do you guys have a spare this period or something?" she asks.

"Yeah," we both say.

"Me too. I was just going to go get an iced cap at Tims, do you want to come?"

Emma and I both look at each other and nod. "Yeah, sure," we both say.

The three of us walk ten minutes to the nearest Tim Hortons and we all get iced caps with chocolate milk, but Alisha also gets a donut. We sit by the fireplace and start sipping our cold drinks. We talk about music class and what other classes we're all taking, and I tell them a bit about Teague's and my Challenge and Change project. I tell them that we got a sports fan store in the Newmarket mall to donate a soccer jersey to the winner, with a player's name and number on the back and everything. We don't have any stores in town that have items like that, and the store in Newmarket was the first one to say they could donate one. Teague and I will go pick it up together when it's ready, but we'll let the winner pick which jersey they want first.

"Alisha, aren't you a walker?" I ask.

"Yeah."

"So why don't you just go straight home if you have a spare last period?"

She shrugs. "I like prolonging going home."

"Oh." I don't want to pry so I don't say anything else.

"My parents are constantly fighting. And they both work evenings most of the time so they're always home during the day, just yelling at each other."

"Oh, I'm sorry," I say. "I know what that's like."

"What? You do? Aren't your dads like, super in love?"

"Um, they're my uncles," I say. "And they're not together anymore."

"Really? They're not your dads?"

I shake my head. "No."

"Why do you live with your uncles?"

"My parents died when I was four."

"Really? Oh my god, I'm so sorry, I had no idea."

"It's okay," I say.

"Do you miss them?"

"Sort of. I don't really remember them. But my uncles just broke up a little while ago, and they fought a lot before then, so I know what you're going through."

"That sucks, I'm sorry. I wish my parents would break up."

"They might be happier if they do. But maybe they're trying to work it out for your sake," Emma steps in.

"Well they don't need to. I would be much happier if they were happy."

"Maybe you should tell them that," I say.

Alisha smiles. "Maybe." She sighs and looks at her watch. "I guess I'll go. I'll take the long way home. See you guys on Monday."

Emma and I both leave too, but we head back to school so that we can catch the bus.

I work at Laser Tag all weekend, and it's weird not hearing the air hockey table in use. The sound of the plastic puck hitting the mallets and the sides of the table usually fills the entire room, but now the machine is permanently turned off until it can get fixed. Even when the arcade is busy, it's oddly quiet without it, and it makes me sad. At least I have a bit of a distraction because Teague keeps texting me to tell me how many tickets we've sold for the soccer shoot-out.

"What's that smile about?" Uncle Adams asks after coming out of the arena.

"What? I'm not smiling."

He looks down and sees my phone. "Oooh, I see, you're smiling because of a boy."

"No I'm not," I say, holding my phone behind my back. "I mean, like, yes, it's a boy, but it's not because it's boy. He's just being ridiculous."

"Ridiculous how?"

"He's just counting how many tickets we've sold and instead of counting them all at once he's texting me every time he counts 50 more."

"So he can text you more often," he says, nudging my shoulder with his fist.

"Whatever. I'm just smiling because he's being ridiculous."

"Exactly."

"What? No. I'm not-"

"It's okay Sadie. You're allowed to have a crush on a boy."

"I don't have a crush on him!" I whine.

"Yes you do. But anyway, I'm going to head home. Have a good rest of the night."

❤❤❤♡♡

"We've sold 250 tickets!" Teague yells from down the hall on Monday. "Zed!" He waves his hands in the air as if I can't see him, but really I just want to get closer before I answer him. "Zed! 250! And fifteen participant tickets! Zed! Why aren't you excited!?"

"Only because I already know!" I yell back. We're getting closer to each other and I notice that everyone in the hall is looking at us.

"But now you know in person! Throw your hands up in the air!"

I put my hands up and Teague high fives them both when we meet. "We're going to ace this project!"

"I'm happy for you, Teague. Good job."

"No, for us!"

"You sold all the tickets."

"No, you sold some, didn't you?"

I shrug. "Some. And the office sold some. You sold most of them."

"Well whatever. We're going to have so much money to send out these soccer balls!"

"It's going to be amazing!" I say, trying to be as excited as Teague. I'm not sure why I'm not as excited as he is, to be honest.

I'll probably get excited on the day of the shoot-out when we see all the people filling the bleachers in the gym.

"Anyway, we should probably try to set up a schedule for the shoot-out, eh?" Teague says.

"Maybe closer to the date, in case we sell more," I say.

"Yeah, good idea. We could even get together the night before and work it out."

"Yeah, sure," I say. "We also need to work on our presentation."

"No, we have so much time for that. That's not until the end of May."

I don't even realize it until we're there, but he walked with me to my locker. I don't even know where Emma is, and I feel bad that I sort of left her. Or did she leave me? I have no idea. He leans his shoulder against Emma's locker while I open mine and get my binders for my morning classes.

"I guess it'll be easier to write it when we know what the outcome was," I add, putting my binders in my bag.

"Yeah, totally. We can even put foreshadowing into it."

I smirk at him and zip up my backpack. "Okay, so you can take care of that." I shut my locker and keep my eyes on him as I put my lock back on it. He's just smiling at me, leaning into Emma's locker, and for a minute I feel like we're friends. Like we're not just two people working on a project together, but two people who actually maybe enjoy each other's company.

"Shall we?" I ask.

"We shall." And with that, we talk to class together.

He smiles at me when he sits down at his desk and I continue to my desk farther back in the room. Gavin gives him a nod and Teague nods back, but I don't try to listen to what they're saying.

"Emma!" I say, meeting her at our lockers in between first and second. I don't need to get anything from my locker but I was hoping to catch her there before Music so I'm glad I did. "I'm so sorry I left you! I didn't even realize what I was doing, Teague was just all excited and then he was high fiving me and we were walking and talking and then we were at my locker and you were gone! I didn't mean to!"

Emma giggles. "It's okay, you didn't leave me. I left basically right after he high fived you."

"Oh. Why?"

"Because I wanted you guys to have your moment."

"We didn't have a moment," I say.

"You sort of did. He was really excited. And he was really excited to share it with you."

"Oh. Well that's nice of you, but you didn't have to do that. You can be excited with us, you know."

"I know," she says with a smile. "But I didn't want to. I wanted you to have it."

"Okay," I say slowly, still feeling like I left her behind in the halls. I mean I didn't even notice that she was gone, so a part of me feels like I'm to blame for it.

"Seriously," Emma says. "Even if you were the one who left me, I would have forgiven you."

"Really?"

"Yes! He was excited and trying to get you excited! It happens. If you started to constantly blow me off, or if you always left me in the halls, then that's a different story. But you got excited once. You're allowed to get excited about cute guys sometimes, Sadie."

"I don't think he's cute," I say, but I can feel myself blushing.

"Whatever helps you sleep at night." She winks at me and we start making our way to Music class, but there are a bunch of people talking in front of the stairwell doors. "What are you doing!?" she yells at them. "Why do you think a doorway is a good place to have a meeting!? MOVE!"

"Emma," I say, "you could just say excuse me."

"But if someone yells at them, they might think twice about gathering here again in the future. Am I right!?" She directs the last part to the group as we squeeze our way through.

Teague comes into Laser Tag to play in the arcade with his little sister that night. He smiles and gives a small wave when they walk in and I wave back, but let them do their thing. They seem disappointed that the air hockey table is turned off, but make their way over to *Dance Dance Revolution*. After about half an hour, his sister comes up to the snack counter to buy some pop and a chocolate bar for them to share. She's really shy but pretty cute, and says thanks as she takes their treats over to Teague.

"Did you tip her?" he asks.

"What's that?"

"When someone in a service job does really well, you have to tip them. With a little bit of extra money."

"Oh."

He hands her something and she comes running back up to the counter. I try to busy myself and pretend I didn't hear their conversation, but I'm not sure if it's believable or not.

"Here," she says, handing me a loonie.

"Thanks," I say, taking it from her.

I look up and see that Teague is watching, and he gives me a smile.

"You're welcome!" she says, skipping back to her brother.

It's the night before the soccer shoot-out and Teague is on his way over so that we can work on the schedule. We basically just have to pair up all the people so that the best person in each round can move on to the next one. He walks through my apartment door with Bristol board, Sharpies, foam board, glue, and Velcro, and I have to ask what he plans on using it all for.

"It's so everyone can see the standings," he says. "We'll make our own score board, basically. And we can put each person's name on Velcro, and we can move them up for each spot."

"Wow, you really put a lot of thought into this," I say.

"Yeah."

We move the coffee table out of the way and get to working on the floor of the living room.

"Did you have fun with your sister at Laser Tag the other day?" I ask after we've got a lot of the board done.

"Oh yeah, I always have a good time with her," he replies.

"Was it a special occasion?" I'm not sure how subtle I'm being but I hope he doesn't catch on to the fact that I'm trying to find out why neither of his parents were at her birthday party.

"No, we just needed to get out of the house for a bit."

"Ah." Now I'm afraid to say any more.

"Can I ask you a question?" he says.

"Sure."

"Do you remember your parents?"

I'm a little taken aback, but I've never really been asked that question before. I've been asked if I miss them, and when I am I always say I don't remember much of them, but I've never actually been asked if I remember them to begin with.

"Um," I start. "Not really."

"What do you remember?"

I lean back into the bottom of the couch that's behind me. "Well…" I take in a breath. "I remember the smell of my mom's hair when she tucked me in at night. Or I mean, at least I think I remember it. And I remember my dad's laugh. I remember it so well that I can still hear it if I think about it. And I remember this one time that I tried to pour my own cereal and I spilled the milk all over the floor and I cried, but my mom kept telling me that it was okay to spill things. The rest of the memories I'm not sure if they're real or if I made them up myself from looking at pictures and stuff. Like I feel like I remember going to Wonderland with them and meeting Sponge Bob, but I can't remember recalling it before looking at pictures of it. Every time I look at pictures or videos I want to say that I remember whatever it was, but..." He nods slowly, but doesn't reply, so I keep talking. Maybe if I open up, he will too. But there's also something about him recently that's made it easy to talk. That's made me *want* to talk. And not just to anyone, but to him.

"But I don't know," I continue. "I think I just *feel* like I remember things. But really I just remember pictures." He nods, but stays quiet, so I keep going. "You know what I remember the most?" I say.

"What?" he asks.

"I remember missing them. My biggest memory of my parents is after they already died. I remember crying a lot. I remember crying into Uncle Adam's chest, and I remember falling asleep on the couch and waking up in bed. I remember telling Adam that I wished my mom was here, that he wasn't the same as my dad, that his house wasn't the same as mine. I remember yelling at him for not being my dad. I remember feeling so alone every night that I went to bed and not letting Adam leave after he tucked me in. I don't really remember them, but I remember... I remember *remembering* them."

"That's sad."

"Yeah," I say with a sigh. "It is." I've never really thought about the fact that I don't remember them. Any time I say that to someone, they leave it at that, and it feels normal. But tonight, telling Teague the details about it makes me so sad that I almost can't breathe.

I watch quietly as Teague glues the last piece of Velcro to the last participant name. I clear my throat and hope that he can't tell I'm trying not to cry.

"Why do you ask?" I finally get the courage to say.

"I was just curious."

"Teague, if you need to talk to me about something, you can."

"I know."

But he doesn't.

Teague and I are allowed to use our Challenge and Change period to get everything set up in the Gym. The Gym classes that day even accommodate us and have Gym outside. The bleachers have already been opened and pulled out from the wall when we get there, and we're both relieved because neither of us know how to do that. We set up our board in the corner by the main doors and go together to the office to borrow one of their foldable tables.

"Oh I brought a table cloth the other day because I knew I would forget it at home today if I didn't. I'll just go to my locker and get it," Teague says.

I nod at him and set the table on its side so I can pull the legs out. He's not gone long, and before I know it, we're accepting tickets at the door and letting everyone in. Teague hands out brochures and walks around with a jar collecting extra donations while I take tickets from everyone and tell them to have fun. I tell the participants to line up against the wall opposite the bleachers and they all excitedly make their way over.

The principal hands Teague a microphone once everyone is settled in on the bleachers, and I watch him as he speaks to everyone and explains what it is we're doing. He talks about the kids in Mozambique and Niger, and what they use for soccer balls and that we're sending them brand new ones, but they have to be deflated, so we also have to send them pumps. He explains the rules, that every shoot-out is the best three out of five, but if no one wins in the first five shots, the first person to get a goal after that moves on to the next round. "Otherwise we could be here all day," he jokes. "I know, I know, you would all rather watch people kick a soccer ball around all day than go to the rest of your classes, but Sadie and I won't be very popular with the teachers if we let that happen." Everyone in the bleachers laughs and all I can think about is how nice it is when he uses my real name. It sounds so lovely coming off his tongue.

Teague calls the first two participants over and they wave to the audience before Teague asks one of them to pick heads or tails. He flips a quarter and the first person is chosen to start. The first person takes their first shot and gets it in the top left corner of the net. They take turns taking shots and when they've each taken their five shots, we have the first winner. I move the first name on our board to the next round, and then we call the next pair of participants. Summer is in this round and she smiles at me as she walks up.

"Good job guys," she says to us. "This is amazing."

"Thanks," I say.

It's really fun to hear everyone cheer when someone makes a goal, and I smile every time I move someone to the next round. The bell signaling the end of the period goes off, and some people get up and leave, but most people stay, which makes me happy. I see some people pull food from their bags and eat it on the bleachers while they continue to watch, and some people not even bother. I spot Emma sneaking her way back in halfway through lunch, carrying a small thing of fries.

"Here," she says. "I thought you might be hungry."

"You're the best," I say.

"I know." She smiles and shrugs, and heads back to the bleachers.

I take a step back and start eating the warm fries, and Teague takes a few without asking, but I don't mind.

We finally come to the final two players when there's about twenty minutes left of the lunch period. And it's Summer against

Carter! Summer wins the coin toss and chooses for Carter to go first. He takes his first shot but the soccer coach deflects it with both his hands. Summer grabs the ball and puts it on the floor in front of her, kicks it gently between her feet a few times before dribbling it ahead a little bit and then shooting it just above his head. His hands miss it by centimetres and everyone cheers once the ball goes in. Carter smiles and shakes his head, takes his shot and gets it in the top right corner of the net. Summer's turn next. She tries to deke him but Mr. Reynolds isn't having it; he blocks it easily and throws the ball back out for Carter to take his next turn.

They've both taken their five shots and each have gotten in only one goal. This is it. Down to the wire. Whoever gets the next shot in, wins. And because Summer chose for Carter to go first, this may be how she loses. He takes his shot and hits the post! I want to cheer, but that's not cool, and I hold it in. Summer might win this! She takes in a deep breath, closes her eyes as she lets it out, and then runs towards the net with the ball. She does a double deke and confuses the goalie just enough to slip it right past his left leg and into the net. Everyone left in the bleachers stands up and cheers, and I run over to Summer to give her a hug, but Carter is already doing that. I stay back and let him congratulate her, and I'm happy to see that he seems to have a genuine smile on his face.

"We're amazing!" Teague says, coming up to me and giving me a hug.

I'm a little taken aback at first; I wasn't expecting him to actually hug me, but I let myself relax and squeeze my arms around him..

"I know, right!?" I screech, as I let go and pull back from him.

Everyone starts filing out of the gym, but Summer comes over to find us, Carter closer behind her.

"So?" she asks excitedly. "Do I get a soccer jersey or something?"

"Yes," I say with a bit of a laugh. "But not yet, because you get to pick the team and player name. We'll order it for you."

♥♥♥♡♡

"Does your fourth period teacher know that you'll be late?" Teague asks as we start taking down the soccer net.

"I have a spare," I say.

"Oh, lucky."

"You don't have a spare this semester?"

"No," he says. "All my classes got messed up this year. I'm not even taking any of the classes I wanted."

"What? Why not?"

"I had a bunch of conflicting classes. I couldn't take Advanced Fitness because it was at the same as Challenge and Change, and I couldn't take Metal Tech because it was at the same time as University Math. I had to take a two-credit class last semester and that only counts as one credit when you're applying to university, and it was just this huge mess. So I don't have a spare this semester." He shakes his head and pulls the netting off the rods of the net.

"So what are you going to do? I mean you have the right credits to graduate, right?"

"Yeah," he sighs. "But I'll probably do a victory lap and take the classes I couldn't take this year."

"But wouldn't you just want to go away to school?" I ask.

"I don't know if I can. Go away for it, I mean. I don't mind staying here, at least for a year while I figure it all out. Lots of people do victory laps; it's no big deal."

"Of course it isn't a big deal. I'm not going to school right away, either. I'm taking a gap year to work."

He stops with the net and smiles at me. "Oh yeah?"

"Yeah."

It doesn't take us too long to finish clearing everything away, and Teague hands me the jar of donations. "You can count it if you want."

"Sure," I take the jar from him and watch him leave the gym.

"See you on Tuesday, Zed. Have a good Easter." He turns back just a little as he walks.

"Yeah, you too."

I go to find Emma so she doesn't have to be alone for the rest of fourth period, but all I can focus on is that I completely forgot it was Easter this weekend. I would have come to school on Friday only to find the doors locked and no one around. Or I guess I would have gone to pick up Emma and she would have been really confused as to why I was at her house so early on a day off.

"I forgot that it's Easter this weekend," I say when I find her in the caf.

"Really? But aren't you doing something with your family?"

"I guess not," I say. "Adam hasn't mentioned anything."

"Well don't you usually go to your grandparents?"

"Yeah," I say slowly. "Maybe Adam doesn't want to go without Mat?"

"Your grandparents know they broke up, right?"

"Yeah," I say. "I mean I think they do. Adam's parents know for sure. I think."

"You sound really sure about that," Emma jokes.

"Well they have to. I mean, I haven't talked to them in a while, so I don't know... I actually haven't talked to any of my grandparents in a while."

"Maybe you should."

"Yeah but I can't be like 'hey grandma, have you talked to your son recently? Did he tell you that he's single now?' That's his business to tell, not mine."

♥ ♥ ♥ ♡ ♡

Adam's just getting home at the same time I am, and we meet in front of the elevator.

"Hey!" I say.

"Hey! How did your soccer thing go today?"

"It was amazing! So many people came, and we got extra donations, and I think everyone had fun."

"Ah, that's awesome!"

The elevator pings and we both go inside, but then Adam's phone pings too. He looks at it and frowns. He looks at me, then back to his phone, then back to me.

"Hmm," he says.

"What?" I ask.

"It's Mat."

"Really?" I say a little too excitedly. "What did he say?"

"He wants to know if he can take you to his parents' for Easter on Sunday. He wanted to ask me first before he asked you."

"Oh," I say, my heart thumping against my ribcage. The elevator opens and we both walk to our apartment. I'm too shaky to unlock the door and I'm glad that Adam does it first.

"Just oh?" he asks. "Don't you want to?"

"Well, I mean…"

He looks at me like he's waiting for me to continue, but then his phone pings again and he sighs a little when he reads it. "Oh," he says, and then he laughs a little as he continues. "He says he's hoping it's okay with me since I've been okay with you guys hanging out already."

No. No no no. This can't be happening. This isn't how I wanted it to go. I wanted to tell him, I wanted him to hear it from me, not like I was keeping a secret. I mean, I was keeping a secret, but I didn't want it to come across that way. Everything is spinning and I need to sit down. I slip my shoes off and make my way to the couch, but when I see Adam sit on the other couch I notice that he's crying. I made him cry. Why am I such a terrible person?

"I'm sorry," I say with a cracking voice. "I wanted to tell you but I didn't know how you would take it and I didn't want to hurt your feelings and I'm-"

But he cuts me off. "Why are you sorry?"

His question catches me off guard and I'm not sure what to say. "Because. Because I just said-"

"Why do you think that seeing your uncle is something you need to keep from me?" Even though his eyes are teary, his voice is pretty strong and confident.

"I don't… I don't know."

He wipes his eyes with his hands but then he starts to cry a little harder. He takes a shaky breath and lets it out slowly, keeping his head down so I can't see his face. I haven't seen him cry many times and seeing it happen now is hurting me. If he's okay with me seeing Mat then why is he crying? What's bothering him so much?

"I can't believe it didn't even cross my mind," he says through a crack in his voice.

"What?" I ask.

"Of course you would want to see him. He helped raise you. Just because we broke up shouldn't mean that you don't get to see him anymore. He's- He's just as much your uncle as I am." He wipes at his face again and takes in another deep breath, and this time it doesn't seem to quiver when he lets it out. I can still tell in his voice that he's trying not to keep crying, though. "I'm such a terrible parent. I can't believe that even after you asked me if I was okay, I didn't ask if you were okay. I didn't ask you if you wanted to go see him. It didn't even occur to me. I was just wrapped up in my own blanket of grief about it that I didn't stop to see what you wanted. God, Sadie, I'm so sorry. I'm sorry that I made you feel like you needed to keep Mat a secret from me. I'm sorry." He puts his face in his hands and sobs a little.

I slowly get up from the couch and make my way to him and sit down next to him.

"I'm sorry I thought you couldn't handle it," I say quietly.

He laughs a little bit and I put my arms around him.

"You're not a bad parent," I add.

"I'm the worst," he says quietly.

"No you're not. I don't know what I would do without you."

"Oh please, you don't need me. You could make it so far on your own. I'm a wreck. I don't know how to be a dad!"

"Well it's a good thing you're my uncle," I say.

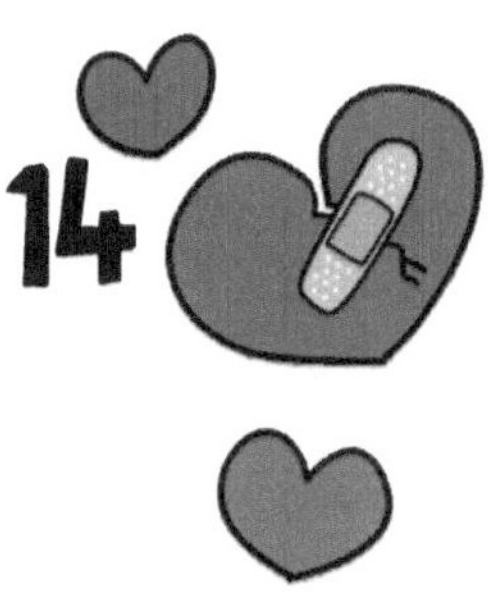

Adam gets his sniffles out of the way and we end up watching the rest of our show. After the last episode ends and Netflix starts playing trailers for other movies and TV shows, Adam squeezes my leg a little and I look over at him.

"So do you want to have Easter with Mat then?" he asks quietly.

"Not if you don't want me to," I reply.

"What's that supposed to mean? Of course I want you to. If you want to."

"I only want to if you want me to," I say.

"Stop that. I think you should continue to see Mat any way that you would have if we were still together. If we were your dads instead, we would be working out times for you to see him. This is no different."

I want to say that I had been thinking that myself earlier, but I don't say anything because I don't want to tell him that I had been confused about it.

"Yeah, okay," I say. "That makes sense. I just don't want to leave you here on your own," I say.

"Don't worry about me, I'll be fine."

"Will you go to Grandma and Grandad's?" I ask.

"They never invited me, so they must not be doing anything this year."

"You could still go see them. They're your parents."

"It's alright. I'll give them a call, how's that?"

"I think they would appreciate it if you stopped by."

He smiles and gets up from the couch. "What do you want for supper?"

I let him avoid the topic and suggest that we make spaghetti. I haven't had spaghetti in forever. He agrees and I get up from the couch to help him in the kitchen. I get the water boiling while Adam starts cooking beef to put in the sauce. We just have sauce from a jar, but it'll do just fine. We joke around the whole time and laugh and act like goofs, but I can't help but wonder if this is all an act that Adam is putting on. If he's trying to act like he's happy for my sake.

"I don't have to go see Uncle Mat," I finally say as I stir the pasta.

"Why not? Why wouldn't you want to see him?"

"I do want to see him," I say, "but I don't want you to be hurting."

"Why would that hurt me?"

I just shrug.

"Sadie, I'm not going to deny you from seeing him. In fact, I encourage it. I *want* you to see him."

"But you're still sad. And you were so sad and trying not to show it, that you didn't think of the fact that we would still want to see each other."

He sighs and tilts his head back a bit. "I knowww," he drags the word out in a bit of a whine. "I feel terrible. I don't want you to think that I don't care about you, or that I'm putting my own feelings ahead of yours."

"I know, and I'm not upset about that. And I don't think you're putting your feelings first, I just want you to be okay. I don't want you to be trying so hard at *acting* okay that it's making you not okay."

He's quiet and he looks at the pot of pasta on the stove. I can tell he's trying not to cry again and I'm not sure what to do. I don't want him to cry. I don't want him to have to cry in front of me, because even though I don't think it's embarrassing, I think he might be embarrassed about it anyway. He's not only my uncle, but he's my legal guardian, he's basically my parent, and he's supposed to have it together. No, that came out wrong. He doesn't have to have anything together; he's a human being and he's allowed to have moments, days, hell, even weeks. He's allowed to be a mess. He's allowed to not know what to do, or how to feel, but because he's basically my parent, I get the impression that he thinks he's not allowed to have those things. Media and magazines and famous people and all that show that if you're a parent, or even over 25 years old, you should have it together. You should know what you want in life or own your own business or be the manager of something, or have three kids who are all perfect and go to private school. I know these are all ridiculous things, and as a seventeen-year-old I feel like I will never have any of that. I feel like I will never be able to achieve any kind of greatness and show it off gracefully. But if I had a younger person in my life I was trying to set an example for, I wouldn't want to cry in front of them, or make mistakes in front of them. I would want them to think I'm perfect. I wouldn't want them to think that I have no idea what I'm doing, because then maybe they wouldn't trust me, or take me seriously. But I know that's not true. I would never think less of Adam for showing his emotions, or letting them get the best of him sometimes. Never.

But there is something stopping me from saying that out loud to him.

I turn the stove off and grab the pot to drain the spaghetti. The steam hurts my hands as I pour it all into the strainer and I drop it all into the sink. Most of it lands in the strainer, but then the pot tips the strainer over and all the spaghetti goes everywhere.

I step back and squeal as I shake my hands out, and Adam grabs the pot and puts it on an element of the stove that's turned off.

"Dammit," I say, but tears are already on their way and I feel like I can't hold anything in. "I ruined it," I cry.

"No you didn't," Adam says confidently, grabbing the spaghetti from the sink and putting it in the strainer.

"It's all over the sink," I blubber.

"The sink is clean, Sadie, it's fine." Once he has all the pasta in the strainer, he turns the water on and swishes it around a bit.

"I ruin everything," I mumble as I leave the kitchen and head to my room.

"Sadie," Adam says with a sigh. "Come back, it's fine!"

I have no idea why spilled spaghetti is bothering me so much and now that I'm alone in my room, I can't stop crying. I'm not alone for long though, because Adam makes his way in less than two minutes later.

"Sadie," he says slowly. "What's up?"

"I ruined dinner!" I grab my comforter and bunch it up in my arms so I can hug it.

"You did not ruin dinner. And even if you did, this can't be what's bothering you."

I sniffle and take in a shaky breath, looking for my stuffed narwhal. He's usually in my covers somewhere, or under my bed, but I can't find him. I hang off the edge of the mattress and look under the bed frame but he's not there, so I start fluffing up the blanket, hoping he'll fall out of it, but he's not here.

"What are you doing?" he asks.

"I'm looking for Whally!" I cry.

Uncle Adam smiles just the tiniest bit, and walks over to my bed. I watch him, confused, as he gets closer, but then he leans over me and grabs him off my pillow from right behind me.

"Oh," I say quietly as he puts him in my lap. I squeeze him against my chest and press my face into him a little bit.

"So what's going on?" Adam asks again, gently sitting on the edge of my bed.

"I told you," I say, but I'm not sure how well he can understand me because I'm talking directly into Whally's head, his horn sticking up beside my cheek.

"We both know this is not about the spaghetti," he says gently. "Is it about me and Mat? Or me? I don't want to put any pressure on you about this weekend and I'm sure if Mat thought that would happen, he never would have asked."

"It's not that," I whisper.

"Then what?"

I take in a deep breath and hold it for three seconds. I pull my face up from my narwhal stuffy and look at Adam. My breath is shaky as I let it out, and I feel like I'm going to cry even harder if I say out loud what seems to be on my mind. I guess it's been on my mind since I talked to Teague about it yesterday, but it's been in the background and I haven't let myself actually think about it. But it's been there, asking to be thought about, talked about, but I didn't want to. I don't want to. It makes it too real if I talk about it.

"I don't remember Mom and Dad," I finally say.

"What?" He shifts closer to me, pulling his legs under him on the bed. "Of course you do, why would you say that?"

"Because I don't!" There it is. I'm crying again. "I don't think any of my memories of them are real. They're manufactured, from stories you've told me, or from pictures and videos I've seen."

Adam lets out a deep breath and looks away for a couple seconds. "Maybe that's true," he starts. "But you were little when they died."

"I know… But I wish that when I thought about them, I could actually have things to think about."

"Do you think you would be less sad if you could remember more of them? Or do you think it would just make you miss them more deeply?"

"I don't know," I say with a bit of a shrug. "I'm sure they didn't want me to have no memory of them. That's terrible."

"Of course they wouldn't want that. But they also wouldn't want you to be sad."

"I'm sure they also didn't want to die. Just like you didn't want me to come live with you."

He pulls back a little bit. "Excuse me?"

"I completely overhauled your life."

"Well to be fair, my brother and his wife overhauled my life. But I don't like that word. Changed, yes. Of course. But not in a bad way. I couldn't imagine my life without you."

"But you didn't want a kid."

"So? I wanted *you*."

"That's not what you told Mat."

"What?"

I squeeze Whally a little tighter and dare to say the next words. "I heard you," I say quietly. "You told Uncle Mat that you didn't even want me."

"Oh Sadie," he says, moving closer to me again. "That's not... I didn't mean it like that. And also we were fighting, and I was upset... I didn't... I didn't mean it like that, not at all."

I nod, because of course I know that. I know. I just want to hear it from him. "What did you mean, then?"

"I meant..." he sighs, thinks about his answer. "I meant that I never planned for you. I never had children in my life plans, it was never something I particularly wanted in my life. But I love you, I've loved you since the first second that I held you.

"And you know you almost went to live with your grandparents because they thought that I was too young and not prepared enough to take care of a child? But I was twenty-four, it's not like I was a teenager. And it's true; I wasn't prepared. I had a studio apartment, I worked two retail jobs because I couldn't get full time anywhere, and I had only been with Mat for eight months at the time. I had no idea what I was doing. I was afraid. I was afraid that I would mess up your life, but at the same time, I couldn't imagine not being there for it. I couldn't let my *parents* raise you. I knew I was the better choice, even if I didn't want to have kids. I didn't want to have kids, but you were different. I already sort of had you."

I'm still crying, but the tears are silent now, and mixed with some happy relief.

"I just meant that it was never something that had crossed my mind," he continues. "The thought scared me, it scared me so much, and I was afraid that I wouldn't have the right time for you, or that I wouldn't know how to talk to you about serious things. But I wanted you specifically, more than I wanted my own kid, because you needed me. And in a way, I needed you too. I lost people too, when your parents died."

I wipe my tears on Whally and nod. "I'm sorry," I say.

"For what?"

"That your brother died."

He gives me a small smile. "Thanks. But I never *didn't* want you, Sadie. Please don't ever think that I didn't want you. I know I used those words, but I swear that was not my intent. I wasn't thinking clearly. Also, I'm sorry that you heard that. I didn't know you were home. You said you weren't home."

"I lied," I say softly. "I didn't want you to know… that I heard."

He chuckles quietly and leans in to give me a hug. Whally is squished between us, and when we pull away, Adam takes him from me and gives him a squeeze.

"I always liked this thing," he says.

"You lived in a studio apartment?" I ask, ignoring his comment about the stuffy.

"Yeah, you don't remember?"

I shake my head.

"You slept in my bed and I slept on the couch, although…" he pauses, tilts his head from side to side a little bit. "We did share the bed an awful lot the first month or so. You didn't like me so much when it was time to eat, or have a bath, or go to school, it was always 'mom does it like this,' and 'dad lets me do this,' but at night… night time was hard, for the both of us."

I take Whally back from him and he relinquishes him easily. "I remember that," I murmur. "But I don't remember it being in a different apartment."

"You don't remember looking at apartments with Mat and me?" he asks. "You liked doing that. 'oh please, Uncle Adam, let's get this one!' you'd say. For every one that we saw. Every one. We thought at first about keeping your parents' house but we thought it might be too hard to move on. We thought maybe if there was less reminder, it would be easier for all of us. Maybe that wasn't a great idea. Maybe if we didn't sell the house you would have stronger memories of them. There would be things tied to it."

"I remember…" I say, suddenly seeing boxes, and knowing that I've had this memory before. An apartment, this apartment, but bigger, empty, floor and walls and ceiling that go on forever, with boxes all over. Boxes piled and stacked, and me hiding behind them, trying to push them around the room but not being strong enough. Adam and Mat jumping over them, leaning across them to kiss as they emptied them. "I remember moving into this apartment."

"Yeah?" he says with a soft smile.

I nod and smile back. "My timelines are all messed up though, I always thought that happened first. But I think it was a good choice. Selling the house. Instead of letting me hold on to things I could never really touch anymore, I got to reach for new things. Plus I still have Whally."

"Yes," he says. "That's what counts."

"Well, if supper wasn't ruined before, it definitely is now."

"You're so dramatic," Adam says. "The pasta is rinsed and covered and the sauce is keeping warm on the stove. Supper is fine."

Uncle Mat meets me downstairs on Sunday morning and gives me a hug in the lobby. It feels good seeing him now, knowing that everyone is okay with it. Knowing that I'm not sneaking around and keeping secrets, or worrying about how everyone else will feel.

There's a box of Timbits in the car already, even though the drive to Mamie and Papi's house is only an hour. I'm not hungry, but I open it as soon as we pull onto the road and eat a chocolate one.

"Hand me a sour cream glazed," Mat says, holding his hand out. I oblige and take one for myself as well. "So you kept a secret, did you?" he asks after swallowing his Timbit.

"What?"

"Adam told me."

"I didn't know you guys were talking again," I say.

Mat shrugs. "We're not. But after I asked him about today, I guess it was pretty natural for him to bring it up. You know you didn't have to do that, right?"

"Yes," I say with a bit of a sigh.

"Okay, good. Now hand me a honey dip."

"Hand you a honey dip, what?" I ask.

"Hand me a honey dip right this second." He smiles and holds out his hand again.

"You need to learn some manners, sir."

"I do? Me? Really? Whatever for?"

"Well, for a Timbit, for starters."

He laughs, and I hand him a honey dip.

It's really nice seeing Mamie and Papi, and it's only a little awkward when they ask me about Uncle Adam and my Grandma and Grandad. I tell them I'm pretty sure he's having dinner with them, but he wasn't decided by the time I left. They tell me to give him their best, and I say I will, but I just wish they could do it themselves. It's terrible that because two people break up, they don't get to see so many people anymore. Mat can't see Grandma and Grandad anymore, because they're not his parents, they're Adam's parents, and now Adam can't see Mamie and Papi, because they're Mat's parents. But they were a part of each other's lives for so long, and just because Adam and Mat aren't a part of each other's lives anymore, a bunch of other family members have to take part in that too.

I'm surprised when all the stops are pulled out for lunch, and wonder how I'm going to have enough room for supper. But as we're eating the ham and scalloped potatoes, and I try not to be annoyed every time they slip into French conversation, I clue in that we aren't doing dinner. And as we leave their house at three in the afternoon, I realize that maybe Mat has something else planned.

"Ok so I have some exciting news," Mat says as we pull out of the driveway.

"What?" I ask.

"I got a dog."

"What!?" I screech. "When!? How!? Where?"

Mat laughs a little. "A friend of a friend on Facebook actually just got this dog, but then she found out that she's pregnant and she doesn't want to raise her first baby with a young dog. The good part for me is that he's already house trained and knows how to sit and come."

"Wow," I say. "That's so exciting! It's sad for them, though. I'm sure they could raise a baby and a dog."

"Oh yeah, of course they could. But they don't want to. And that's fine, too. And I would love a dog."

"More than you want a kid?"

"No, not more than I want a kid. But adopting can be a long process."

"Are you going to wait to adopt until you get another boyfriend, or are you going to do it yourself?"

"Well I've already started filling out application forms, so I guess I'm not waiting to get another boyfriend."

"Do you want another boyfriend?" I ask.

He's quiet for a minute before he answers. "Eventually."

♥♥♥♡♡

We pull into the driveway of a brick bungalow and Mat smiles at me as he undoes his seatbelt. We get out of the car and walk together up to the front door. Mat rings the doorbell and it's answered less than a minute later by a tall woman with dark, wispy hair.

"Hey," she says. "Come in, come in. This must be Sadie."

"Yeah, hi," I say a little sheepishly.

"I'm Kara. Pasta's out back."

"Pasta?" I ask. "The dog's name is Pasta?"

"Yeah," she says. "My husband thought of it, and I thought it was cute."

I can hear the little barks as we walk through to the back of the house, and I almost squeal when we step outside and I see a light-furred Corgi. Oh my goodness gracious, Pasta is a corgi! This is the best day ever! Scalloped potatoes *and* a corgi!?

"Pasta, come!" Kara says, making him look up from his play time with the man who must be her husband. He runs over to us and because he's still small, but clearly on his way to growing up, he's excited and clumsy. Mat and I both bend down to pet him, but any time our hands go near him he tries to lick us. He spins around and yelps happily, trying to lick our hands instead of letting us pet his soft fur. He ends up climbing into Mat's lap and eventually calms down, letting him stroke his back. I pet his head and after a few minutes, he's fast asleep.

"I think he likes you," Kara says, wiping a tear away.

"No, he loves me," Mat says.

"Oh, yes, sorry. He loves you." She smiles, and starts walking into the house. Mat gets up, keeping a hold of Pasta in his arms as he follows her.

"Thank you for this," Kara says at Mat's car.

"No, thank you."

"No really, I was worried about finding him a good home. I know he'll be happy with you."

Kara's husband comes out of the house with a big bag of dog food in one hand and a plastic kennel in the other.

"How much for the food and stuff?" Mat asks.

"Oh don't worry about it," Kara's husband says. "You're doing us a really big favour."

We transfer Pasta to my lap so Mat can drive home, and he wakes up, but must still be sleepy because he stays calm for most of the drive. When we're about twenty minutes away from town, Pasta is up and looking out the window and barking at cars and people as we pass. I keep a gentle hold of him so he doesn't jump around the car, and we both laugh.

The backyard of the basement apartment Mat lives in is free for him to use and he made sure he can have the dog out there, so we immediately throw a ball for Pasta once we get there. The yard is fenced, which is perfect because he will only need a leash for walks. We stay in the backyard and play with Pasta until seven in the evening, and then we bring all of the dog's stuff inside. There is a leash and some toys inside the kennel, so we take them out and find a spot in the bedroom for it. We hang the leash up by the door and then take Pasta with us for the drive back to my place.

"You can come visit him any time you want," Mat says before I get out of the car.

"You mean I can come visit *you* any time I want," I correct.

"Well, yeah. But maybe you can drive over and keep him company after school some days, until I get home from work. Emma can come too."

"Okay, well any day that I have the car, I will come visit Pasta. And maybe I can stay for dinner before going home?"

"That sounds great," Mat says.

❤❤❤♡♡

I'm afraid to tell Uncle Adam about Pasta because I don't want him to think that Mat is moving on so quickly, but then I realize that I'm doing the exact same thing as when I wouldn't tell him about seeing Mat.

"How was it?" Adam asks when I step through the door.

"It was good. Mat got a dog."

"Really? I thought he wanted a kid." He sounds a little bitter when he says it, but I don't think he means for it to show.

"He does. He's already started applying to adopt. But his friend needed someone to take her dog, and you know, he's lonely, so…"

Adam nods and smiles. "What kind of dog is it?"

"A corgi!"

"Cute," he says with a smile that actually seems genuine. "Like Cheddar from *Brooklyn Nine-Nine*."

"Yeah," I say. "And guess what his name is!"

"Mozzarella," he tries.

"Pasta!"

"Ha. That's adorable."

"I know."

"That's good. I'm happy for him. I hope he gets what he wants."

"Me too," I say slowly.

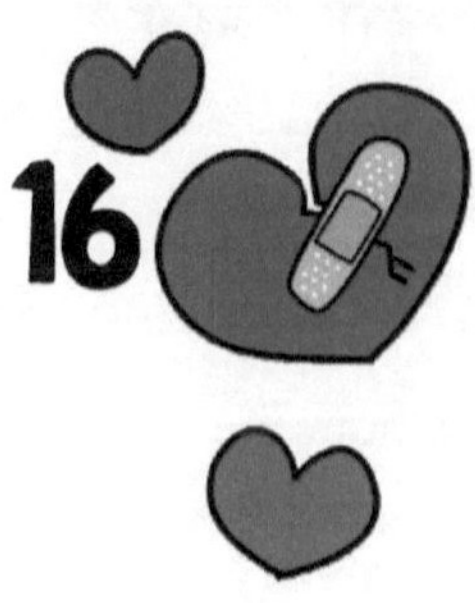

16

I pick Emma up for school on Tuesday morning and tell her all about my weekend, minus my weird breakdown over spilling spaghetti in the sink. I don't tell her about my conversation with Adam, but I tell her about Sunday with Mat and all about Pasta.

"Ugh, I'm jealous," she says, leaning her head back into the seat behind her. "I played board games with the family all weekend. All. Weekend. All weekend, Sadie! It was my parents, my brother, and my grandparents, all weekend, playing Monopoly and Risk."

"You didn't play anything else?" I ask.

"Oh sorry, we also played Clue."

I shrug. "It doesn't sound too terrible."

"It wouldn't have been if it was a Friday night, but it was all! Weekend!"

I chuckle. "Okay, I guess that would get pretty boring. Did you guys have a nice dinner? Or eat Easter chocolate or anything?"

"Yeah we had Turkey and mashed potatoes, so that was good. Anyway, can we go see this dog after school?"

"Yes," I say with a smile. "Mat gave me a key to his apartment so we can go right after school and let ourselves in. Maybe we can take him for a walk!"

"Oooh, yes, let's!"

Teague pulls his chair over to my desk as soon as we're instructed to work on our projects during first period. We already did our event, so now we have to figure out actually getting the soccer balls and shipping them to a whole other continent.

"So I called the sport store in town and they said they would give us a discount on soccer balls," Teague says.

"Really? That's awesome."

"Yeah, it's great. Also we should be able to pick up Summer's jersey tomorrow, so do you want to go together after school? We can stop for food on the way if you want. We can get something that you approve of putting ketchup on." He winks at me and my stomach flutters a little bit.

"Oh, I approve of putting ketchup on very few food items," I say.

"So no ketchup on Kraft Dinner?" he asks.

I shake my head. "No! It's so cheesy and delicious already, why would you ruin it with ketchup?"

"Why do you think ketchup ruins everything, Zed? And it's not real cheese, you know that, right?"

"Let's just work on this," I say, trying not to laugh.

"What do you like to put ketchup on?" he asks.

"Teague, get out your notes."

"Will you put ketchup on a burger? On hotdogs? Regular fries?"

"Teague," I say.

"What? I'm just trying to understand you."

"You will never understand me," I say with a smile.

Emma practically runs to Adam's car after school because she's so excited to meet Pasta. I'm excited to see him again, but for some reason I seem to be slightly less enthusiastic about it.

"Come on!" she calls, after making it to the car before me. "Let's go! It's puppy time!"

I laugh and unlock the doors with the fob so she can get in before I make it there. I slide into the driver's seat and look at Emma, who is bouncing in her seat. "You'll have to calm yourself when we get there or he's going to go bonkers," I say.

She just grins. "Excellent."

♥♥♥♡♡

As soon as I open the door to Mat's apartment, Pasta starts barking, but it's definitely an excited bark. We take our shoes off and make our way into Mat's room where his kennel is. He waits while I open the door and let him out and then he spins around and wags his tail as we pet him.

"Do you want to go for a walk?" I ask him.

He barks and runs around the room, making Emma and I both laugh.

"Come on, then," I say, walking back to the front door.

He follows us and I grab his leash. He sits right away and I attach it to his collar, and then we put our shoes back on, and we're off! Walking the adorable, not quite grown up corgi! He does a pretty good job of not pulling, but I have to tug on the leash a few times and tell him to heel, although I'm not sure if he's learned 'heel' yet. I say it every time I tug on the leash and hope he catches on. He looks up at us with his mouth open as he trots along beside us and he's basically the most adorable thing I've ever seen.

We walk him for about forty minutes but he's still really energetic when we get back. He runs around the apartment about three times when we get inside, but then he plops down on the floor against the couch curls up in a little ball. Emma and I both watch him for a few minutes as he falls asleep and then turn on the TV so we can watch something while we wait for Mat to come home.

I texted Uncle Mat and told him that Emma and I were there, so he brings Pizza home on his way back from work. We eat it together at the kitchen counter peninsula, which I really like. I've always wanted a peninsula or an island in the kitchen, especially one you can eat at. We hang out for a little bit after we're done eating, but Emma announces that she has homework, so we say our goodbyes and I drive her home.

"Mat seems pretty happy," she says in the car.

"Yeah, I think he is," I reply.

"That's good."

"The dog helps, I'm sure," I say.

"And probably the fact that he's seeing you again," Emma adds.

I just shrug as I drive.

"I'm serious," she says.

♥ ♥ ♥ ♡ ♡

"You ready, Zed?" Teague asks, coming up behind me at my locker on Wednesday.

"Yup," I say. I turn to Emma and say bye to her, and she pouts over dramatically to make me feel bad for making her take the bus by herself. I shake my head and smile at her as we both leave.

"Do you put ketchup on your eggs?" Teague asks as we head down the stairwell.

"Ew no," I reply.

"You're no fun! Do you not put ketchup on anything?"

"I put it on normal things, like hamburgers and hotdogs."

"Everything else is normal, too," he says defensively, but in a joking way.

"I like ketchup chips, does that count?"

"No, that does not count. Ketchup chips don't even taste like ketchup."

"Sure they do," I say. We step outside and I blink as some random rain drops fall on my face and get under my glasses. We walk a bit quicker through the parking lot and once we get to the car, it starts to downpour.

He narrows his eyes at me after doing up his seatbelt. "You only like Lays ketchup chips, right?"

"Ketchup Pringles are good, too," I say.

"Okay, I'll accept." He starts the car and backs out of his space. I'm glad that he's the one driving, because I would be having a panic attack right now if I had to navigate my way through this rain.

"I would have been okay even if you didn't accept," I say.

"Fine then I don't," he laughs. "You wanna get food on the way there or the way back?"

"The way back," I say. "'Cause then it'll be like a celebration of sorts."

"Of sorts," Teague mocks.

We run through the parking lot and into the closest entrance of the mall and continue to joke around about putting ketchup on food as we wander the quiet halls to find the store.

"Wow this mall is really dead during the week," Teague says.

"Maybe everyone's afraid to go out in the rain."

"Yeah," he says, "maybe."

The soccer jersey looks amazing, and it looks like it'll fit Summer great. The guy behind the counter puts it in a bag for us and tells us that we did a great job coming up with our project idea. He said his boss was really excited about it as soon as Teague called, and he immediately checked to see what kind of donations budget he was allotted from head office. Teague smiles and lets the clerk tell him the story even though he already knows it. I know it too, but Teague didn't relay it to me in as much detail as this guy is doing, so I enjoy it too.

There's a restaurant in the mall so we decide to just go eat there before heading home. Maybe the rain will die down while we're eating. I'm not super hungry for some reason so I get chicken fingers and a Caesar salad, while Teague gets chicken parmesan. We don't say much while we wait for the food to come, but it doesn't feel weird or awkward. I actually enjoy looking at him from across the table.

"What?" he finally asks.

"Nothing," I say.

He squints at me. "Doesn't seem like nothing."

I raise my shoulders a little and lean back into my chair. "Well it is."

I swear I never thought he was cute before. Even when we were friends when we were kids, it was never something that crossed my mind. And even throughout high school, I thought girls only had crushes on him because he was popular. I didn't think it was because they actually thought he was good looking. But now that I've gotten to know him more and I actually find myself getting excited to hang out with him, and joke with him, I dunno. He's cute now. Is that a normal thing? To think someone is cute later? Does that happen to everyone?

It's still raining when we're done eating and making our way back to the car with the soccer jersey, but it's not as bad as it was a few hours earlier. We still run to the car to avoid getting as wet as possible, and shake out our chills once we're inside.

"Summer's going to be stoked about the jersey," Teague says.

"Yeah, it's really nice quality," I agree. "I was afraid when you said the store was donating one that it was going to be a cheap, crappy one or something."

"Me too, to be honest."

An *Infinity Pool* song comes on the radio so I lean forward and turn the stereo up a little bit. Teague sings quietly to it, but I don't have the guts to do the same. I hum a little to the chorus, but that's all I can allow myself to do.

"Oh shoot, can you do me a favour?" Teague asks when the song is over.

"Sure," I say.

"Can you draw me some insulin?"

"*What?*" I ask.

"I left it in the car so I couldn't take it in the restaurant unless I came all the way out here to get it."

"So, you could have taken it before we left."

"Yeah, but I didn't. Come on, it's easy, I'll walk you through it."

"And then what, you're just going to give yourself a needle while you're driving?"

"No, you're going to do it."

"*What?*" I say again.

"Come on, Zed, please?"

"I'm not giving you a needle while you're driving."

"Why not?"

"Because what if I make you crash!?"

"Why would you make me crash?" he asks.

"Because I'm poking you with a needle!?"

"So? It doesn't even hurt and there's no way you can mess it up; the needles are so small." He grabs his little pouch from the cup holder and hands it to me.

"No," I say, refusing to take it. "I can't. Plus I can't draw the insulin, I don't know how to do it!"

"I'll tell you. Please? It's so easy."

"You only think it's easy because you've been doing it since you were eight, Teauge!"

"Okay, fine." He puts the pouch back in the cup holder and checks his side mirror. He turns on the blinker before checking his blind spot and pulling over.

"What are you doing?" I ask.

He puts the car into park and turns his four-ways on. "I'm doing it myself. I can't do it myself while I'm driving, Zwicker, that's why I asked you to do it."

"I'm sorry," I say quietly.

"Why?"

"I don't know."

He smirks his weird little half-smirk that I now think is ridiculously cute, and unzips his pouch. He pokes his finger and puts a drop of blood on his little blue meter, and then puts his finger in his mouth, sucking away the rest of the blood. I can imagine the metallic taste and I shiver a little at the thought.

"Can't you get one of those arm things that checks your blood for you?" I ask.

"Don't like having things attached to me, remember?"

I nod. "Right."

I watch him as he reads the result and then puts the needle into the insulin bottle.

"I'm sorry if not wanting to do it for you made you mad," I say.

He stops and looks at me, the orange needle cap between his teeth. "You think I'm mad?"

"No."

He takes the cap out of his mouth so he can speak more clearly. "Then why are you sorry? Do you think I'm bummed that I had to pull over to do it myself?"

"I don't know," I say slowly.

"You're cute," he says, and I try my hardest not to blush. "It's okay that you didn't want to do it. I just thought you wouldn't mind. And then I thought I could convince you," he continues with a growing grin. "But you're allowed to not want to give someone a needle, especially while that person is driving a car."

"Yeah, okay," I say.

He lifts his shirt to put it in his abdomen but I hold a hand out.

"Wait," I whisper.

"Yes?"

"Can I do it now?"

"Hell yeah you can," he says, handing the needle to me.

"Okay, okay," I say, getting nervous. "I don't know how to do this, where do I put it?"

He raises the sleeve of his t-shirt. "Just grab a bit of fat from my arm and shove it in there."

"What if I hurt you?"

"You won't."

I hold the needle in my right hand and lean over the middle console to grab some of his arm. It's quiet except for the sound of the rain pounding down on the roof and windshield, and the occasional car driving by. It's calming, and my heart isn't beating nearly as fast as I thought it would be.

"You're fine," he says. "Just don't put it in the muscle."

"What?" I screech, moving away. "Why not, what will that do?"

"Um, hurt like hell."

"But you just said I wouldn't hurt you!"

"You won't! As long as you don't put it in the muscle."

"Well now you're making me nervous!"

"No, I think you're making yourself nervous. Just grab a chunk of fat." He crosses his left arm over his chest and taps at his right arm. "Right here."

"You don't have much fat," I say.

"There's some right here," he says again.

"Okay." I lean closer again and bunch the fat between my fingers with my left hand. There really isn't a lot to grab, but the needle is so tiny, so I guess there doesn't really need to be much. "Right here?" I ask, and he just nods. "Okay, I'm putting it in."

"Okay," he chuckles.

I stick the needle into his arm and squeal a little bit. Oh my god. Now what? How slowly do I press the plunger down? Or am I supposed to do it quickly? Does it sting if you do it quickly? Why did I agree to this? I put my index finger on the plunger and depress it, feeling like I'm doing it a little too slowly, but I do it. I slide the needle out of his skin and let go of his arm.

"Did I do okay?" I ask, handing him the needle.

"You did amazing." He puts the cap back on, puts everything in his pouch, and checks over his shoulder before pulling back onto the road.

"Do your other friends ever do that for you?"

He laughs pretty loudly. "No," he says quickly. "Absolutely not." He stops at a red light and looks at me for a second. He looks back at the lights ahead of us, and then back to me, and I keep my eyes on him the whole time. "Besides nurses and my parents," he continues, "you're the only person who has ever done that for me."

The light turns green and I'm trying to think of what to say to him. I guess I should be flattered; it's probably a really intimate and personal thing to let someone give you a needle. He clearly asked me out of convenience so he didn't have to stop the car, but there was something about it, something about the way he looked at me when I asked if I could do it once we were parked. Did he let me do it because he likes me? Do I like him? No. Of course I don't like Teague. It's probably just not a big deal to him since he's been doing it for so long; it's like letting someone tie your shoes for you. Or maybe it isn't. I don't know.

My mind is still moving in so many directions, but when I open my mouth to reply, everything is shattering. I don't know how else to explain it, except that my head is shattering, my chest is shattering, the car windows are shattering. Everything goes black for a second, or I don't know, maybe longer, and my head is pounding, and I almost can't breathe. I try to take in a breath but my chest hurts and I have to stop, taking shallow gulps of air that don't satisfy my lungs. What happened? Did someone hit us?

"Sadie?" Teague asks. "Sadie, are you okay?"

It worries me that he's using my first name instead of his nickname for me, and I wish I could think it was endearing like when he used my name back at school. But it scares me. Am I okay? I don't think I'm okay. I try to breathe normally again but it hurts and I can feel tears pricking my eyes. I want to say something, but I'm afraid.

"Sadie," he says again, and I can hear the panic in his voice. But then I can hear sirens, and I hope that means we're going to be okay.

"Sadie, I'm right here." His hand slips into mine and I squeeze it, not wanting him to let go. "Should- Should I get out of the car?"

I want to tell him to wait for the paramedics to get here, but I can't do anything without my entire body erupting with pain. I can't even turn my head to look at him. All I can do is stare ahead at the broken windshield. I want to tell him not to leave me. I can hear myself wheezing and it scares me more than the pain of trying to breathe. His other hand gently presses against my face, and the sound of the sirens are coming closer. They're getting louder. Everything is getting louder.

"I'm right here," he says again.

"Don't leave," I manage to whisper.

"I won't, I promise. I'm right here."

"Sadie?" That voice doesn't belong to Teague and I'm worried that I've passed out. How long has it been? Am I still in the car? No. The rain is pounding down all around us, onto my face, into my mouth. I can't open my eyes because of the water in my eyelashes. Where are my glasses? But we're moving too, and then the rain stops, and I can only hear it the same way that I heard it while I was working myself up to giving Teague his insulin.

"Sadie, can you hear me?" the paramedic asks. How does she know my name?

I nod my head, and I want to answer, but all of a sudden my painful breathing seems to be so much worse. I can't breathe at all; it feels like someone is sitting on my chest, not allowing me to inhale. I grab onto her hand and she squeezes it. Her face comes into view and she gives me a soft smile that comforts me. Her dark, wet hair is falling into her face, but she seems friendly.

"I can't breathe," I rasp.

I shut my eyes tight and try to pretend that none of this is happening. I don't want to hurt anymore and I just want to be able to breathe. I feel her touching me and I hear her talking, but I can't focus on it anymore. It sounds like she's talking to someone on a walkie talkie but I can't figure out what they're saying. It's all doctor talk.

"Sadie?" The sound of my name on her calming voice brings me back a little bit. I open my eyes again. "Sadie, your lung collapsed," she says. "The doctor can fix that when we get to the hospital, but I'm going to put a needle in your chest so it's easier for you to breathe, okay?"

I try to nod but I have a neck brace on, so I can't. I don't think she was looking for permission anyway, just letting me know.

"Okay, little pinch," she says.

I would call it more than a little pinch, and for a second I think I won't be able to handle it. I don't know what to do. I don't know what's happening. What happened? Did someone go through a red light? Teague didn't, I saw the light turn green. I saw it turn green before he moved into the intersection, so it isn't Teague's fault. He didn't do it. But before I can finish my thoughts, I can breathe. I couldn't breathe before, and now I can, and something about it feels weird, but I'm breathing, and it's amazing, and even though I'm still in pain, I can *breathe*, and suddenly I don't feel as scared.

I feel wobbly when I wake up in the hospital. My head is filled with cotton and a wet wheezing sound seems to be perfectly in sync with each breath that I take. The rest of the ambulance ride and what happened in emerge is all a bit of a blur. I remember bits and pieces, but not enough to put it all together and make a clear picture. A part of me wants to recall it all, but another part thinks it's probably best if I let it stay lost. I turn my head to the side and almost gasp when I see Mat and Adam sleeping in the chairs across the room, pulled close together so they can lean on each other. Their heads are pressed against one other's and their fingers are linked together. Mat is noticeably fitter, and his tattooed arm looks strong holding Adam's hand. I want to say something, but again I feel like I can't. My mouth is so dry and my throat is sore, and I'm dizzy and don't feel like myself. But Adam wakes up and immediately shakes Mat when he sees me. They get up from their chairs and come to either side of my bed.

"Sadie," they both say. Adam grabs my left hand and Mat takes my right on the other side. Both my hands have tubes coming out of them or wires attached to them, but it doesn't hurt when they touch them.

"Hi," I manage.

"How do you feel?" Uncle Adam asks.

"Weird," I say.

They both laugh softly, probably just relieved to see me awake and talking.

"I don't..." I stop and try again. "I don't know... I don't know what happened."

"You were in a car accident," Mat says.

Well yes, that part was obvious, but what I can't seem to voice is that I don't know *how* it happened. I don't know how long it took for the ambulance to come. I don't know which hospital I'm in.

"Teague," I say.

"He's fine," Adam assures me. "Barely a scratch on him, actually. They made sure he didn't have any internal injuries or anything, and he's already been discharged."

"But he's in the waiting room," Mat adds, "if you want to see him."

"No," I say. "Not yet." A part of me really wants to see him, but a bigger part of me just wants to feel safe with my uncles for now. I'm glad that Teague's okay, but I think I'd rather see him when I'm feeling a little less rattled. "Don't tell him I didn't want to see him, though," I say. "I don't want him to think-"

"It's okay," Mat says, "We'll tell him you're not feeling well and want to sleep. He'll understand."

I smile and nod, unsure of what else to say. I'm hooked up to so many machines, and they're all so noisy. I wish I had a pair of headphones to block it all out. "Do I look like death?" I ask.

"You don't look too bad," Adam says. "The side of your face is a little bruised, but most of your injuries are to your chest. You cracked three ribs, and your lung collapsed."

"Yeah," I say. "I was there when that happened." The memory of the doctor inserting a tube to drain my chest flashes by. Or inflate my chest? I'm not really sure how it works, I just know that they shoved a tube between my ribs while I was awake. She froze it first, but I remember it hurting anyway. I guess it felt more uncomfortable than painful, but in the moment everything was jumbling together, and it all just felt like pain to me.

Adam rubs the back of my hand beside the tape holding in the IV, and then squeezes it gently. "I've never been so scared in my life," he whispers. "I thought I was going to lose you."

I don't notice until that second that Mat isn't holding my hand anymore, because he's across the room, bringing one of the chairs over. He sets it behind Adam so that he can sit in it, and once he's sitting down, he pulls the chair even closer to the bed and leans onto the mattress.

"So did I," Mat says, sitting on the armrest of Adam's chair.

"So did I," I say. "I had no idea what was happening, it all happened so fast. It just came out of nowhere."

"Well you're okay now," Adam says. "But you have to stay here for a few days, until your lung is better."

"At least they give me pain killers here," I say as a joke, even though I'm half serious.

"So the pain isn't too bad?" Mat asks.

"It's okay," I say. "A lot better than before. But I don't know how I'm going to get comfortable enough to sleep with this thing sticking out of my chest."

I fall asleep and the next time I wake up, Adam and Mat are gone. Did they go home? Or are they just getting something? The machine next to me is beeping, and another machine is wheezing, and the light in the hallway floods into the room making it too bright to fall back asleep. The clock on the wall across the room reads 4:25. It must be 4:25 in the morning. What time did we even get here at? I don't know. I want to curl up and pull the blankets over me but there are too many things attached to me, or coming out of me and everything hurts. Do I have my phone? I look around and see it sitting on the table beside the bed. I reach over and grab it, wincing a little at the pain in moving. The screen is broken, spiderwebs of cracks all over the glass. I turn it on anyway and check to see if I have any messages. There is a flood of beeps and pings that don't seem to stop for a while. I can't focus as well without my glasses, and the broken screen doesn't help either, but it seems that most of them are from Emma and her family, and a few people from music class. I scroll through all the messages of well wishes until I find Teague's name. He didn't text me, and I wonder if he has his phone or if it broke in the crash. I hope the jersey is okay.

Are you ok? I text to him.

He replies almost instantly. **Yeah. Are you?**

I guess.

I heard they put a tube in your chest while you were awake.

Ya I'm a badass I say.

Of course you are.

I can't sleep I type.

Me neither.

I'm about to reply to him when my phone starts ringing. Is he calling me? Why is he calling me? I tap the answer button on the screen and put the shattered phone to my ear.

"Hello?" I say, slightly confused.

"Hey," he says.

"Hi."

"So the car's a write off," he says.

"Can you guys get a new one?"

"Oh yeah, for sure, but the car isn't worth enough for the insurance to give us enough for one that isn't used."

"Right. But you can get another car, I mean."

"Yeah."

"So you didn't get hurt?" I ask.

"Not really," he starts. "The guy hit us on your side so I guess you took most of the impact. I still don't really understand what happened. But it could have been bad. What if he was going faster, or hit you more directly? You could have died."

"That's scary to think about," I whisper.

"Then let's think of something else."

"Okay," I agree.

"How are you doing?" he asks.

"I'm okay. I'm sorry you couldn't come in to see me earlier."

"Oh that's okay, I just wanted to make sure you were alright. I'm not offended."

"Are you sure?"

He chuckles. "Yes, I'm sure. You'd just woken up after being in a serious car accident; that's a lot to handle. Plus you needed to rest."

I sigh. "Okay."

"So, do you have a TV in that place?"

I look around and notice that the turned off monitor coming down from the ceiling is actually a TV. It's on a swinging arm so I can position it any way that I want, except that it's too far for me to reach.

"Not one that I can reach," I say.

"That sucks. You don't have to share a room with anyone, do you?"

"Not yet at least. But it looks like my bed is the only one in here."

"Well that's a plus. Do you want me to stay on the phone until you fall back asleep?"

"Okay."

"What do you want me to talk about?" he asks.

"Anything," I say.

"Alright," he starts. "Emma and I want to come see you tomorrow, if you're up for it. She's going to drive us both down."

"What about school?" I ask.

"What about it? We can't visit our friend in the hospital?"

"Of course you can," I say. "When did you and Emma decide this?"

"She messaged me on Instagram tonight after I posted about being home from the hospital."

"You and Emma are following each other on Instagram?"

"Yeah, don't you two follow each other?"

"Yes, Emma and I follow each other, I mean me and *you* don't follow each other."

"And why's that?" he asks.

"I don't know, because we weren't friends."

"You don't have to be friends with someone to follow them on Instagram."

"Well why do you follow Emma and not me?" I ask.

"I don't know, Emma followed me in like, grade ten, so I followed her back."

"Oh."

"Did you follow me?" he asks.

"No," I say quietly.

"Then that's why we don't follow each other on Instagram."

"You could have followed me first," I say.

"Yeah," he agrees. "But you could have too. And you didn't."

"Because we weren't friends."

"Exactly."

"But…"

I can hear him laughing so I stop talking. "Do you want to be Instagram friends?" he asks, still laughing a bit.

"No," I say. "And Instagram doesn't even sound like a word anymore."

"So is it okay then, if Emma and I come visit you tomorrow?"

"Yes," I say. "That would be great."

"Ok good. Now go to sleep."

"I can't, it's too noisy and bright."

"So close your eyes."

I close my eyes and turn my head to the side, away from the door.

"Are your eyes closed?" he asks.

"Yes," I say.

"Okay good. Now just focus on my voice instead of all the machines making noise in your room."

"Okay."

"Okay so I'm trying to do this math homework, but it's really stumping me. You're not any good at math, are you Zed?"

"Call me Sadie," I say quietly.

"You don't like it when I call you Zed?"

"It's fine," I say. "But I like it when you say my name."

"You only like it because I hardly ever do it. If I called you Sadie all the time it wouldn't sound special anymore."

"So just say it right now, then."

"Alright," he says softly. "Are you good at math, Sadie?"

I sigh and find myself smiling. "No."

"Well you're no help."

"I know." My eyes are getting heavy again and it's hard to keep the phone up against my ear.

"My phone is dying," he says. "But I'll stay on until it cuts us off."

I nod, but I can't bring myself to answer him.

"Are you still there?" he asks after a few minutes.

I nod again.

"Sadie?"

"Hmm?" I manage.

"My phone is dying."

"Mhmm," I say.

"But I'll see you tomorrow, okay?"

I nod again, the phone starting to slip out of my hand.

"Goodnight, Sadie."

A nurse wakes me up at 6am sharp, checking all my vitals. I groan a little and she apologizes, saying there was a shift change. I nod and let her check my breathing and everything. Then a doctor comes in and does the same thing. She asks me how I slept and I lie, saying I slept fine. She looks at all the machines and the nurse changes the IV bags and then the doctor pulls a rolling stool up to the side of the bed.

"How's your pain?" she asks.

"It's okay," I mumble.

"On a scale of one to ten?"

I shrug. "A five, I guess."

"And when you take deep breaths?"

"I don't take deep breaths," I say.

"Why? Because it makes the pain what number?"

"An eight, I guess," I say.

"Okay. And can you tell me what day it is?"

"I have no idea," I say. "Thursday?"

She nods and looks at a tablet that may or may not have my vitals information on it that the nurse just checked. She looks at the tube coming out of my chest and then nods and smiles one more time. "I'll check in on you a bit later," she says as she gets up from her stool.

Adam and Mat come right after I'm brought breakfast, which I don't eat. It's still on the tray over my bed when they come into the room and I smile as soon as I see them.

"Not eating?" Adam asks.

I shake my head. "I'm not hungry."

Adam shrugs and picks up my fork, stabbing it into the scrambled eggs. "They're not bad," he says with a mouth full of food.

"Adam, that's Sadie's!" Mat says, irritated.

"She just said she didn't want it."

"But she needs it. Stop being a child."

"Okay, I'm not being a child." He puts the fork down and pulls a tote bag off his shoulder. "I brought you stuff from home," he says. He pulls out Whally first and hands him to me. I take him right away and squeeze him.

"Thank you," I say.

"Of course." He takes out my old pair of glasses, one of my zip-up hoodies, a pair of soft pyjama bottoms, and a new pair of underwear.

"You went through my underwear drawer?" I ask, appalled.

"I didn't *go through* it, I just grabbed a pair from it. Do you not want it?"

"Yes, I want it," I say, defeated.

Adam laughs. "That's what I thought."

"What did the doctor say?" Mat asks.

"Nothing really," I reply.

"Can we go find the doctor?" Mat says to Adam.

"Yeah, of course."

"She said she was coming back," I try.

"Let's go." Mat takes my things from Adam and hands me my glasses and gently places the rest of the stuff on the rolling stool that's still by my bed.

"Okay, we'll be back," Uncle Adam says to me.

I nod and watch them leave, disappointed that I still can't reach the TV.

❤❤❤♡♡

Emma and Teague show up before Adam and Mat come back, and Emma gasps way too dramatically when she sees me. I roll my eyes and smile a bit, and she steps towards me, her hands over her mouth.

"Are you okay?" she asks. "Does it hurt?"

"I'm okay," I say. "Better than yesterday, I think."

Teague is hanging back, still near the door, and I notice a few stitches above his left eyebrow. There's a bruise creeping around the outside of his eye, and he isn't wearing his glasses, but other than that he looks unharmed.

"Is the food really bad?" she asks, looking at my eggs.

"I don't know, I'm just not hungry."

Teague finally comes in closer to us and I give him a nod. "Hey," he says.

"Hey."

"Can I eat your Jell-O?" Emma asks, picking it up off the tray.

"Go for it," I say.

She takes the foil cover off and takes it with her to the chair on the other side of the room. Teague steps in even closer to me and smiles. "Hey, I remember this guy."

I don't know what he's talking about at first, but then I realize that I'm still clutching Whally, and I'm utterly mortified. He wasn't supposed to know that I still have him!

"Oh, yeah, Uncle Adam brought him for me, he thought I would want it." I loosen my grip on him and let him fall beside me on the bed. It hurts me inside a little to do it and I feel like I've just destroyed Whally's feelings.

But Teague grabs him and tucks him in under his arm before walking around the bed and carefully climbing onto it. He makes sure he's on the side with less things attached to me, and he's in danger of falling right off, but he does it, slowly, gently. I'm not sure how I feel about him getting onto the hospital bed that I am currently occupying, but I let him do it.

"I'm sorry," he whispers.

"For what?"

"For almost getting you killed."

"It wasn't your fault," I say.

"I should have been paying more attention. I should have noticed that he wasn't stopping."

"Teague, it's fine," I say.

"That looks cozy," Emma says.

Teague laughs briefly but it mostly just comes out as breath through his nose, and I can see him smiling. "Does it hurt anywhere?" he asks, putting a hand lightly on my arm.

"My chest hurts," I say.

He nods and lays his head down next to mine. "Emma, turn on the TV, will you?"

She nods and gets up from her chair to turn it on. Then she pulls her chair over to the side of my bed so we can all watch Dr. Phil together.

Emma eventually gets up and I lift my head from the pillow a little bit to ask where she's going.

"I'm going to find you something to eat."

"I told you I'm not hungry," I say.

"I know, but there's always *something* you will eat, and I'm going to find it."

I watch her leave and then put my head back down. Teague rubs my knuckles with his thumb and it sends goosebumps up my arm. I want to ask him why he's acting like this all of a sudden, but the thought of it makes my throat close up. I don't dislike it; it's actually rather comforting, so I don't say anything and I just let him keep doing it.

"I wish I could move over and give you more room on the bed," I say quietly.

"I'm fine. You need more room," he replies.

"You're going to fall off."

"I'm fine." His words come out so gently that it almost catches me off guard.

"Okay," I say. "As long as you're fine."

"I am. Are you?"

I smile at him and move my hand away so that he can't stroke it anymore, and then I link my fingers through his. "I am," I say.

Emma comes back into the room with her left hand in the air. "Look at what I found!" She's got a handful of single serving Kraft Peanut Butter packets, and she carefully places them in my lap.

"Peanut butter?" Teague asks with a hint of amusement in his voice.

"Yes," I sigh, looking over at Emma. "Emma, you're the best."

She smiles and puts her hands on her hips. "I know. It's too bad you can never find those things in crunchy, otherwise I would be the best-times-infinity."

I smile at her and take my hand from Teague's so I can pick up a packet. I carefully pull back the green seal and leave it attached on the edge so I don't have to throw it away.

"You don't have anything it put it on," Teague says.

I smile and put the tip of my finger in it, scooping up the sweet, smooth peanut butter. I put it in my mouth and suck it off my finger before getting a little more.

"Okay," Teague laughs. "Apparently you don't need anything to put it on."

"Nope," I say, shaking my head.

They take the chest tube out on Sunday evening and I get discharged on Monday afternoon. I'm told to take it easy for the next week, and we all agree that means no school or work, although I am supposed to get up and walk around for at least twenty minutes a day. They wheel me out to the parking lot with Mat while Adam goes to get the car. He meets us at the doors and immediately gets out and walks around the car to help me in. Mat sits in the back and we drive home in silence. I think I fall asleep.

After Adam helps me out of the car and Mat gives me a hug, Mat starts walking away from the building.

"Uncle Mat?" I ask.

He stops and looks back at us.

"Where are you going?" I ask.

"I have to get home," he says apologetically. "Pasta needs to get out."

I nod once. "Right. Will you come back?"

"I don't think so. Not tonight."

"Tomorrow?" I ask.

His lips pull into a tight line. "Maybe."

"Okay," I say.

"Go rest, Sadie."

Uncle Adam puts his arms around me and keeps me steady as we walk across the parking lot and into the building. We're quiet in the elevator and we're quiet getting into the apartment. He helps me lie down on the couch and he kisses my head before turning on the TV and handing me the clicker. I smile at him and he goes into the kitchen, but I fall asleep before he comes back out.

He wakes me up and helps me sit, hands me a mug of chicken noodle soup. I thank him and blow on it a few times before taking a careful sip. I watch the TV but I don't really pay attention to it. I'm thinking about how Adam and Mat came together to the hospital every day to see me. Not once did they come separately, and for a split second I thought they were getting back together. I thought the grief and worry that they shared brought them back, made them realize that they were being silly. That they still loved each other. But they were just doing it for me.

I sleep a lot over the next few days, and Adam and I walk around the halls of our building a bunch of times for my twenty minutes of exercise. I'm still pretty slow, but Adam doesn't mind. On Wednesday he takes my phone to a repair shop and gets a new screen installed for me, and even buys me a new case. It's got The Millennium Falcon on it and it's shiny and awesome.

Teague comes over on Thursday after school, and by that point I feel a lot more like myself. Luckily I showered earlier that day so I don't look so terrible when he comes in. He's got a fancy new pair of glasses, and I tell him they look really good.

"You think so?" he asks.

"Yeah, I like them better than your last pair."

"Me too."

We watch *Brooklyn Nine-Nine* for a little bit before he grabs the remote and starts looking for something else.

"Hey," I say.

"Hey what?"

"What's wrong with what we were watching?"

"Um, nothing except for the fact that you've watched it about a billion times."

"So?"

"So, we're watching something else." I open my mouth to suggest something but he cuts me off before I can even get a word out. "Not *Star Wars*," he says.

"How do you even know that's what I was going to say?"

"Was it?"

I try my hardest not to smile. "No."

He smirks at me and scrolls with the remote a little. "What about that *Neighbourly* show? They just added season four to Netflix. Have you seen it?"

"I have."

"The new season?"

I smile and nod.

"Fine," he huffs, and for a second I think I've won. "Let's go for a walk."

"No," I say, shaking my head. "I want to lie on the couch all day."

"It seems you already have," he says, looking at his watch. "It's 5pm. Did you even get your exercise for today yet?"

"Yes," I lie.

"Oh yeah? Did you do that alone? While your uncle was at work?"

"Yes," I say.

"Nope. I don't think so. Come on." He stands up and holds out his hands. "Let's go. Time to walk."

"But my ribs still hurt," I whine.

He laughs. "I'm sure they do. That's why you move slowly." He grabs onto my hands and gently pulls me to a standing position. "See?" he says. "That was easy, right?"

"No."

He smirks as if he knows I'm being difficult on purpose, and he leads me to the door where my shoes are.

"Can you put them on?" he asks.

"I don't know, I haven't put on shoes myself since before the accident," I say.

"Okay." He bends down in front of me and slides the first shoe on. I grab onto his shoulder so I don't lose my balance and then he puts the other shoe on. He looks up at me briefly before tying them, and I can't help but feel like this moment is more intimate than it probably looks. Sure, he's just tying my shoes for me, but it's somehow so much more than that. And then, ending the moment so quickly, he's standing again, holding out his hand for mine.

We move slowly and deliberately to the elevator, and I lean on him a little while we wait for it to take us to the ground floor. He puts his head on top of mine and I wonder at the same time when this closeness started, and when it really ended the first time.

We walk around the parking lot once before his phone rings. He keeps his hand in mine while he uses his other hand to get it out of his back pocket.

"What's up?" he says into the phone. "No, I'm at Sadie's." A pause while the other person is talking. "Shayla, you're fine… Well you know how to make Mr. Noodles, right? Just with the kettle." He sighs and tilts his head back a little. "Then don't answer it." He squeezes my hand and smiles at me. "Shayla, you're twelve, you can be at home alone for a few hours. I'll be home before it gets dark, okay? … Okay, bye. … I love you too." He pockets his phone. "Sorry about that."

"Is everything okay?" I ask.

"Yeah, of course."

"Why is your sister home alone?"

"Because my mom's out," he says quickly.

"You can go if you need to," I say slowly.

His eyebrows shoot up. "Do you want me to go?"

"No," I say. "Of course not. I love that you're here."

He smiles and tugs on my hand a little as he walks ahead. "Good. Then let's keep going."

I'm still off from school on Monday, because walking through the crowded halls scares me. At this point my ribs feel more uncomfortable than painful, but it still hurts enough to take my breath away if I inhale too deeply or touch them. Adam understands and says we'll wait until I have my checkup with the family doctor on Tuesday to figure out what we're going to do. He takes me to a one-hour glasses place in Barrie though, so I can get a new pair of frames. I hold my breath every time we drive through an intersection and I find myself scanning the roads for cars that aren't slowing down fast enough.

"You okay?" he asks.

"Yeah," I say through an accidental deep breath that makes me wince.

"Are you sure?"

A nod is the only answer I give him.

"Do you want to drive on the way back?" he asks.

"Um, no," I say.

"Okay, just checking. I thought maybe you would feel safer if you were the one in control."

"No, that scares me more," I say.

Infinity Pool plays through the stereo but I'm too anxious to pay attention to it. Adam turns the volume up and sings along, tapping his fingers on the steering wheel, but all I can do is grip the door beside me and look out the window.

I feel better once we're inside the store, and I start trying on frames right away. Adam asks if there is any room for a last-minute appointment and they squeeze us both in, which is really nice of them, and we both have healthy eyes. My prescription didn't change, so that's nice too. I come back out of the exam room and continue looking for frames that I like and after about an hour, finally settle on a plastic pair that is a similar size and shape as my last pair, except the frames are black with white on the insides. I think they're really sharp and I'm excited to come back and get them after Adam and I go get some food.

We slowly walk across the street to the McDonald's and sit and talk long after we're done eating. Uncle Adam glances at his watch and is shocked at how fast the time went by, so together we get up and make our way back to the glasses store. They adjust the frames to fit my face properly, and I wear them out with a smile.

The drive home is a little better and I'm able to relax a bit easier. I'm still nervous every time we drive through a set of lights, but we make it home and I'm just happy that I can go inside and relax.

There's no one to work for Uncle Adam the next day during my afternoon doctor's appointment, and an office has reserved the laser tag arena for some kind of team building exercise, so Mat leaves work early and takes me instead. My ribs seem to be healing nicely and the pain I'm still having is apparently totally normal. He can't hear anything wrong with my breathing, so he gives me the all-clear to go back to school. I'm still nervous about it. Sometimes if I hit my chest with something by accident it makes my eyes stings with tears and I feel like I can't move. My entire rib cage spiderwebs with pain and that's all that will happen to me in our crowded halls at school. People will literally be constantly banging into me. You have to walk through a literal mob of teenagers to get my locker.

I talk about it with Adam when he gets home and we decide that I will take one more day off from school, and he'll call tomorrow to tell them I have to be late to all my classes so I can walk through empty halls.

Uncle Mat comes over with Pasta that night, but I stay on the other side of the room until he's calmed down and not jumping all excitedly anymore. I make my way to the couch and sit next to him and he immediately curls up into me, putting his head in my lap as I pet him. What a good dog. Mat and Adam whisper in the kitchen and I know they're talking about me, but can't make out what they're saying. Mat raises his voice a few times, but always realizes it and fixes himself after only saying a few words. I sigh and turn the TV volume down and all of a sudden they stop talking.

"What are you talking about?" I ask.

"Nothing," they both say at the same time.

"Then come in here and watch a movie with me."

"I should go, actually," Mat says.

"But you just got here. And Pasta is so comfortable in my lap."

"He can stay the night if you want," Mat suggests.

"Um, no," Adam says. "I'm not taking him out to pee."

"Okay, then I'll bring him back to visit tomorrow." He comes back into the living room and kisses me on the top of my head. "Pasta, come on," he says as he makes his way to the door.

Pasta lifts his head and tilts it to the side in curiosity, and Mat has to call him again before he gets up from the comfort of the couch and my lap. He trots over to the door and Mat hooks his leash on his red collar.

"See you tomorrow," he says.

"Bye," I say from the couch, leaning over the armrest a little bit.

Uncle Adam sighs as he sits on the other couch, and I stare at him, trying to figure out what they were arguing about. He watches the TV and I don't think he even notices that I'm glaring at him.

"You want a snack?" he finally asks.

"Popcorn? And Oreos with peanut butter?"

"Sound good. You pick a movie while I do that." He gets up and walks in front of my couch to get to the kitchen, which is definitely the long way around, and tousles my hair on his way.

♥ ♥ ♥ ♡ ♡

"I picked up all the balls and pumps yesterday," Teague says on the phone the next day.

"What? Without me?"

"Well there was a lot; I couldn't ask you to help with that. You're all injured and stuff."

"Fine," I say, rolling my eyes a bit. "I get to help you ship them at least, right?"

"Sure. So when are you coming back to school?"

"Tomorrow," I say with a sigh. "But I have permission to be late for all my classes so I can wait until the halls are empty."

"Really? Maybe I'll get permission to be the person who walks with you."

"I don't think that's a thing," I say.

"Oh I'll make it a thing. I'll come pick you up tomorrow."

"I'm way out of your way, Teague."

"So?"

"Okay fine, but we have to pick up Emma."

"Fine."

♥ ♥ ♥ ♡ ♡

Teague pulls up in a red Toyota Corolla the next morning and before I even get the chance to walk up to the car, he gets out of the driver's side and runs around to open my door for me.

"Thanks," I say.

He gently slips my thankfully mostly empty backpack off and then grabs onto my hand and helps me in the car. "You're welcome." He makes his way back around the car and gets in, stops and looks at me. "Your glasses are nice."

"Thanks," I reply.

"It's too bad we aren't twinsies anymore, though."

"Yeah," I say. "That's the real shame in all this."

"Totally."

Emma gets in the back seat when we go to pick her up and she reaches up to the front to hand me a Kraft peanut butter packet. "It's good-luck-on-your-first-day-back peanut butter," she says. Then she faces Teague. "Hi Teague. Nice car."

"Thanks. It's new."

"You don't say."

Emma gets out of the car when we get to school, and she wishes me luck again. We watch her go into the school, and I open my peanut butter. Teague reaches over and sticks his finger in, taking a scoop for himself. I laugh and put my own finger in.

"Are you nervous?" he asks.

"A little."

"What about?"

I look down at the peanut butter, afraid to look him in the eye. "I don't know, people talking. Or people asking me questions."

"What kind of questions do you think they'll ask?"

"I don't know. People probably didn't even know that I was gone."

"Summer did. She asked about you a few times in Challenge and Change."

"Really?" I ask.

"Of course. People care about you, Zed. I know you think they don't, but they do."

"Alright, well not a lot of people do."

He narrows his eyes at me. "You think a lot of people care about me?"

"Well yeah. Everyone knows who you are."

"So? That doesn't mean they care about me. Nobody at school knows me, Sadie. I mean, no, okay, like, Carter, and Gavin, and Candace know me, and you know me, and I guess now Emma knows me a little bit, but nobody else knows me. All the people I party with, they don't know me. Most of the guys I play soccer with, they don't know me."

"But they still care. If you didn't come to school because you were in a car accident, everyone would be worried."

"Except that I did miss school because I was in a car accident. Guess what? My friends were the only ones who cared."

"Really?" I ask, not believing him.

"Really. I went to school on Friday and everyone just wanted to know if all the rumors people had been spreading were true. They didn't want to know if I was okay. They wanted to know if the guy who hit us died. They wanted to know if I watched them put a tube in you."

"That's terrible," I say.

He shrugs. "My friends cared, though. That's my point. Carter and Gavin, and Candace, they all cared. They came to my house on Thursday night when Emma and I got back from visiting you, and they brought me gummy sharks and flowers."

"They brought you flowers?"

"Yeah. Because they're my friends and they care. There will always be people who care. And the people in your life who don't care, don't deserve to be in your life."

"No one brought me flowers," I say quietly.

"It doesn't matter," he replies, shaking his head. "They came. They showed up. Your uncles who are currently going through a break up came to see you every day, together, because they care about you. They probably didn't bring you flowers because they were so worried about you and all they were focusing on was getting to see you. Going shopping was the last thing on their mind."

"Yeah, you're right," I say.

"Of course I'm right."

The bell rings behind us and I turn slightly to look at the school, as if I can see through the walls or something.

"We'll give it a few minutes," he says.

Once we're sure the halls are cleared, we get out of the car and make our way across the tarmac. He grabs a hold of my hand and squeezes it a little, and I squeeze back. The announcements are currently playing when we walk through the doors, and we slowly walk up the main staircase. We go to Teague's locker first and then to mine, but Teague doesn't let me switch out my books myself.

"Which binders do you need?" he asks, taking my bag from me.

"The yellow one and the purple one," I answer. He takes my lunch bag out of my backpack and sets it on the floor of my locker, and then gets out the right binders and puts them in my bag for me. I try to take it from him once it's zipped up and my locker is shut, but he won't hand it over.

"You can't carry my stuff for me," I say.

"Sure I can." He smiles and starts making his way to class. I have no choice but to accept it and follow him.

20

We stay sitting in class after the bell rings to end first period, but when the next class starts filing in, we stand off to the side of the room. The bell for the start of second period goes off, so everyone should be in their next classes by now. Teague thanks our teacher and we leave together, slowly making our way downstairs to the music room. He smiles at my music teacher and grabs a saxophone off the shelf for me.

"Will you be okay to play this?" Teague asks.

"I don't know, I guess I'll find out soon."

He takes the case over to my seat and everyone, including my teacher, just stares at him. I try really hard to hold in a giggle, and when he finally looks up and sees that he's the center of attention, he just waves.

"Just taking care of my injured friend," he says. "Have a great music class everyone, hope you play something fun." He backs out of the room and a few people laugh. I can feel my cheeks warm as I open the case and can feel everyone watching me. I try my best not to care, to just be me, but then I move a weird way when I pull out my saxophone and I yelp a little bit. Now I definitely can't ignore everyone's eyes on me.

"I'm okay," I say.

I notice Emma at the front looking back at me, and I give her a little smile. She returns it, but it seems sad, and then turns back to the front to look at her music.

Playing the saxophone hurts. It never occurred to me before Teague asked about it that it would hurt. I don't know why I didn't think of it. Of course it would hurt. Playing this instrument is basically all about taking deep breaths. I feel tears welling up in my eyes but I'm too embarrassed to say or do anything about it, so I just pretend to play. I wish silently that he thinks the saxes sound great and doesn't have to hear any of us play on our own. When he starts getting different instruments to play certain sections without the rest of the class, I get nervous. I don't know why I'm nervous; no one is going to judge me for not playing an instrument while I have not-yet-fully-healed ribs. But something inside my head is telling me that I'm wrong. That everyone is going to judge me. That I was stupid even thinking I could come back to school. That everyone is going to think I'm stupid for thinking I was ready. I don't want him to know that I've been pretending. I can picture it now; I can see him asking the saxophones to play the last few bars because it sounded off. I can imagine him squinting at me as he sees me moving my fingers but no sound coming out. He'll know. He'll know that I'm not really playing and he'll figure it out in front of the whole class. While he's working with the flutes I start to pack up my instrument.

"Sadie, are you alright?" Mr. Calvin asks.

Everyone turns to look at me, but I only notice Emma.

I can't speak out loud. I can't or my voice will crack and I'll start to cry and I cannot cry in front of everyone. So instead of answering him I just shake my head and grab my backpack and carry it out into the hall with my left hand. I walk down the hall and into the stairwell and sit on the bottom stair, wondering how I'm going to shake this. I can't take deep breaths. And because of that, I start to take deep, wheezing breaths that I can't control, and it hurts, and it makes me cry.

The door to the stairwell opens and my head snaps up to see Emma. She doesn't even say anything; she sits right next to me and puts her arms around me. I hug her back and cry as softly as I possibly can, which is not very soft at all.

"What's wrong?" she finally asks. "Are you okay?"

"I just feel like I shouldn't be here yet. I thought my ribs were okay but I've just been sitting at home. I haven't been doing anything, and I can't play an instrument! Why did I think I could play an instrument?"

"Why wouldn't you? You've been at home for two weeks, you haven't been thinking about that kind of thing."

"I thought that if… I thought that if I stayed at home longer, people would think I'm weak or something." I didn't even know I thought that until the words come out of my mouth.

"Why would people think you're weak? You're trying to heal your ribs. If someone breaks a leg, they can put a cast on that. It's impossible to move it and it's easy to let it heal, but you can't have a cast. Your ribs are constantly moving every time you breathe. I don't think anyone would think you're weak for that."

"Well how am I going to pass music, now?" I ask.

"It's already May. What do you need to do to pass Music?"

"Um, play an exam."

"Mr. Calvin isn't going to make you do a playing exam, Sadie."

"So what am I supposed to do? I have to do something."

"He'll probably just grade you based on your grade now. Or maybe you can play the xylophone or something."

"I don't know how to play the xylophone."

"Then maybe you can learn, and do a grade nine exam."

"You want me to learn a new instrument in a month and take a grade nine exam for it?"

"No," she says. "And I said maybe. Maybe you can learn. I don't know. But you need to talk to him about it. You can't just run away and cry. You have to tell him that you can't play. He'll understand and the two of you can work something out."

I lean my head on her shoulder without saying anything.

"You'll be fine," Emma adds. "I promise."

"I want to go home," I whisper.

"Maybe Adam can come get you."

Teague is supposed to come get me before second period is over so that I can get to my locker before the lunch rush starts. I forgot to text him and tell him that I left class, but he finds Emma and me at the bottom of the main stairs.

"Hey, where are you going?" he asks.

"Home," I reply.

"What? Why? What's going on?"

"I don't feel good."

"Well let me drive you," he says.

"It's okay, my uncle is coming to get me," I say.

"Can I wait in the parking lot with you?"

"Emma's going to wait with me, but thanks."

He nods slowly. "Emma," Teague says, "Come find me if you need someone to eat with."

"Okay," she smiles.

"Feel better, Zed." He sort of half-waves and walks away without another glance.

"I think you hurt his feelings," Emma says as we turn towards the doors.

"What?" I ask. "Why?"

"Emma's going to wait with me, but thanks." She uses an unnecessarily high tone of voice, like she's mocking me.

"Okay first all, I don't sound like that. And second of all, um, it's true!"

The bell rings and people immediately start filling the halls.

"So? You were supposed to tell him yes!" Emma cries.

"And ditch you? No way?"

"Him coming doesn't mean that I have to leave, silly."

"Right. I guess. I don't know. How was I supposed to know he actually wanted to wait with me? I thought he was just being nice!"

Someone almost walks into me and Emma opens up her arms to him like she's ready to fight. "Watch where you're going!" she shouts. "You wanna break her ribs a second time?" Then she turns back to me with a smile. "Of course he was being nice. But nobody is nice just because they feel like they have to be."

I scrunch my eyebrows at her as she holds the front door open for me. "Why not? I am."

"You offer to wait with people for their rides for no reason other than you think you should?"

I half-shrug. "I don't know. I mean, if they were crying, or it was dark out or something I would."

"Okay, but you're not crying and it's not dark out."

"So what are you saying?" I ask. "That he likes me?"

"Of course he likes you!"

"No," I say, shaking my head. "We're just friends. It's like how it used to be when we were little."

"Sure."

Uncle Adam pulls up then and Emma smiles at me. I don't know what to say to her, and I let her open the car door and put my bag on the back seat for me.

"It's true, *Zed*," she says with a wink.

I roll my eyes and let her shut my door.

Uncle Adam puts a movie on Netflix for me when we get home and he tucks a blanket around me after I've settled on the couch.

"I have to go back to work," he says after leaning down and kissing me on the forehead.

"Is no one there for you?" I ask.

He shakes his head as he stands back up. "And there's a booking right when we open so I have to go get ready."

"Uncle Adam," I groan, "You didn't have to drop everything to come get me. I would have been fine. Now you're going to be rushing."

"I would much rather know that you're okay. I'm fine. Call me if you need anything."

I must say I'm disappointed when Teague doesn't text me all afternoon. I keep turning my phone screen on, hoping he texted me and I had just missed it. But he doesn't. I open our conversation a few times and think about texting him first, but I get too nervous thinking about it, so I text Emma instead. She just tells me that school still sucks without me, and lunch was sort of weird. She hung out with Teague and his friends, but she didn't really take part in the conversation. She wished she just ate lunch alone or with people from music like she did when I was at home the last two weeks. I tell her I'm sorry I left early and she tells me not to be sorry.

Uncle Adam is on his phone later that night in his room with the door closed and a part of me wants to go to the washroom or my room just so I can be closer to his room and hear his conversation. I know I shouldn't; he's in his room because he obviously doesn't want me to hear, so I don't. I try to focus on the TV show I'm watching, but then Adam raises his voice a little bit.

"No, I'm not asking her, Mathieu!"

I scrunch my face a little in confusion and turn my head a little bit towards the hallway. I've almost never heard Uncle Adam call him Mathieu before, and I wonder if he's using his full name like that because it makes him feel further away from him. Like using his full name is more of a professional thing than a personal thing.

"I told you!" His next sentence is quieter and I'm back to not hearing what he's saying. But then he's yelling again. "Stop it! You always think that I'm being childish and right now you're being the most—" It sounds like Uncle Mat has cut him off, and when Adam starts talking again, it's soft enough that I can't make it out. I feel a little awkward and can't help but think they're arguing about me. What does Mat want me to do?

The door buzzer goes off and I jump in surprise, but Adam comes out of his room and goes to the intercom before I manage to get off the couch.

"Hello?" he says into it.

"I have a delivery for S Zwicker," the intercom says.

"Okay, come up," Adam replies. He buzzes him in and then looks at me with twisted eyebrows. I shrug at him, because I didn't order anything, and he shrugs back.

"Are you okay?" I ask him quietly.

"Of course I'm okay. Why?"

"You were arguing with Uncle Mat."

"It's fine, Sadie, don't worry about it."

The knock on the door seems to startle us both for some reason, and when Adam opens it, there's a man in the hallway with a giant bouquet of colourful daisies. Adam takes them and says thank you, the man nods and smiles and turns to leave. Adam smiles and hands them to me as I start to get off the couch.

"What?" I ask, dumfounded. "Flowers? Who on earth would get me flowers?"

He raises his shoulders and smirks at me, but says nothing. I open the little card attached to the flowers and almost start to cry.

I care about you, Z
-T

"Who are they from?" Adam asks.

"Teague," I say quietly.

"That's cute. Is he your boyfriend?" He asks it with a playful tone.

"No," I say, shaking my head. "He's just... It's because of something we talked about this morning. He's just... Cares."

"He's just cares," Adam says, mocking me. "Makes sense."

"Shut up," I joke. "I'm getting all flustered."

"I know. Because you want him to be your boyfriend."

"No I don't!" I yell light-heartedly, as I head to my room.

"But he's just cares, Sadie!" he calls after me down the hall. "That sounds like boyfriend material to me!"

"You know what I meant!"

I shut my door and carefully lie down on my bed, still clutching my flowers in my right hand. I can't stop smiling, or looking at all the colours on the soft petals. I touch them gently with my left hand, I smell them, and I look at them again. I finally grab my phone and start to text him, but then I decide to call him instead. My nerves start to get the best of me and I almost hang up on the first ring, but I hold my breath and force myself to let him answer.

"Hey," he says after the third ring.

"Hey," I say through a big grin.

"What's up?"

"Nothing." Why am I afraid to mention the flowers? What's wrong with me?

"Nothing?"

"Well a man showed up at my apartment with a bouquet of flowers… not sure what that was about…" I'm still smiling.

"Hmm, that's weird," he says. "Does it say who they're from?"

"No, it just says it's from the letter T."

"I wonder who that could be," he says.

"Me too. It's weird, I don't think I know anyone who goes by that."

"Yeah, me neither. Let me know if you figure it out."

It's quiet for a minute. "Thanks," I finally say.

"Of course." It's quiet again, and I'm about to break the silence, but he speaks first. "I mean it," he says. "Okay?"

"Okay," I reply.

"Are you going to school tomorrow?"

"Yeah," I sigh. "But I can't play the sax."

"That sucks. Have you talked to your teacher about what you're going to do?"

"Not yet. I'm nervous about it, though."

"Why? I'm sure he can just give you an independent study to do."

"Yeah," I say. "Yeah, I guess."

"Can I pick you and Emma up tomorrow?"

"That would be great."

"Cool."

"Teague?"

"Yes?"

"I'm sorry about today," I say nervously.

"Sorry for what?"

"Well when you said you could wait in the parking lot with me and I said no."

"Why are you sorry for that?"

"I don't know."

He laughs. "Okay. So you're not really sorry, then."

"Well, it's just that Emma said that I probably hurt your feelings. That you wanted to wait with me."

"Of course I wanted to wait with you; that's why I offered. But you didn't hurt my feelings. You're allowed to not want me there."

"It's not that I didn't want you there," I try. "I wanted you there."

"Then why did you say no?"

"Because Emma was there. I don't know. I didn't think of it. I guess…" I stop and take a breath, bracing myself for what I'm about to say. "I didn't know that I wanted you there, I guess. But now I do."

"Now you want me there?"

"Yeah."

"Good."

"Anyway," I say. "Thanks for the flowers."

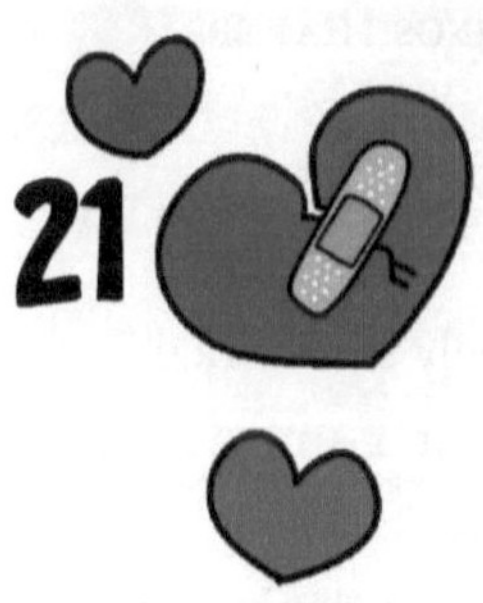

The rest of the week goes by pretty smoothly. Teague picks Emma and me up for school, I talk to my music teacher about not being able to play my instrument and he gives me a research project to do instead, and Teague and I take all the balls and pumps to the post office. We've been conversing back and forth with the people who are with the organizations that'll be accepting them in the two countries we picked in Africa, and they seem really excited about it all. Teague comes over twice so that we can work on our presentation, and Mat comes over on Friday with Pasta.

Teague stands up as soon as Mat comes into the apartment, and I'm not sure if he feels uncomfortable or something. "I'll see you later, Zed," he says.

"You don't have to leave," I reply, watching him walk to the door.

"It's fine, I have to be home for my sister anyway."

"Alright," I say quietly. He leaves and I turn my attention to Mat. "Hey," I say.

"Hey." He smiles and sits down on the opposite couch, dropping Pasta's leash. "I wanted to ask you something."

"Okay," I say, scrunching my eyebrows a little at him. Pasta leaps onto my couch and I pet him, but push him back a little, since having my ribs bumped still hurts.

"Pasta, off," Mat says, irritated.

"It's fine," I say.

"No it's not." He gets up and picks the dog off the couch, carries him back to the other side of the room.

"So what's up, then?" I ask.

Mat opens his mouth to answer me, but the front door opens and Uncle Adams walks in.

"Hey," Adam says to us both.

"Hey," Mat says, a bit of disappointment in his tone.

"Is everything okay?" Adam asks.

"Yeah, I was just bringing Pasta by to visit. You just missed Teague."

"I ran into him in the parking lot," Adam replies. "Do you want to stay for dinner?"

"Me?" Mat asks.

"Yeah."

"Oh. Oh, no, that's okay. Thanks for offering, though. I should really get going."

I'm confused, but before I can say anything, Mat subtly shakes his head at me. I'm even more confused now, but let him stand up from the couch and put Pasta back on the ground. He grabs onto his leash and heads into the hall.

"That was nice of you," I say to Adam after Mat has left. "To invite him for dinner."

Adam shrugs.

I retreat to my bedroom after dinner when Teague won't stop texting me. I lie on my bed and smile at my phone as we talk in short sentences and emojis.

Are you going to prom? he asks after a while.

Ya. Are you?

I think.

Neither of us says anything for a few minutes, and then Teague responds with a pondering face emoji.

What does that mean? I ask.

We could go together.

I'm going with Emma. We have a whole date thing planned.

Cute. he says.

I know.

Well maybe we can sit at the same table he tries.

Ya that would be fun. I don't know how they plan the seating though.

I know people on the prom committee he says. **I can hook us up.**

❤❤❤♡♡

By the time we do our presentation in the last week of May, my ribs feel basically normal. I could most certainly do my music playing exam in three weeks, but I've already started my project, and I'll have less time to practice the song than everyone else. I feel like I need to keep pretending that my ribs still hurt so I don't get guilted into doing the playing exam, but Teague changes my mind.

"You need to let them heal properly," he says. "I know you think they're all better, but I see the way you move, you know. I can tell you're still being careful."

"I am?" I ask.

"Maybe you're doing it subconsciously, but you are. And if you go around and take a bunch of deep breaths for an hour every day, they're not going to heal properly."

"Okay," I say.

"Well, that makes sense, doesn't it?"

"Yeah, I guess."

The bell rings for first period to start, and my nerves start to get the best of me. My mouth is suddenly so dry that I can feel it on my tongue, and my hands are shaking so bad I'm sure the people at the back of the class will be able to see.

But once we get up there and start talking, and Teague makes everyone laugh, I start to feel a bit better. I'm still nervous and I can still hear my voice quiver, but it's easier for me to get through it. The rest of it breezes by pretty quickly, and when we head back to our seats I can't help but smile.

"You did amazing," Teague says quietly before he sits down.

"Thanks," I say, making my way further back to my own desk. Summer smiles at me when I sit down and I smile back.

"I have an idea," Teague says at the end of class. "How about we get a group of us together the night before prom and go to Laser Tag?"

"Yeah, okay," I say. "That might be fun. I'll see if anything's already booked, and if it isn't I'll reserve the whole arena for us."

"Okay text me as soon as you know. And let me know how much it costs. We can all split it so it'll be cheap."

There is an air-hockey-table-shaped hole in my heart. The first thing I notice when I walk into work after school, is an empty space in the middle of the arcade where the air hockey table should be. Okay, so I guess I'm being a little dramatic, but the air hockey table is gone!

"Um, Uncle Adam?" I march towards the snack counter where he's standing, watching me with his eyebrows raised. "Where's the air hockey table?"

"The technician couldn't fix it."

"So you just got rid of it?" I can't believe I'm actually fighting off tears right now.

"There's no sense in keeping a big broken machine, Sadie."

"But I didn't even get to say goodbye to it!"

His face falls a little. "I'm sorry. It all happened so fast. They let me do a trade-in to get a deal on the new one."

"We're getting a new one?" I ask.

"Of course."

"Well good," I say shortly. "But still. I'm going to miss that one."

He smiles softly at me. "Me too."

We're quiet for the next few minutes and then Adam nudges my shoulder with his.

"We can have a memorial service for it if you want," he suggests.

"For an air hockey table?"

He shrugs. "Hey, you're the one who said you didn't get to say goodbye."

"It's fine," I say with a bit of a whine. "It's fine."

He smirks at me. "Okay."

I take a seat on the stool behind the counter and start booking the arena for everyone at school while Uncle Adam tidies up. He comes to grab his bag before leaving and catches the booking screen on the computer before I finish.

"Wow, how many people are coming?" he asks.

"Um, well it's just a rough number so far, but twenty-two?"

"Wow, that would be a great game. What's it for?"

"Um, pre-prom," I say, not sure why I sound hesitant about it all.

"Are these your friends? Are you a part of this?" I can tell he's excited but also trying to act like he isn't.

"Yeah," I say as calmly as I can.

"Sadie! That's so cool!"

I shrug. "They're all Teague's friends."

"Okay, so? It's pretty exciting to be in a game with that many people. You'll have so much fun!"

"Yeah," I sigh.

"It's okay if they're not your friends, Sadie. You can still have fun. It's pretty cool that Teague invited you, right?"

"Yeah," I reply. "It's pretty cool. Emma's going too. And I'm friends with another girl who's going."

He squeezes my shoulder for a second before walking around the counter to leave. "Just so you know, I would be excited for you if you were booking the arena for just you and Emma. It's not a requirement for you to have twenty-two friends. I was just excited about you being a part of something."

"I know," I say with a smile.

"Just breathe," Emma says. "Look into my eyes, and take in a deep breath. No wait!" she cuts herself off and holds her hands out to me. "Just a regular breath. I don't want you hurting yourself."

I roll my eyes at her and smirk. "I can take slow deep breaths," I say. "But I don't think it's going to work."

"Then just get over yourself. This is going to be fun."

"But it's all the popular people," I whine. "It's going to be weird."

"It's not going to be that weird. I'll be there. And Teague will be there. And Summer. You're friends with her aren't you?"

"Yes," I say. "But everyone's popular except for us."

"I'd say there are varying degrees of popular people going."

"How come you don't think it'll be weird? You said lunch with them was weird."

"It was, because you weren't there. We'll be on the same team, and it's going to be amazing."

I force a smile and Emma laughs at me.

"How can you not be excited?" she asks. "We're going to play laser tag and then it's prom tomorrow!"

"That part I'm excited for," I say with a genuine smile.

"I have to pee." Emma gets up from my bed and hops into the hallway. I know she's going to fuss with her makeup while she's in there, so I pull out my phone to check the comments on our Challenge and Change project. Written projects are all submitted through Google Docs and our teacher said she'd have the marks and comments on them by now. I have to keep pinching the screen and zooming and moving it around to read everything properly so I make my way to the living room to check it on Uncle Adam's laptop instead.

But I don't even open the internet browser because a word document in the task bar catches my attention.

Mat's Recommendation it says. Mat's Recommendation? Recommendation for what? Should I read it? No, of course I shouldn't read it. But what's it for? No, I couldn't possibly read it. I couldn't possibly move the cursor over the tab and click it on it. I couldn't. Except that I did. And now it's open, taking up the whole screen, staring at me. It's basically begging me to read it.

No, I can't read it.

"Sadie?" Emma calls from down the hall. "Where'd you go?"

"In here," I say, still staring at the word document, but not letting myself focus on the words.

"What are you doing? We should leave soon."

"Look," I say, pointing to the screen.

"What is it?" She leans into me so she can see the screen too, and then she gasps and backs up. "Oh my god, Sadie, you can't read that!"

"I know!"

"Then why is it open!?"

"It was already open!"

"Really?"

"Well, no, it was minimized, but it was there! Easily readable by anyone who uses this laptop! And Adam knows I use it for school!"

"I'm sure he meant to close it."

"But it's nothing bad," I say. "I don't think. It's a recommendation." And then it dawns on me. "Oh my god!" I screech. "It's for Mat's adoption thing! He wrote him a recommendation letter!"

"Oh my god, read it!" Emma half shouts, sitting next to me and shoving me a little on the couch.

"No! You just said I shouldn't!"

"That's when I thought it was something personal!"

"This *is* personal! This is probably the most personal thing he's ever written. No, I can't read it. It's like going through his drawers or something. This was probably really hard for him to write. If he wants to share it with me, then he will."

"You're right," Emma says. "I'm sorry I tried to make you read it. I'm a terrible person."

"No you're not. But both of us will be terrible if we're late to laser tag."

♥♥♥♡♡

Almost everyone is there when Emma and I arrive but we're still waiting on Carter and Summer, and two of their friends. Teague waves to us as soon as we walk in and he heads over to us, leaving Gavin and Candace by the snack counter.

"I'm so excited!" he says when he meets us in the middle, where the air hockey table used to be.

"Me too," I say. "It's going to be fun."

"So are you going to give the speech to us before we start?" he asks.

"No," I say shortly. "I'm not working."

"Yeah but you do it so well."

"My uncle will probably do it," I say with a small smile.

"Or you could do it."

"Come on," Emma says. "It'll be more fun that way."

"Why does it look so different in here?" Teague asks.

"It doesn't look different," Emma says.

"The air hockey table is gone," I tell him.

Emma laughs. "Right, of course."

"How did I not notice?" Teague asks.

"You're actually standing where it once lived," I add.

He looks down at his feet and then back to me. "I feel like we should step to the side. Be more respectful."

The three of us laugh a little, and then Carter and Summer walk through the doors, so we get everyone's attention so we can get this game started.

♥♥♥♡♡

Everyone piles into the front of the arena and puts on their vests, and my heart feels like it's going to shoot out of my mouth. Teague smiles and winks at me as people start to sit, and Emma squeezes my hand before taking a seat at the end.

"Okay everyone," I say as loudly as I can. Some people are still talking, so I try again. "Hello! You need to listen right now!"

"Calm down," Gavin says with a laugh. I want to curl in a ball and die. But I don't actually want to die, so really, I sort of just want to run away and pretend that I don't exist until everyone forgets how much of a loser I apparently am.

"Gavin, shut it," Teague scolds.

I can't help but smile at that, but I try to hide it as quickly as I can. Now that everyone is staring at me and actually giving me the attention I wanted, I don't know what to do. I feel like now everyone is listening because they don't want to get into trouble or something. Or like they feel like they need to be nice to me because I'm not as popular as they are. I shake my head and let out a slow breath. *No one is actually judging you*, I think to myself. *It just seems like they are, but no one cares. No one cares.*

I give my explanation, and it turns out to feel the same as it does when I'm working, so my nerves go away almost instantly. Nobody has any questions when I'm done, which is nice. Well, Gavin raises his hand, but I ignore him because I know he's just going to say something inappropriate, and we file into the arena. Emma and I run off right away, but Teague catches up to us pretty quickly. We're heading for our favourite bridge when he sneaks in between us.

"We need someone on defence," he says to us just as our vests start their low chime.

"Okay," Emma and I say in unison.

"We all voted Emma and Summer."

"We weren't a part of this vote," I say.

"You guys ran off pretty fast." He looks around him and then crouches down, motioning for us to do the same.

"I don't want to be on defence," Emma says.

"But it's such an important job. And it's fun! You get to shoot all the people who are trying to get to our base!"

"Keep it down," I say.

"Sorry," Teague whispers. "But really, Emma, you'll have so much fun. Plus Summer's really cool."

"I know she is," Emma says.

"Come on. Please?"

Emma huffs and Teague gives her this weird stare, and all of a sudden she's all smiles. "Okay, see you guys later. Good luck getting to blue team's base." She gives us a two fingered salute and runs off, but someone is hiding behind a glowing tree and shoots her in the back. She turns around to shoot him back, but she can't see him. Teague grabs my arm and pulls me around a post.

"How many times can we get shot again before we need to respawn?"

"Five," I remind him.

"Okay good, so Emma can still make it."

I shrug. "She probably won't. It's going to take her forever to get there. She'll definitely get shot again on her way to our base, and the checkpoints are in the middle of the arena and back at the door. It's a total inconvenience."

"As it should be." He smiles and nods his head in the opposite direction. "Come on."

I follow him around the post and towards a fake tree with glowing leaves. He looks back at me and smiles, and reaches out to grab my hand. He pulls me in next to him and keeps me close.

"Do you see anyone?" he whispers.

"Not yet. They must be good at hiding."

He gasps and sort of pushes me behind the tree. I yelp in surprise and he pulls me down to a crouch with him. "There's someone there," he says. "Sorry, did I hurt you?"

"No," I whisper. "I'm okay."

"Okay. I'm going to go out and kill them."

"I can come," I say.

"No, you have to keep guard in case someone comes the other way. We have to get to their base together without dying."

"Okay," I agree. I turn to face ahead, my back against the glowing tree, my gun in both my hands, ready to shoot if I need to. I look around and see glowing blue and red vests in the distance, but they're only focused on each other and not close enough to us to care about what we're doing. I hear someone behind me whine and I turn a little to peek around the tree.

"Aw come on!" Gavin says. He turns around looking to see who shot him, but he can't spot Teague under the bridge, in the fake stream. I can see him from where I am, since I'm at a lower level, and I smile as I watch Gavin get shot a second time, and then a third. Why he isn't running away is beyond me, and when Teague shoots him again and it doesn't make a noise on Gavin's vest, we know he's been shot five times. Now he has to find a checkpoint if he wants to stay in the game and shoot anyone else, so he starts to walk away. I holster my gun and look around and crawl out from behind the tree, slowly making my way towards Teague. I squeeze in next to him, keeping myself up, propped up on my forearms and elbows. There's just enough room for the two of us under this bridge, and when he turns to look at me, our faces almost touch.

"I got Gavin," he says.

"I saw," I reply with a smile.

"How much farther to Blue's base?" he asks.

"It's not far," I say. "But they probably have people guarding it. We need a plan."

"Yeah, they'll probably surround us when we get there. One of us needs to go first, so they focus on that one person while the other one sneaks in and gets a shot on base."

"Okay." It's quiet for a little bit and we are just lying there under the bridge, on top of the fake, glowing stream with rushing water sound effects, staring into each other's eyes. "We'll probably both die," I whisper.

"As long as we go down fighting."

"As long as we get at least one shot in," I add.

He smiles at me and then inches himself a little closer. I watch his mouth as he closes the gap between us, and then I look into his eyes and I'm afraid and excited all at once about the possibility of him kissing me. Is that what he's doing?

"Sadie?" he asks quietly.

"Yes?"

He smirks again, but says nothing. He continues to look at me, or at least I think he's looking at me, but I'm not really sure because I'm looking at his mouth again. And then his face is even closer to mine and I can taste his minty breath.

"Can I kiss you?" he asks in a whisper.

I smile and bite my bottom lip in a bit of nervousness, but then I nod. "Yes please."

And then his lips are pressing against mine, and we're kissing. It's very nice, and soft, and quiet, if that makes any sense. But after about four seconds I get paranoid that I'm doing it wrong, that he'll judge me and laugh about me to his friends after, so I pull away.

"Oh, sorry," he says.

"Wh-what?"

"Did I do something wrong?"

"No, I was afraid that I was," I say.

"What do you mean?"

I shrug, afraid to admit that I had never kissed anyone before. I mean, I kissed Freddie Kaiser in grade eight before he moved away, but that was nothing. We were thirteen and incredibly naive and innocent and when we were dared at a birthday party to kiss for ten seconds, we literally pressed our lips together for ten seconds without opening or moving our mouths. I thought we were so grown up for doing that, and now I just laugh about it. Except now, here with Teague, it makes me nervous. I've never had a real kiss before and Teague has surely had many. I have no idea what I'm doing.

"I just got nervous," I finally say.

"Oh." He looks down in front of him and plays with his gun a little that's lying under his glowing red vest.

"I think a little bit of nerves are normal though, right?" I ask.

He looks at me and smiles. "Yeah, I think."

"Are you nervous?"

"Well I am now," he says with a bit of a chuckle.

"I'm sorry."

"Why do you always say that?" he asks.

"I don't know. Because I am."

"You don't have to be sorry because of something I feel. That's silly."

I shrug. Now that I feel more confident that he's not going to judge me, I want him to kiss me again, but I'm too afraid to ask him to, or to lean in and do it myself. Why can't I just get over myself and do the things that I want to do?

"We should go," he whispers.

"Now?" I ask.

"Yeah… Why not?"

"Well, we have the arena for two hours," I say, trying my hardest. "And there are other people on our team who are trying to get to the base. They don't really need us… right now…"

His smile is slowly growing. "Oh, is that what you think?"

"Yeah, that's what I think." I'm smiling too, and I can't make myself stop.

"Well, what should we do, then? Just hide here under this bridge? This fake water won't get us wet if we stay here for too long, will it?"

"It definitely won't," I say, shaking my head.

I hear someone run over the bridge above us, followed by someone else and Teague and I both flatten ourselves into the ground below us, staying as quiet as we can. We both look up at the underside of the bridge above our heads, and then at each other, as we wait for them to pass, afraid they are from the Blue team. Mostly I'm just afraid of any people at all, and that they'll ruin my moment with Teague.

"I think they're gone," he whispers with a sigh of relief, relaxing a bit. "How are your ribs?"

"They're fine," I say.

"And how are your nerves?"

I find myself smiling again. "They're fine."

"Mine too, I think."

"That's good."

"So Zed, I have a question for you."

"Okay." My nerves are making their way up again but I try not to let them get the best of me. I'm not nervous of Teague, I'm just nervous of the situation and I know it's silly or normal or both, so I try to swallow and keep myself as calm as possible as I wait for him to ask me the thing I think I know he's going to ask me.

I think he's nervous too, because he takes a second to talk. He licks his lips and looks away for a bit, playing with his gun again. What changed? He didn't seem nervous when he asked if he could kiss me, and now he's afraid that I'm going to tell him I don't want to do it again? Do I make Teague Tremblay nervous?

"Before you got nervous," he starts, without looking at me, "were you happy that you were kissing me? I mean, did you…" He finally looks at me and I can tell that he's having a hard time getting his words out. "I mean, did you like it?"

"Yes," I say quietly.

"So now that you're less nervous… Do you want to do it again?"

"Yes," I whisper.

He moves closer to me, and this time I'm not nervous. I can feel him smile against my mouth and I let him kiss me again. Teague is beginning to feel like a safe space for me, and now that I know he doesn't have all the ulterior motives I thought he had, I trust him. I feel like this is right. And that even if I'm not good at kissing, Teague won't tell his friends. His mouth opens a little and I reciprocate, letting him lead. His lips are so soft and warm, and I just want to melt into him. I press myself closer but it's hard with our vests and because we're still on our stomachs, holding ourselves up on our elbows and forearms. Our necks are craned to the side as we kiss slowly under the bridge, but his hand finds mine in front of me and our fingers link together. And in this moment, I don't want to be doing anything else other than sitting here in this secret little world with Teague and his magical kisses.

22

My first instinct is to run and tell Emma about finally having my first real kiss, but of course I can't, because we're playing laser tag and I still want to win. When we finally stop kissing, we giggle a little and stare at each other, and then we kiss a little bit more, small, soft, quick kisses in a row, and then he tilts his head to the side and tugs on my hand.

"Come on," he says. "Let's go destroy the other team."

I follow him through the glow-in-the-dark arena and hide behind pillars and rocks and trees any time we see someone. I shoot someone from behind an orange rock which prompts them to swear out loud. Teague and I laugh quietly and wait for the person to leave before we get up and make the rest of our way to the base.

There are three people guarding the base when we arrive, and we watch them from behind a log, wondering how we're going to get in.

"Hey," we hear from behind us, jumping in surprise. It's Carter, and he crouches down next to us, his red vest letting us know he's on our team.

"Hey," we reply in unison.

"How's it going?" he asks.

I resist the urge to yell, "AMAZING! I JUST KISSED TEAGUE UNDER A BRIDGE SURROUNDED BY GLOWING COLOURS, I'LL BET MY NIGHT IS BETTER THAN YOURS!" and instead say, "Okay."

"We have three shots on them so far," Carter says. "I just respawned and managed to make it back here without getting shot again so I've still got full life."

"Us too," Teague says.

Carter looks at me. "Sadie, if Teague and I go first and try to shoot them all, do you think you could rush in and get a shot on their base?"

I smile and nod, but then come up with an even better idea. "Is there anyone else on our team nearby?" I look around for some red glowing vests, but we're in a pretty covered area so it's hard to see any kind of distance. "If we kill the three people guarding, we can get as many shots as we want while they run to a checkpoint."

"We'll try to kill them, Sadie, but they might get us first. And you might have to sacrifice yourself in the process."

"Okay," I say slowly. "But if we get another team member here first -"

"We'll do this first, and then we'll find more people on our way to a checkpoint," Teague says.

"Okay," I agree. "Good luck."

"You too." Teague smiles and the two of them stand up and hop over the log, making their way to the blue base, guns out and blazing.

As soon as they all start shooting each other, I creep out myself and try to get in undetected. They are all shooting one another, trying not to get killed themselves, so I sneak up behind Carter and take a shot on the base. I get us another point, and then someone shoots me. My vest makes a noise and I know I have to focus on the base before I get killed. There's no time to shoot back at whoever is trying to kill me; I have to get us more points before I go down. I get one more shot on base before two people shoot me at once so I turn around to shoot back and get one of the blue vests. I get shot again by everyone it seems like, and I'm suddenly out of the game until I get to a checkpoint. I turn around, feeling more accomplished than defeated and start heading towards the middle of the arena. Teague and Carter are waiting for me close by and they each give me a high five, which makes me feel super awesome.

"That was amazing!" Teague half shouts. "You rock!"

"What can I say? I'm just that good."

♥ ♥ ♥ ♡ ♡

We beat the blue team by 5 points, and I must say I'm quite disappointed when our two hours are up. I smile at Emma on our way out and she nudges me in the arm with her elbow, but I decide to keep quiet until we get back to my place.

"See you tomorrow, Zed," Teague says with a smile and a head nod.

"Yeah," I reply. "See you tomorrow."

Emma and I help my uncle sanitize all the guns and vests and then make our way back to my apartment. I tell Emma about my kiss with Teague, and how magical it was, and she squeals and jumps up and down practically the whole time that I'm talking. I shove her a little bit but she's too excited to care.

We get into our PJs as soon as we get in, and make a batch of popcorn to eat while we watch a movie. The whole time that the movie is playing though, my eyes keep wandering to Adam's laptop. I know I shouldn't read it, I know I shouldn't. But I'm just so curious. No, I can't. I shake my head, trying to convince myself that it's terrible to even think about wanting to read it.

Adam comes home halfway through our movie and immediately grabs the laptop off the coffee table.

"Evening, ladies," he says with a smile. He tucks the laptop under his arm and heads to his room.

"Off to write more secret things about Mat, I presume," Emma whispers.

"Don't even," I say.

"I'm just kidding."

"I know. But still. I really want to know what it says and you're just making it even more difficult."

"How?" she chuckles.

"By mentioning it."

She shoves me into the armrest of the couch and I laugh a little.

♥♥♥♡♡

"IT'S PROM TODAY!" Emma is on her knees, bouncing next to me on my bed. "IT'S PROM TODAY!" she yells again.

"Oh my god, yes, yes, it's prom!" I say, rubbing the sleep out of my eyes and looking for the time on my alarm clock. "Emma," I whine, "It's not even 8:00!"

"I can't sleep anymore; I'm too excited, it's like Christmas!"

I smile and slowly sit up in bed. "Should we go out for breakfast, then?" I ask.

"Okay! Let's invite your uncle."

"But it's prom breakfast. We can't have my uncle at prom breakfast."

"Okay, I guess you're right. But if he comes, he might pay for us."

"You're such a slime sometimes," I joke.

"Hey!"

"Well you are," I laugh. "Only inviting someone hoping they'll pay for us."

"But we're poor high school students," she says with an over exaggerated pouty lip.

"We're actually high school students with a disposable income because we both have jobs and no bills to pay."

"Not true! I pay for my phone," Emma says.

"Yeah so do I. But Uncle Adam pays for my food and most of my clothes, and the rent, and the streaming services, and the internet…"

"But we need to save for university."

"Just get changed, Emma, we're paying for our own breakfast. It's not like we're buying a new TV or a laptop, or -"

"Hey, you guys are up," Uncle Adam says, opening my door a little.

"Oh," I reply, a little surprised. "Yeah."

"You want to go out for breakfast?" he asks. "My treat."

Emma just beams at me.

❤❤❤♡♡

"So how's Mat's adoption thing coming?" I ask as I cut into my eggs benedict, watching the yolk mix in with the hollandaise. I almost don't ask; my throat closes up every time I think of it, but finally once I look away from him, it just comes out.

"I don't know," Adam says with a shrug. "You talk to him more than I do."

I take a bite of my delicious meal and try to wait for my nerves to calm down a bit before I even think of an answer. "Seems like you guys are talking a lot lately," I finally say. "On the phone, and in the kitchen…"

"Why don't we talk about this later, Sadie," Uncle Adam says.

I glance at Emma who shrugs subtly, and I sigh. "Okay," I say.

"How are your eggs?" he asks.

"Really good," I reply.

"How are your pancakes, Emma?" Uncle Adam asks.

"Delicious," she says with her mouth full. She chews a bit more and swallows. "Thanks for taking us out."

♥♥♥♡♡

We're all ready. Well, I'm ready. I'm still in the washroom, staring at myself in the mirror, afraid to come out. I did my hair the way I've always secretly wanted to, by just messing it up a bit while it's still damp and putting mousse and hairspray in it. I think it looks awesome. But what if I'm just weird and it actually looks stupid? I'm afraid to open the door and show Emma. I'm afraid she's going to ask me what I plan on doing with my hair, or something equally as innocent that will make both of us feel like crap when I say that I already have my hair the way I want it.

"Are you almost done?" Emma says through the door.

"Yes," I say hesitantly.

"What's taking so long? I heard you turn the shower off forever ago. Are you stuck in your dress? Do you need help?"

"No," I say. "No, I'm fine. I'm in my dress. I'm just afraid that I look stupid."

"Why would you look stupid?"

"I don't know," I say slowly.

"What do you mean? Come out so we can take pictures!"

I let out a deep breath and open the door.

"Oh. My. God," Emma says. "Your hair looks amazing!"

"Really?"

"Yes! Wow, girl! It's so hot!"

"Really?"

"Yes!"

"You think it looks hot?" I ask, unsure of myself.

"Hell yes it looks hot! Don't you think you look hot?"

"I don't know, I thought maybe… cute?"

"Nope, definitely hot."

I feel myself blushing but allow myself to smile. "You look great, too."

"I know." She smiles and puts her hand on her hip. "And we look amazing standing next to each other, don't we? With our matching accessories!"

"It's like we're dating," I giggle.

"I know, right?"

We take a bunch of selfies and post them on Snapchat and Instagram, and then Uncle Adam takes a few nice pictures of us in the living room before we leave. It's nice and sunny out, and it's the perfect temperature, about 18 degrees. Nice enough for us to not be too cold without a sweater, but not so hot that we'll sweat. The evening might be a different story, but for now we're excited about everything. We get into Adam's car and I back out of our space, and then Emma starts squealing.

"What oh my god!?" I shout, slamming on the breaks.

"Sorry, I'm just excited."

"You can't do that! You can't do that when I'm driving!"

"I'm sorry," she says. "But you're just backing out of your spot."

"It doesn't matter, I'm way more nervous about driving than I used to be, Emma."

"You're right, I'm sorry. But you'll be fine. It's not far anyway."

"Yeah," I sigh.

♥♥♥♡♡

"Where do I park?" I ask as I pull into the marina.

"I dunno, wherever," Emma says with a shrug.

"But like, is there a place I'm supposed to park?"

"In a spot."

"But some spots are reserved for people who have boats here, right?"

"I don't think so. Maybe. There would be signs if there were. Just park in this one," Emma says, pointing to a spot to the right. I pull in and put the car in park.

Emma looks at me and squeals, so I squeal too, getting more excited now that we're here. I carefully step out of the car and put my keys in my little yellow clutch, and smile at Emma as she comes around to my side of the car.

"Shall we?" she asks, hooking her arm through mine.

"We shall."

Together we walk across the parking lot and to the other side of the building that I'm not actually sure what its purpose is. There's a patio overlooking the water with sailboats along the dock, and the slight wind seems to make them sing.

"I think we have to go inside," Emma says.

"Why weren't there instructions on our tickets?"

"Maybe there are," she says with a bit of a laugh, flipping her ticket over.

We make our way up the steps of the patio and across the wooden flooring towards the double doors in the middle. Someone is propping them open as we come closer and she stops and smiles at us.

"Are you here for the prom?" she asks.

"Yes," Emma replies, immediately handing her ticket to her.

The girl laughs and holds her hands up. "I'm just letting people know where to go. You two are actually the first ones here. I'm supposed to go to the front and direct people back here, so good job guys, you made it on your own!" She gives us a thumbs up and I'm not sure if she's joking or not. She's probably joking.

"Yeah, we're pretty smart sometimes," Emma says, tapping the side of her head.

The girl winks at her and then holds her arm out into the doorway. "It's just right in here, ladies. Have a great night." She smiles and then makes her way across the patio where we had just come from.

"I can't believe we're the first ones here," I say. "We're not that early, are we?"

"I thought we were late…"

"Maybe everyone else is trying to be cool… by being really late," I suggest.

"That must be it."

We step into the building and almost immediately my breath is taken away. It didn't look like much from the outside, but inside, it's amazing. It looks like a fancy wedding. There are rose gold table cloths and chair covers, bows and napkins in this very soft, almost steel blue colour. Flowers poking out of tall glass vases in the centre of each table, and fairy lights strung from the wooden rafters in the ceiling. It's magical. The windows let in a soft light that warms the room, and the open doors to the patio provide a fresh breeze and sounds of birds chirping happily.

"Let's find our table." Emma jolts me from my mesmerized gaping and I follow her to the seating chart.

It's laid out just like a wedding, with table numbers and names listed underneath in fancy script. Before we have a chance to find our names, a few other people show up, a boy and two girls whose names I can't remember. They are laughing and don't even pay any attention to us as they come in.

"Were they at laser tag?" Emma asks.

I just shrug and go back to the seating chart. It looks like we're sitting at a table with Teague, Summer, Carter, and Gavin. Hmm, it's sort of weird that Candace isn't sitting with Teague, Carter and Gavin, but I guess since Carter's dating Summer now, there isn't room. Emma and I find the table together and sit down where our names are placed. Before Emma sits down she grabs Gavin's name and immediately switches it with Summer's.

"But now Summer isn't sitting next to Carter," I say.

She huffs a little and switches Carter's name so that now Gavin is in between Carter and Teague, I'm on Teague's other side, and then Emma is next to me.

"That's better," she says with a smile. I smirk at her as she sits down, and we both look around the room in awe as we wait for more people to show up.

A server comes by with a pitcher of water and ice and we immediately pour ourselves a bit to drink.

"Should we go take pictures outside?" I ask.

Emma smiles and nods, and together we make our way back out to the patio. Teague and Gavin are outside and Teague smiles at us as soon as we emerge.

"Hey!" he says excitedly.

"Hey," Emma and I say in unison.

"You two look amazing," Teague says.

"Thanks," I reply. "So do you."

"I love that you guys match," Gavin says.

"Thanks," Emma says quickly. "We're each other's dates, so we thought it made sense."

We take selfies and group pictures in front of the water and when Summer and Carter show up, we do it all over again. People from yearbook snap a group picture of us at the edge of the balcony, and when it looks like most people have shown up, we head inside to our table.

Candace is sitting at a table next to us, and when she sees us sit down, she immediately gets up and stands between Teague's chair and mine.

"Hey Teague," she says. "I'm bummed we're not sitting together."

"Yeah, it sucks a bit, but there's only room for six people at each table."

Candace shakes her head. "Some tables have eight."

"Oh. Well I don't know, then. I just said I wanted to sit with Sadie, and they knew that Sadie and Emma came together, but that's all I can say."

"What do you mean that's all you can say?" she narrows her eyes at him.

"I just mean that's all I know. I don't know why they didn't sit you with us. But you're friends with all those guys."

"Yeah, but Ashley Castor is sitting at my table."

"So?"

Candace sighs. "So nothing, never mind." She turns around and smiles at me. "Hi Sadie. Your hair looks really good."

I'm caught off guard and almost stumble over my words. "Oh. Thanks."

"Of course." She smiles again and heads back to her table.

"That was weird," I say to Emma.

"Was it?"

I shrug a little and Emma laughs.

Dinner is served and we all laugh and joke about school and work as we eat. There's time for more pictures before dessert, so we all rush outside to get some good shots in front of the sunset. The pink and red glow of the sky is gorgeous, and there are a lot of low, whispy clouds that add to the texture of the sky. Teague gets in real close to me and holds his phone out in front of us and I watch the screen as he tries to place us in the frame so that you can see the glowing sky behind us. When he finally has it the way he wants, he puts his arm around me and kisses my temple. I can't help but lean into his lips a little, and I'm a little embarrassed that my smile is giving away too much about how good it feels to be here with him.

"That's a great picture," he says, his arm still around me.

"Yeah it is," I say, studying it. My smile is fine; I don't think it gives too much away. Or maybe it does, but because Teague is kissing me, it fits. It's pretty cute, actually. We look like we belong.

"You really do look beautiful, you know," he whispers into my hair.

"Oh. Um, thanks."

"Okay," he chuckles. "Do you think I'm lying or something?"

"No. I don't know why I said it like that," I say, shaking my head. "Thanks." I smile at him. "You look really good, too. And not… not just tonight."

The corner of his mouth curls and he wraps his arms around my waist. "Can I kiss you right now?" he whispers.

"In front of everyone?" I ask, slightly horrified.

He laughs quietly and looks around. "No one's paying attention. But even if they were, would it matter?"

"No, it doesn't matter. It's just sort of…" I trail off, because I actually don't know what I was going to say.

"Sort of what?" he asks.

"I don't know."

"Come here." He gently pulls me in closer so that our chests our touching, and then our noses, and then our lips. I close my eyes and let myself melt into him as we kiss. His mouth is like magic, I'm telling you. My arms and legs are turning to jelly, but I don't want to pull away from him.

But then I pull away from him because someone whistles and it makes me feel uncomfortable.

"Come on," he says, grabbing my hand and walking back to the hall. "They're probably serving dessert."

Emma and I get up to dance as soon as the lights dim and the music starts to blare. We don't even care what we look like, or if we're good at it, well, I care a little bit, but Emma helps me to loosen up. We've danced a lot in my room or in her room, and if I don't think about it or pay attention to everyone else around us, it's basically the same. Just like driving. Driving alone is just like driving with other people, and dancing in a room full of people is just like dancing alone with Emma. When the slow songs come on, we hold hands and place our other hands on each other's backs, and gently spin around, occasionally throwing in a twirl here and there. When we're tired and starting to sweat, we head back to our table for water, where Gavin and Teague are lounged in their chairs, their suit jackets off and ties loosened. I smile at Teague, but let him keep talking, and Emma and I sit in silence as we catch our breath. After about ten minutes, another slow song comes on and I'm about to grab Emma's hand but Teague is already standing next to my chair, an intense but very cute glare cutting into me.

"Yes?" I ask, looking up at him.

"Will you dance with me?" he asks.

"Oh, why yes of course," I reply with a smile. I take his hand and let him pull me to my feet, and together we walk to the middle of the dance floor. He pulls me in close to him like he did before we kissed on the patio, and butterflies erupt everywhere inside of me. I wrap my arms around his shoulders, and then he pulls me closer. We spin around in circles so slowly that we're barely moving, and I can't stop thinking about his hands on my lower back.

"Are you having fun?" he asks.

"Yeah, are you?"

"Yeah, it's alright. The place is set up really nice."

"And dessert was good," I add.

"Yes, the waffle bar was definitely a genius idea."

I can feel his pants buzz and he steps back a little bit from me, but still keeps a hand on my waist as he pulls his phone out of his pocket.

"Sorry," he says, "but it's probably my sister." And then he puts the phone to his ear. "Hey, what's up?" He takes another step back and lets go of me completely. He looks at me with this sharp pain in his eyes, and then turns away, putting his head down as he talks to Shayla. "Well is she breathing? Listen to me, it's fine, this has happened before, she just… Hold on, okay?" he turns to me with a pinched expression. "I'm really sorry, but I have to go."

"What's wrong? Is everything okay?" I ask.

"I don't know. Just give me a second, okay?"

I nod, and watch as he runs outside, his phone back against his ear. I stand alone on the dance floor, unsure of what to do next. Emma comes up behind me but I don't even flinch.

"What happened?" she asks.

"I don't know. It sounds like something bad."

"Oh my god, really?"

"He said he'd be right back, but I don't know, I'm worried."

I start to head for the door and Emma grabs onto my elbow.

"What?" I ask, looking at her fingers gripping my arm.

"He said he'd be right back, right?" she says, letting go of my arm.

I look towards the doors that Teague left through, and then back to Emma. "Yeah," I say slowly. "But I have a feeling he was just saying that."

"You don't think you're over stepping?"

"Sometimes people need someone to overstep, Emma," I say. "You're always telling me how I'm not paying attention to the people around me, like the signs of Teague liking me, and well, now I am. I'm paying attention, and I think Teague needs my help. Even if he doesn't tell me what's wrong, he needs to know that someone's there for him. That I'm there for him."

Emma nods, her face serious. "You're totally right. I think I need to learn from you, now."

"We can all learn a little bit from each other." I wink at her, but then remember what we're talking about, and I shake my head. "Okay, I'm going to go make sure he's okay."

Emma nods, and all of a sudden I'm walking towards the exit. What am I doing? Is this even the right call? He always seems so embarrassed when it comes to stuff with his sister. He clearly cares about her, but he keeps that part of his life so private, it's like he doesn't want anyone to be a part of it. He needs it to be a secret, and I don't want to force him to share it with me if he doesn't want to. But I'm walking through the doors now, and Teague is leaning forward with his hands on his knees, taking deep breaths.

"Teague?" I call out.

He stands up right away but he doesn't look good.

"Are you okay?" I ask.

He just shakes his head and says nothing.

I take a step towards him and he looks at his phone. Checking the time? A text message? A wind comes across the water and gives me goosebumps.

"I need to go home," he says.

"Are you okay to drive? You don't look great."

"I don't know," he says slowly. "But I didn't drive here, Gavin did."

"I can take you."

He takes a deep breath and then finally nods once. "Yeah, okay."

"Okay wait right here, I just need to get my purse."

He nods again and I run inside, almost twisting my ankle even though my heels are so small. I grab my clutch and quickly tell

Emma that I need to drive him home but that I'll be back. She tells me to go and before I know it, Teague is in the passenger seat of my uncle's car and I'm driving us away from prom.

23

I want to wait in the car but something is forcing me to go up the walkway with him. He doesn't tell me not to, but some part of me thinks he doesn't want me to see what's going on. But maybe another part of him does, and that's why he doesn't tell me not to go with him. I'm nervous for him, and I feel like I'm about to barf up my heart. He opens the front door pretty quickly and his sister is already there, frantic and crying. Teague pulls her into his chest and wraps his arms around her, stroking her back and gently shushing her.

"Where is she?" he whispers.

"She's in the bathroom upstairs, and I think she puked, but she's just lying there and-"

"It's okay," Teague says. "Stay here with Sadie; I'll go check on her, okay?"

Shayla gulps and nods, and Teague heads up the stairs that are right in front of us in the entrance. I suddenly feel more awkward than nervous, and I have no idea what to say to Shayla. What do you say in a situation like this? What's wrong with their mom? Is she sick?

"She's probably dead," Shayla says, making her way into the living room.

I slip my heels off and follow her. "Why would you say that?"

"It was bound to happen sometime," she sniffles.

"Is your mom sick?"

Shayla sits down on the couch so I sit next to her. "Not really," she says.

"Well your brother's upstairs making sure she's okay." I hope that's the right thing to say. I don't want to tell her that she'll be fine, because what if she isn't?

Teague comes bounding down the stairs and into the living room with his phone in his hand.

"I called an ambulance," he says. "Shayla, I'm going to call Anna's mom and see if you can spend the night at their house."

"What, no, I want to be with mom!"

"Mom's going to the hospital, so you can't!"

"I can go to the hospital with her!"

"No you can't, you can't sleep there."

"Well then why can't I stay here with you?"

"Because I'm going with her and I'll be back late."

"I can stay up late, too."

"Shayla, you're just going to be bored. I'm just going to be sitting in the waiting room and then when she wakes up I'm going to yell at her."

I really wish I knew what was going on, and why Teague wants to yell at his mom for being sick, but I stay quiet on the couch and let them figure everything out. Teague dials a number on his phone and then leaves the room to talk. He comes back a few minutes later and walks deliberately over to me, stops and stares at me like he's afraid to tell me my cat died.

"I need you to do me a huge favour," he says quietly.

"Sure, whatever you need."

"The ambulance is going to be here soon… and Shayla's friend is expecting her… And I need…"

"Do you want me to take her to her friend's house?" I ask.

"Could you?"

"Yes, of course. Do want me to help her pack a bag?"

"No, it's okay. Or, yes, that would be great. Just… don't go in the bathroom. Actually, I need to go up there and stay with her anyway, I'll follow you up. Shayla, come on."

Teague's sister reluctantly follows us up the stairs, and as I run my hand along the banister I'm transported back to when Teague and I were kids. The pictures on the wall are mostly the same; Teague and Shayla as babies and toddlers. My feet drag on the carpet once we get to the top, and I remember which way the bathroom is, so I make sure not to head that way.

"My room is right here," Shayla says, coming up behind me and opening her door before I have a chance to step any further.

Her room is all decked out in pink and black; a hot pink comforter with black throw pillows and black curtains, a furry area rug near her desk that's got pink sparkles in it. She opens her white dresser and pulls out some pyjamas, a new change of clothes, underwear and socks. She looks at me for a second and then at her bed, back to me, and then she quickly grabs a stuffed unicorn that has definitely seen better days, from her bed.

"I have a narwhal," I say.

"What?" she puts the unicorn in her bag and zips it up.

"You have a unicorn. I have a narwhal."

"What's that?" she asks.

"You don't know what a narwhal is?"

She shakes her head and sort of leans on her mattress a bit, waiting for me to tell her.

"It's basically a water unicorn. But they're real."

"What? No way."

"Yes way. They're like whales with horns on their heads, just like a unicorn."

"But they're real?"

"Yeah." I smile at her and she smiles too.

"I need my toothbrush," she says quietly.

"Oh. Right. Um. You know what? I'm sure it's fine for just one night. Or maybe your friend has a spare at her house."

"Yeah, maybe." She sighs and heads out of her room, so I follow her and shut the light off before I leave.

❤❤❤♡♡

"Is this your car?" Shayla asks once I back out of the driveway.

"No, it's my uncle's."

"Why is it your uncle's?"

"What kind of a question is that?" I ask with a bit of a smirk and sideways glance in her direction.

"I mean why are you driving your uncle's car instead of your mom's or your dad's?"

"I don't have a mom and dad. They died when I was four."

"Oh." I can see out of the corner of my eye that she's fiddling with her nails.

"It's okay," I say. "You don't have to be embarrassed or feel bad or anything."

"So you live with your uncle?" she finally asks.

"Yeah."

"Do you like it?"

"Yeah, I do. He's great."

"That's good."

"Yeah, it is."

It's quiet for a minute and all I can hear is the car blinker as I wait for traffic to clear so I can turn left.

"Not all families are perfect, I guess," Shayla says softly.

"Of course they aren't. I don't think any family is."

She lets out a deep breath and nods. "Some of them seem perfect, though. Like, they have a mom and dad, and siblings, and they have barbeques in the summer and stuff."

"You think that's the only thing that makes a family perfect?"

"I don't know," she says with a sigh. "Oh, that's her house right there." She points to the right and I pull into a driveway of a house that almost looks just like hers.

Shayla opens the door but stops before jumping out. "Thanks," she says with a soft smile.

"Of course," I say.

She gets out of the car and I wait to make sure she makes it inside before I drive away. I make it back to prom and pull into the same spot I was in before. I check my phone before going back in, in case Teague still needs me.

I'm getting a cab home in a bit. Will you come over? he had typed.

I can come get you from the hospital. Is your mom ok?

It's fine, have fun with Emma and just… if you just want to come here after, that would be cool.

Are you ok? I ask.

I think so.

I stare at my phone screen, thinking about what to say back. He only *thinks* he's okay? That means he's not okay. What happened? I can't have fun anymore knowing that Teague's mom is sick and he's at home by himself, worrying. Either way, I have to tell Emma what's going on. I put my phone in my purse and head inside, shivering a little on the way.

I find Emma sitting at our table, talking with Summer. It looks like a lot of people have already left; the dance floor only has about 20 people on it.

"Hey, is Teague okay? What happened?" Emma asks as soon as I sit down.

"I don't know," I say, shaking my head. "He had to call an ambulance for his mom."

"What? Oh my god, what happened?"

"I don't know. But he asked if I would go to his house after prom is over; he's going to be there alone."

"Oh my god, are you ready to do that?"

"Do what?" I ask.

"Um, hello, no one else is going to be there?"

"No, it's not like that. He just needs someone. He's worried about his mom."

"Okay, if you're sure that's all it is."

"I'm sure that's all it is," I say.

Emma and I try to dance and have fun for the rest of the night, but it's hard with Teague on our minds. We end up going outside to look at the boats on the water and all the lights around the marina illuminating it in glowing spotlights. The boats rock gently when the wind comes, and Emma and I just hold each other, trying to keep each other warm. A few other people come out to talk, or take pictures, or just admire the view, but mostly we're alone and mostly it's quiet.

"We can go if you want," Emma finally says.

"In a bit. Let's just sit a little longer."

When the cool summer air is finally too much for our bare arms, we go in to say goodbye to Summer and Carter, and then go back to the car. I drive Emma home and then text Uncle Adam.

Something happened to Teague's mom and she's at the hospital. I'm going to go to Teague's.

When do you think you'll be home? he replies.

I don't know. But I really think he needs someone to be with him right now.

Okay stay as long as you need. I love you.

I love you too.

♥ ♥ ♥ ♡ ♡

I can feel my heartbeat in my throat by the time I get to Teague's and I have to take a few minutes to breathe deeply before I get out of the car. I fidget with the rearview mirror and the sun visor. I open the glove compartment and make sure the car insurance and ownership is there. I don't know why. I'm just stalling going in for some reason. I pull out my phone and look at the time: 10:47pm. Prom ends at eleven, so besides me leaving for a bit in the middle, we stayed for most it. Not that it matters, anyway, what matters is that Teague is okay. I finally grab my stuff and force myself out of the car. I can do this. I need to do this. Teague needs me.

I knock on the door first, and wait a minute or so. He doesn't answer the door so I knock again and then text him.

I'm at your door I type.

No response. Is he even home? His car is in the driveway, but he said he was getting a cab home, so he must have gone with his mom in the ambulance. What if he's not home yet? What if he thought I was going to stay at prom until it was completely over and he wasn't expecting me until later? Should I go home and change first? But then I notice that a light is on; I can see it through the window beside the door. I let out a deep breath and decide to just try opening the door. Maybe his phone is dead and he didn't hear the knock. I turn the handle and push the door open easily.

"Teague?" I call.

I hear a weird choking sound coming from around the stairs and I startle. What is that? And then I hear a moan, and a sob, and I realize that Teague is crying. But he's not just crying, he's like, bawling. I'm afraid to walk in on him because I have a feeling he doesn't know that I'm here, but I don't want to just stand at the front door or go back to the car while he's clearly upset. I can't leave him alone. He's all alone.

"Teague?" I call again, hoping to give him some warning. I slide my feet out of my shoes and set my clutch down on the bottom stair and slowly walk around the entry and into the kitchen. Teague is leaning forward, his arms stretched out to the edge of the counter, with his head lowered between his shoulders. And every time he takes a shaky breath and lets out with another wail, it makes me want to cry myself. He's not wearing his tie anymore, and his collar is open a few buttons, his shirt untucked from his black pants.

"Teague?" I force myself to say one more time.

He startles a little and turns his head towards me, but keeps his posture leaning on the counter. He sobs again and I let myself step closer to him. He wipes his face and then steps back, leaning his back against the counter behind him.

"Do you… Do you want me to leave?" I ask, pointing my thumb behind me at the door.

"No," he chokes, shaking his head. His eyes are red and his cheeks are puffy, wet with tears. I haven't seen him cry since we were kids and it worries me a little. His face and neck are all red and splotchy. "Just give me a minute," he says, turning away. He strides across the linoleum and sits at the small kitchen table, putting his head in his hands. I want to sit next to him, but I'm afraid his "give me a minute" means that he doesn't want me to see him like this. So instead I stand awkwardly in the entrance of his kitchen while he calms down at the table. His sobs quiet down quickly and he takes a few deep breaths before getting up and slowly walking towards me.

"Sorry about that," he says.

"Don't be," I reply. "Is your mom okay?"

"Yeah." He shrugs.

"… Do you want to tell me about it?"

"Do you want to get out of that dress first?"

I almost gulp and look at him with what I'm sure is the most horrified expression ever.

"Oh my god," he says quickly, "I just heard how that came out. Oh my god, I didn't mean it like that. I just meant… Ugh, oh my god, I'm sorry. I meant do you want some pyjamas to wear? Something more comfortable?"

"Oh." I gulp again because now I'm extra nervous, but I nod and smile. "Yeah, sure. Thanks. I was going to go home and change, but then … Um, I didn't."

I follow him upstairs to his room and he grabs a t-shirt and pair of plaid pyjama pants from his dresser and hands them to me. He grabs some for himself and leaves, saying I can use his room to change. I hang my dress on the back of his computer chair and pull on the pants he gave me. Because Teague isn't much bigger than me and I have hips, the pants are a little tight, but they'll do. I open the door a crack when I'm done so he knows that he can come back in when he's ready, but he still knocks anyway.

"Come in," I say.

He steps into his room with a sheepish smile and I smile back. I don't know what to say.

"So about my mom," he says slowly.

"Yeah?"

The redness on his face and neck is already almost gone. He scratches his head a little and then sits down on his bed. He curls his feet under him and leans his back against the wall.

"Um, so my mom's not very good at dealing with things," he starts.

I nod, and slowly make a move to sit on the bed too. I feel weird about it, but let myself get comfortable on the end of the bed, facing him.

"Mostly it's when good things happen to my dad," he continues. "Like when he first got remarried. She was a mess. And when he had a new kid. Terrible. And…" he runs his hand through his hair and sighs. "Over the past two years or so, he hasn't been keeping touch or wanting to see us."

"Oh, I'm sorry," I say.

"It's okay. He's kind of a jerk. Or I mean, he was already a jerk before that, I mean, so it's not really a big deal. I mean, yeah, it's a big deal, but I would rather not talk to him anyway. But my mom doesn't deal with it well. And since he's been refusing to see Shayla, or I mean, not really refusing, more like, just, not caring to, she's been so upset about it. It hurts Shayla so much, and that hurts my mom, and she doesn't deal with it well."

"So what does she do?" I ask.

His eyes lock on to mine for a second and then he looks away. "She drinks," he says.

I nod slowly. "Oh."

"She's been drinking ever since I was twelve, but mostly she's good at hiding it. I guess I'd call her a high-functioning alcoholic. Is that a term?"

"I don't know."

"Well anyway, usually she just drinks, and yeah, gets drunk, but she isn't always like, visibly drunk, if that makes sense. She doesn't really get sloppy or angry, she's just dulling her pain. But she also goes out a lot and comes home drunk but then just goes to bed and sleeps it off. That or she doesn't come home at all. But sometimes it gets out of hand. Like tonight."

"Like tonight," I repeat, unsure of what else to say.

"She doesn't drive to work or anything, that's why I always have her car. I'm just so afraid that she's going to drink after work and then drive home. Or drink before work. Anyway, if she's having a bad day or week, she usually goes out. She's had a few boyfriends, and I think she just uses them to make herself feel better."

I really wish I had something reassuring to say but I have never been in this situation before and I'm afraid that if I say something I'll make it worse.

"I didn't let her come to Shayla's birthday party," he says quietly. "I thought she would ruin it."

"I'm sorry," I whisper.

"It's fine. I just don't know what to do."

"Can you ask her to stop?"

"I always ask her stop, Sadie. She can't."

"What if she went to a rehab place? Or AA?"

He shrugs and lies down, cuddling one of his pillows. I lie down too, facing him.

"Sadie," he whispers.

"Teague."

"When we were kids… I didn't want you to come over. I didn't want you to come over and see my mom."

"What?"

"That's why I stopped being your friend. My new friends didn't know and I just told them I wasn't allowed to have friends over. I didn't… I didn't know what to say to you. I was afraid that if you came over and saw my mom all drunk, you would judge me."

"Oh, Teague… I never would have judged you. I would have tried to help. Or to at least be there for you."

"I know." A tear seeps out of one of his eyes and runs across his nose. "But I didn't know that then."

I let out a deep breath and nod.

"She's not always bad like this," he says. "Sometimes we have nice dinners together."

"Just sometimes?" I ask.

"Well she's out a lot, with her boyfriends. Most of the time when she's home, she's okay, especially if she comes home right home after work. She's just… not home a lot."

"Teague, I'm so sorry. You make everything seem so easy. I thought … I don't know what I thought. I just had no idea, and I'm sorry."

"Stop being sorry."

"Okay." We're both quiet for a minute, and he closes his eyes, but then I ask a question. "Is that why you're not going away to school right away?"

He nods, but doesn't say anything.

"Have you looked into rehab programs?" I ask. "I can help you."

"Sure. You can help me. But not tonight. Tonight I want to sleep."

"Okay. I should go home, then."

"No, stay? Please?"

"Okay."

We don't say anything else to each other, or even move on the bed. We lay next to each other on top of the covers and fall asleep like it's been waiting all night for us.

"Zed," Teague whispers.

"Hmm?"

"Your phone won't stop going off."

"What?" I wipe my eyes and try to open them, but the room is so bright. "What time is it?" I roll over to see through squinted eyelids that Teague is standing next to his bed, holding my phone out to me.

"I got up to pee and I heard it ding downstairs, and it just wouldn't stop. It's 4am."

I grab the phone from him and am about to open my messages when it actually rings. It's my uncle.

"Hi," I say into the phone.

"Sadie, oh my god, where are you?" Uncle Adam says in a panic.

"I told you I was going to Teague's."

"I didn't know you were staying all night! I was worried sick!"

"I'm sorry, I was going to come home, but we fell asleep." I cringe a little at my lie, knowing full well I could have texted him before going to sleep. But I was afraid he wasn't going to let me stay.

"Well I need the car for work in the morning so when are you going to be home?"

"I can come now," I say, sitting up and letting my legs swing over the side of the bed.

"No, it's too late. Just make sure you're home by eight, please. I have a lot I need to do before I open Laser Tag and I need the car."

"Seriously?"

"Yes, seriously, it's four in the morning, Sadie, and you sound like you're half asleep. I don't want you driving right now, what if something happens to you?"

"Well I'm awake now. I'm not going to crash the car or anything."

"I would rather you stay at Teague's. Is he okay?"

"Yeah, he's okay."

"Good. Let me know what's going on, next time, okay?"

"Yeah, I will. Sorry."

"Okay. I'm going back to bed."

"Okay, goodnight," I say.

"Night." He hangs up the phone and I stare at Teague, who's looking at me with raised eyebrows.

"Are you in trouble?" he asks.

"I don't think so? He told me to stay here."

"That's weird."

"A little."

"Do you want to just go back to sleep?"

"Kind of," I say.

"Yeah, me too."

He gets back in his spot against the wall, but starts to pull the covers so we can get under them. I set the alarm on my phone for 7:30 and snuggle up under the blankets. Teague lifts his arm and I scooch under it, letting him wrap his arm around my back. I press my forehead into his chest and breathe in his scent, falling back to sleep without even trying.

♥♥♥♡♡

I groan when my alarm goes off, but Teague is already up; I can see the bathroom light on down the hall. I get out of bed and grab my dress, and slowly make my way to the door.

"I have to go," I say as I head down the stairs.

Teague comes rushing out of the bathroom. "Me too. I have to go get my mom."

"Do you want to hang out later? And research? Um, AA and stuff?"

"Yeah, okay."

"We don't have to, I just thought-"

"I said yes," he says with a smile. "I've wanted to for a while, but I've been afraid to do it on my own."

"Okay," I say. "Well, just text me, then."

"I will."

"And Teague?" I add.

"Yes?"

"This isn't anything you need to be ashamed about."

"Okay."

"I'm serious," I say. "I'm not going to go telling people or anything, but just… just don't feel ashamed. I feel bad that you felt the need to hide it all this time. People could have helped."

"I know. But it's hard."

"I know it's hard," I reply. "And I get it. But you don't have to hide anything from me."

❤❤❤♡♡

"How was prom?" Uncle Adam asks when I get inside.

"It was good. I mean, besides the whole having to leave because Teague's mom went to the hospital."

"Oh, yeah what happened?"

"Um, I'm not sure if it's something he wants to share. But she's okay."

"I'm glad."

"I didn't… We didn't do anything. At Teague's."

"Oh god," Adam says, throwing up his hands. "Why would you say that to me?"

"Because I didn't want you to think that we did."

"I didn't think that you did anything, Sadie, but now that's all I can think about, and it's weird and wrong and terrible! Make it stop!"

I laugh a little and follow him into the hall. "I mean, I just…"

"You just what?" And then his eyes widen and he gasps. "Is he your boyfriend!?"

"No! I mean, no."

"No you mean no?" he asks, clearly making fun of me.

"I mean I don't know. We kissed."

"You kissed!?" But now he doesn't sound terrified, he sounds happy for me.

"Yes!"

"Well that's really exciting, Sadie! So why isn't he your boyfriend?"

"We haven't talked about it yet. We just kissed, I mean, people kiss without being boyfriend and girlfriend, right?"

He smirks and nods towards the elevators. "I have to go to work. But I'm glad you kissed, and I'm glad you didn't *do anything* at his house. It honestly never even crossed my mind. I knew you were getting a crush on him or whatever, but I didn't…" he stops and shakes his head a little. "Please don't make me worry again. And please be careful and responsible and don't do anything you're not comfortable with. No matter how you think it'll make Teague feel. He's not important, you are." He shakes his head again. "No, he's important, too, but his feelings are not as important as yours. Oh my god, this is not coming out the way that I want. Everyone's feelings are important. But him wanting to do something isn't more important than you *not* wanting to do something. I just want you to be careful."

"Maybe we should talk about this later," I say.

"Right, yes, good call. But I'm-"

"Uncle Adam," I say, "Go to work."

"You've made me all flustered!" he says as he heads down the hall, leaving me at our door. "I don't know what to do now that my niece has a boyfriend!"

"You don't have to do anything!" I call to him.

He says something else but I can't hear him. Probably something about him being worried, or me making good choices or something. He presses the button for the elevator and I head back into the apartment.

♥♥♥♡♡

The recommendation letter is on the coffee table. It's printed, lying face up, on the coffee table. Ready for anyone to come across and read. It's just sitting there. Maybe he put it there on purpose. Like he wanted to tell me about it but didn't know how, so he left it for me to find. Or maybe he just doesn't care if I read it. I can't not read it.

Mathieu Levesque has made me a better person. He is the perfect man for adoption in more than one way, and I found it hard to narrow the reasons down to make this letter an acceptable length.

Mathieu is kind, generous, and selfless. He was only 21 when my niece, Sadie, was put into my care, and he changed his entire life for us. We both changed our lives for Sadie, but Mat and I hadn't been dating an entire year yet, and he knew that he didn't need to help me raise a child if he didn't feel ready for it, but he did. He did everything to help me. And he helped raise a beautiful girl, inside and out, with strong morals and a personality that definitely shows him off.

Mat is loving, and caring, and has always been there for Sadie, no matter how big or small. She knows that he's there for her and always will be. Mat is good at being Sadie's friend while still being her parent, something I always needed help with. Something that I still struggle with. I'm no good at being a parent. I don't know what I would have done if it weren't for him.

And above all, Mat wants *a child of his own. He loves Sadie, and I know he couldn't imagine a world without her in his life, but he wants more. He wants to care for someone from the start, someone who needs him. A child should not be raised by parents who don't want them, and Mat wants them. He wants it so badly that he has decided to do it without me, and I respect him for that. He can do it on his own with no trouble, because he* wants *it. He has his life together, he has a great job, a safe apartment, and a great support system. He has parents a short distance away, an almost-18-year-old niece who I know would love to be a part of this child's life, and he has me. We're not together anymore, but I will always be there for him if he needs it. He has been able to put our differences aside recently when our niece was in the hospital, so that we could both be there for her. He is a good person, and he deserves this. Mat will give a child the perfect, loving home that they too, deserve.*

I sniffle and put the paper back on the coffee table. Adam needs to know that he's a great parent. I can't believe he thinks he's a terrible parent. When he said it back when he found out about me hanging out with Mat, I thought it was just an 'in the moment' thought, not an 'all the time' thought. He actually thinks he's bad at being a parent? Have I made him feel that way? I pick up the letter and read it again, and this time I burst out crying by the time I finish. It makes me so happy to know that Adam doesn't seem to hate Mat, and that Mat must have asked Adam to write it, so their bickering can't be that serious. They still love each other in the same way, or at least care for one another. It touches me in a way I didn't think it would, even though I didn't know what to expect before I read it.

I take a long shower and calm down a bit, thinking of what I want to say to Uncle Adam when he comes home. I brush through my hair and put on a pair of jeans and a hoodie when I get out, and suddenly feel empty. I don't know what to do with my day. I end up eating three bowls of cereal and watching *Brooklyn Nine-Nine* before Teague texts me.

Can't hang out today, sorry.

No worries I reply. **Is everything ok?**

Ya. Can I call you later?

Of course.

He leaves it at that, and I don't push.

Uncle Adam comes home just before 6pm and I look up from studying at the kitchen table when he walks in.

"Hey," he says.

"Hey," I reply, looking up from the table.

"What do you want for supper?"

"Why do you think you're a bad parent?" I ask without thinking. As soon as I say it I want to slap my hand over my mouth and reverse time, but instead I stare at him, sort of frozen.

He shakes his head a little and takes his shoes off without saying anything. He looks at me with an expression I can't place and I'm afraid I've stepped over some sort of line. Is he hurt? Or is he just unsure of how to reply, since he thinks he's a bad parent and all.

"Did I leave the letter lying around?" he finally says, still standing at the door.

I'm too nervous now to say anything so I just nod.

"Sadie," he says slowly. But then he doesn't add anything else.

"You're a good parent," I finally say, looking at him from across the kitchen.

He strides through the room and sits across from me at the table where I've got my binder and text book open across the tabletop. He rests his face in his hands and sighs. "Thanks," he says quietly.

"I'm serious."

"If your parents were still here… your life… they would be…"

"I know," I say. "Everything would be different, but that doesn't mean that this is bad. That you're bad."

He covers his face with his hands for a few seconds and then drops them onto the table. "I let you stay over at a boy's house. *After prom.*"

"So?"

He tilts his head at me and raises his eyebrows.

"I told you, nothing happened!" I say. "We've kissed like, twice, and last night was not about that! He needed someone to be there for him."

"I know, I know," he says quickly. "But a good parent would have thought more about it."

"No," I say. "Most people's parents wouldn't let them stay over at a boy's house, especially the night of prom, and then maybe something bad would have happened. Teague was not doing well. If I couldn't go to his house, he would have…" I shake my head. "He would have been so alone," I add quietly.

Adam takes a deep breath and looks away for a second before landing his eyes back on mine. He opens his mouth to say something, but then closes his mouth again.

"You're a good parent because I can tell you these things," I try. "I didn't lie to you, or sneak around, I let you know where I was because… because you're a good parent."

He smirks a little. "Thanks. But I'm not… I wrote the letter before last night," he says. "It's other stuff. It's just…" He shrugs.

"If you weren't already my uncle, you'd be my dad," I say.

And apparently I just have to see everyone cry lately, because he does a weird little sob thing, like he's trying so hard not to cry but it just snuck up on him, so I get up from my chair and walk around the table to him. I lean over and put my arms around him and he hugs me back, and does another little sob thing.

"I love you so much, Sadie," he says.

"I love you too."

I hear Uncle Adam's phone ring at about 10pm and once I realize it sounds like he's talking to Mat, I try to casually move from my bedroom so I can listen. Not that I think they're going to get back together or anything, but I would love it if they could be friends. If Mat could adopt a baby and Adam could be that baby's uncle, too. I just really want them to get to the point where they want to be at family birthday parties together, or stop to have a conversation if they see each other in the grocery store instead of just nodding and saying hello.

I sit on the couch and scroll through my phone to make it look like I'm not paying attention, but then Adam hangs up and smiles at me.

"What's up?" he asks.

"Nothing," I say with a shrug. I go back to my phone and a follow request pops up on Instagram. I open it up and can't help but smile when I see that it's Teague. I know it's just Instagram, but it still seems like something to me anyway. I hit accept and then follow him back.

"What's that smile about?" Adam asks.

"Huh? Oh, nothing." I get up from the couch and make my way back to my room.

"Where are you going? You just sat down."

"Bed, I guess," I reply.

"You guess? What does that mean? What's going on? Am I missing something?"

"I have school in the morning," I say, but even I can hear the smile in my voice. "I need to sleep."

"Okay," he says, in a tone that tells me he doesn't believe me.

I go into my room, plop onto my beanbag chair and text Emma first.

Sorry I didn't text you after prom I say.

That's ok is everything ok?

Ya I reply. **I told Teague I wouldn't tell anyone what happened.**

But you can tell me right? ;)

Noooooo 😞

That's ok I was just kidding. Is he ok? she asks.

He will be. He just followed me on Instagram.

He didn't follow you on Instagram before?

Ha. No. Anyway, how was the rest of your weekend?

Fine. I just watched TV all day. So is Teague your boyfriend now?

Why do we have to talk about Teague? I type.

Um, why wouldn't we? You guys kissed at LASER TAG and then you went to his house after prom!

But I wanted to talk about you.

Why? I have nothing interesting happening in my life. You're the one who turned the popular boy nice and I want to know about it!

I didn't turn him nice I say. **He was always nice.**

Ok sure.

He was. He never actually did anything to hurt me. He just seemed like a jerk because we didn't know him.

Ok sure.

I call her and she answers the phone with a confused sounding hello.

"I don't want to type anymore," I explain.

"So tell me why you think he was never a jerk, when literally three months ago you were complaining about being his partner for that project."

"I can't tell you all of it, like why he was a jerk when we were kids… but, I mean… we were kids."

"Okay. Fair enough. Kids are jerks. Kids grow up. Why was he not a jerk when he was a teenager? When they usually know a bit better?"

"Because he wasn't a jerk. We just weren't friends. He never said anything rude to me, or made me feel like a loser besides his not saying hello to me. But we weren't friends! You don't say hello to people who aren't your friends, do you?"

"Well, no. But I don't like many people."

"Yeah, I figured that out already," I say with a laugh. "But I dunno. We didn't know each other. I didn't like him because I only knew what I saw in the halls at school, and that wasn't even much."

"What about when he blew you off?"

"Justified," I say.

"He still could have called you."

"Yeah," I sigh. "He could have. But he was in a tough situation. Calling me to say he couldn't study would have been at the bottom of his list."

"Fine. So do you think he's good looking now that you don't think he's a jerk?"

"Well I mean…" I pause and bite my lip, afraid to say it out loud, which makes zero sense since I've already kissed him more than once. Why would admitting that I think he's cute be hard?

"Oh you do," Emma says. "You love him."

"Emma! I do not!"

"Whatever. You like him."

"Yeah," I say slowly. "I like him. A lot." And I'm smiling again. "But I actually meant to text him after I checked in with you. I didn't mean for this conversation to go on this long."

"Oh great, nice to see you care about me," she jokes.

"Bye Emma," I laugh.

"Don't call me back until he's your boyfriend!"

"Goodbye Emma," I say again, and I hang up.

I call Teague and he picks up on the first ring.

"Hey," he says, the recognition in his voice warming my heart.

"Hey," I reply.

"How's it going?"

"Good," I say. "You?"

"It's okay. My mom's going to go to AA."

"Really? That's amazing."

"Yeah, it's a start. We had a really long talk today and we hung out all afternoon and watched movies with Shayla. And after Shayla went to bed, we talked more."

"That's really good," I say. "Was last night… Was last night, like, was it her worst night?"

"Yeah," he says slowly. "I think that's a big part of what made her want to be better. I don't think she realized before, just how bad it was. But when… When you drink so much that…"

"Yeah," I say, letting him not finish his sentence. "It sucks that it had to get to the point for her to realize the damage she was doing to her family, but it's good that she sees it now."

"Yeah," he agrees. "It's something."

"It's something," I repeat.

It's quiet for a few minutes but listening to him breathe is comforting. I want to ask him about our kisses, if it means the same thing to him as it does to me, but I don't really want to do it over the phone.

"Are you working after school tomorrow?" he finally asks.

"Yeah," I say.

"Okay. Um, what about Tuesday?"

"No, I don't work on Tuesday."

"It's cheap night at the movies."

"Yes it is," I say, trying to fight the smile growing on my face.

"Do you want to go to the movies?"

"Is he your boyfriend?" Emma asks when I get on the bus on Monday morning.

"No," I say. "But we're going to the movies tomorrow."

"Ooooh, so he'll be your boyfriend then, right?!"

"I don't know," I laugh. "I hope so."

"Are you nervous to see him in first period?"

"No," I say. "I don't think so."

Oh crap, I'm nervous. I'm afraid to go into the classroom and see him sitting at his desk so I just stand out in the hall. All I can think about is that this weekend everything sort of changed between us, but didn't at the same time. I still felt comfortable with him after we kissed, but now that we're back at school, I feel like I'm supposed to pretend like nothing happened. Like he doesn't want his popular friends to know that he kissed the girl no one cares about. But no, Teague's not like that. Maybe he already told his friends all excitedly, the way I told Emma. Do guys do that? Would he have told Candace? Has he kissed Candace before? Oh my god, he's probably kissed Candace. Candace is probably a way better kisser than I am.

"Hey Zed," Teague says from his desk. Have I been standing in the doorway for a long time? When did I even get to the door? Can people tell that I'm nervous?

"Hi," I say. I practically run past his desk to mine, and immediately start going through my bag. I startle when I look up to see Teague standing over me.

"Are you okay?" he asks.

"What? Yes, of course, I'm fine, why wouldn't I be fine?"

He chuckles and runs his hand through his hair, making it all stick up everywhere. God his hair looks good like that. "You don't seem fine," he says.

"I'm fine, I said I'm fine." I smile at him, but I can tell that he knows it's forced. He leans forward and puts his hands on my desk, bringing his face in real close to mine.

"As long as you're fine," he says gently.

"I'm fine," I whisper.

"I know you are, you just said you were, like nine times." He smiles, but doesn't move his face away from mine. We're so close we could kiss right here in class.

"I know," I say, my nerves not letting up. Is he doing this on purpose?

"Okay," he whispers. And then he kisses me on the cheek, which somehow just makes everything worse, and without saying anything else he turns and goes back to his desk. I can feel my face heat up and it crawls down my neck and I'm so embarrassed and afraid that everyone can see me blushing. Summer sits down next to me with a twisted look, like she has no idea what's going on.

I don't even know what's going on. I slam my forehead against my desk, and when I look up, Teague is half-turned around in his chair, his arm draped over the back, and he's just smirking at me. How is he all calm and cool and collected? How is he acting like the most laid back, cool guy ever right now? This must be why he's popular and I'm not. He's just so cool. Look at him sitting in that chair, acting like he owns it. Like he knows he makes me nervous, and he thinks it's funny. Or cute. Hopefully he thinks it's cute.

Teague waves to me in the hall at lunch, and I wave back, but I eat with Emma like normal, and we hang out in the library during our spare and help each other study for exams. We go our separate ways for last period and I pass Teague in the hall again, and he smiles and says hey, to which I reply with some sort of weird noise. He was already basically passed me by the time I found my voice, and I couldn't form a proper word. I hope he didn't hear me. Why have I turned into a bumbling idiot all of a sudden? Nothing's different. Literally nothing is different, yet I feel like I can't function around him all of a sudden. I just feel different around him when we're at school for some reason.

Mat comes into Laser Tag when I'm working after school and I almost jump when I see him. I come out from behind the counter and give him a hug, which feels better than I thought it would. I haven't seen him in a while.

"I wanted to ask if you could watch Pasta for me this weekend. I'm going away for work," he says.

"Oh. Yeah. Of course."

"If it's okay with Adam, I wanted to ask if you would stay at my apartment so he doesn't have to be in the crate."

"Well I work on Saturday," I say with a sympathetic shrug.

"Oh, right. Okay, well that's fine. He can be in the crate while you work. But if you're there for the rest of the time, that would be really helpful. I can stock the fridge with food and pop for you, and leave money for pizza or something."

"That sounds like fun. Would Emma be allowed over?"

"Yeah, of course. Just Emma, though."

"For sure. Do you want me to ask Uncle Adam about it?"

"No," he says with a little hand wave. "I'll ask him. But you're graduating soon and I thought you would be responsible enough for the job if you wanted it."

"Yeah," I say with a smile.

"Perfect." He smiles and starts to turn to leave but then stops. "It's not busy in here," he says. "I can stay and hang out for a bit. Do you have time to play a game of air hockey?" But then he turns around and sees the empty space where the table used to be. "Oh. It's gone. What happened to it?"

"It broke," I sigh. "We got a new one, but we're still waiting for it to come in."

"Oh man, that sucks. Those things must be expensive."

"Yeah," I say. "But it's okay, people spend a lot of money on air hockey. It was the most popular next to *Clown Fish*."

"Yeah, that's weird, what does everyone love about that game?"

"I don't know, it's fun!"

"Well do you want to play?"

"Yeah, okay. As long as you keep an eye out for customers at the counter when it's my turn."

He doesn't even ask to use my code on the coin machine; he puts in a five dollar bill and a bunch of toonies, paying for us to play. The couple who were playing the racing game for the last half hour get up to leave and they smile and wave as they walk out.

"Thanks for coming," I say to them.

They wave again and say to have a good night just before the door closes behind them.

I let Mat play first and watch him play through the first level, which is swimming as the clown fish and keeping a shell from falling into the abyss below you. He gets frustrated every time he drops the shell and I laugh at him. You're supposed to keep it afloat in front of you as you swim through different caverns and stuff, but if you don't swim at a consistent speed, it's easy to drop it.

"Why won't it let me start over?" he asks.

"You have to get it before it disappears," I say. "Quick! Swim down!"

Aaaand it disappears and he's lost a life and starts back at the beginning of the level. The shell drops down from the surface and he starts pushing buttons and using the joystick to swim the fish along and keep the shell in front of him. But he's pressing too many buttons and keeps making the shell jump and then drop, losing more lives.

"Ah *ben voyons!*" he yells as he tries to swim down and retrieve it before it disappears into the dark waters. He only has one life left, so the pressure's on. He grabs the shell and manages to bring it back up to the pretty part of the water and keeps swimming, keeping it in front of him. He goes a bit of a ways but just as he starts to relax and think he's getting good at it, the shell drops again. He manages to get it in time, but then of course an octopus shows up, throwing him way off.

"What!?" Mat screeches. "Now there's a *pieuvre!?*"

"A what?" I ask, laughing.

"You know what I'm talking about! The *pieuvre!* The big giant *pieuvre!* With all the arms! What's that called in English?" He's jamming buttons and moving the joystick as he yells all this in a panic, trying to avoid the tentacles reaching out for him, but he drops the shell again and the octopus wraps a tentacle around the fish, making the screen turn black and *Game Over* come up on the screen in red letters.

"The octopus?" I ask.

"Yes! The octopus, the octopus! You know what I meant!"

I laugh again, and Mat lets out a deep breath.

"Oh man, that game is stressful," he says.

"It's pretty addictive. People play it all day."

"Maybe we should just play a racing game. I don't even think I can watch you play this, it's too much for me."

I laugh so hard that I actually throw my head back, and Mat giggles a bit too. It's really nice to see him in such a good mood, even if he was just incredibly stressed out from a video game. I could tell he was having fun, even when he was frustrated and forgot how to say octopus, he was smiling the whole time. And even though we've had great visits since he and Adam broke up, we haven't really laughed like this yet. It hasn't been quite so easy and carefree as it is right now. And it's nice.

"We can't play a racing game together, though," I say, "In case someone comes in."

And as if people outside were waiting for the perfect time to come to the arcade, a group of kids from school step through the door.

"Hey guys," I say to them, turning my body towards them. But then I realize that it's Teague, Carter, Summer, Gavin, and Candace, and suddenly I feel incredibly awkward. I just said 'hey guys' to them like they were customers I didn't know.

"Hey," Teague says. He notices Mat beside me and nods to him. "Hi Mat," he adds.

"Hey, how's it going?"

"Alright. We just thought we'd come have a *Clown Fish* contest. See who can get the farthest."

I turn to Mat. "See?"

"Well I'll leave you guys to it. I'm sure you'll do better than I did." He starts to fish the coins out of his pocket. "I'm not going to use these. Do you guys want them?"

"Really?" Teague asks.

"Yeah, of course. You guys have fun." He hands them off to Teague, who then starts giving them to his friends.

"Thanks!" Teague says gratefully.

Mat smiles and nods and then heads to the door. He smiles at me and waves before leaving, and then I make my way back to my stool behind the counter. I notice before I make it all the way there, though, that Teague is following me. I let him, and don't look at him until I'm behind the counter and sitting. He leans his elbows on the counter and smirks at me.

"What?" I ask.

"Nothing. Just thought I'd come say hi."

"Hi." I can feel myself blushing and I wish I could hide it.

"Why do you seem nervous?" he asks.

"I don't know. Because you make me nervous now."

"Why?"

"I don't know, Teague. I don't know!"

He chuckles. "Is it because you don't know when I'm going to kiss you again?"

"Well, it *wasn't*, but now it is!"

"You're cute, you know that?"

"Well I always hoped I was," I try to joke.

"You don't need to be nervous around me, Zed."

"I know I don't *need* to. I don't like being nervous. It's not like I ask for it."

"You're right, that was a silly thing to say. But it's still me. I'm the same person. Just because we kissed a few times over the weekend and you saw me cry doesn't mean I'm going to treat you differently."

Gavin shouts across the arcade and throws his arms up, and then shoves Carter, who shoves him back. Teague looks over at them briefly and then back at me.

"Is it because of my friends?" he asks.

"I don't know, maybe."

"They think you're cool, you know."

"Okay," I say slowly.

"Look, don't worry about them. I know it's hard not to worry when you worry, but just… they don't matter."

"Don't say that, they're your friends."

Summer comes up to us then, and she smiles at me and says hi.

"Hi," I reply. "Having fun?"

"Yeah." She sounds out of breath, like she's been bouncing up and down the whole time she's been here. "Can I get a bag of chips and a Sprite?" she asks.

"Of course." I fill a cup up with Sprite from the pop machine and she grabs a bag of dill pickle chips from the display on the counter and I ring it up for her. She smiles as she taps her debit card on the machine and then hops back over to everyone with her treats.

"You know Summer wasn't really my friend until she started dating Carter," Teague says.

"Of course she was, you're friends with basically everyone."

"Why do you think that? I'm friends with the people in this room right now. Just because I know a lot of people doesn't mean I'm friends with them all. I'm pretty sure you knew Summer better than I did before a couple months ago."

"I don't really know her; we just sit next to each other in first period."

Teague rolls his eyes and leans back, hanging onto the counter with his fingertips. "You need to stop thinking low of yourself. You're way better than you think you are."

"What? I didn't… I'm not-"

He cuts me off. "Confidence, Zed. I know you have it in there." He smiles and heads back over to the *Clown Fish* game.

I'm waiting for Teague to come pick me up for our date and I feel like I'm going to barf. Uncle Adam squeezes my shoulders a little bit as he passes me by the door.

"Is he coming up to the apartment to get you?" he asks.

"I don't know. Maybe I should just go downstairs and wait for him?"

Adam shrugs. "Whatever." But then he laughs. "You look more nervous than you did before your driving test."

"Because I am! This is way worse than a driving test!"

"Why?" he chuckles. "I thought you liked Teague?"

"I do! But… I don't know." I shrug. "I've never done this before. It's scary."

He nods and smiles a little. "Yeah, it can be scary, can't it?"

"Yeah," I say quietly.

"Well Teague doesn't seem like the type to push someone farther than they're comfortable with. I don't think he would make you feel like you have to do things you aren't comfortable with. And if he does… Screw him." His eyes widen suddenly. "I mean leave him. Don't… ah, this is terrible. I'm terrible."

I laugh a little and feel a bit better. "I'm sorry for making you talk about this."

"It's okay. But we probably should talk about it. Parents do that, right?"

"I don't know. Did your parents talk to you about stuff?"

"No. But your dad did."

"Oh." I smirk and raise an eyebrow. "Did he talk to you about stuff and *girls?*"

"Yeah," he laughs. "But it was still helpful. He cared about his little brother. And when I came out he was-" He cuts himself off. "Hey no, we're not supposed to be talking about me."

I put my hands up and back into the door. "I'm not the one who started it!" I say playfully.

"Yes you did!"

"I was just asking if Grandma and Grandad talked to you about it, so you would know if you should talk to me about it."

"Well do you think I need to?"

The door buzzes and I turn the intercom on. "Hey," I say into it.

"Hey. Do you want me to come up?" Teague asks.

"No it's okay, I'm on my way down."

"Okay wait, just wait a sec," Uncle Adam says to me. I stop and wait for him to continue. "I know I said this already, but just... Don't do anything you're not comfortable with. You're allowed to say no."

"I know."

"And, just, ugh, I don't want you to grow up! You used to be so small and innocent and now you're kissing boys, and going on a date..." He looks down for a second, and then looks back at me with just his eyes. "And *if* you don't want to say no..." he adds with a bit of cringe to his voice. "Just please make sure you're being safe. If you're 100% sure that you want something, and you're safe –"

"Uncle Adam," I say, cutting him off. He raises his eyebrows and looks more directly at me. "Thanks, really, but I'm not... I'm not going to be doing anything like that right now. I mean, we'll probably... kiss," I say slowly, embarrassed, "But, I don't want... I'm not..."

"Okay," he says.

I'm glad I don't actually have to finish my sentence and I smile at him, opening the door into the hall.

"Have fun," he says.

"Thanks."

I find Teague standing next to his car, which is pulled up to the walkway in front of the main doors of the building. His arms are crossed and the smile on his face is making my legs wobbly. When did he start doing this to me? I walk right up to him so that our chests are almost touching, trying my hardest to get through my nerves.

"Hi," he says.

"Hi."

"I'm going to kiss you now," he whispers.

"Okay."

When he kisses me, everything from the weekend comes back. Our glowing surroundings in Laser Tag, the sunset and cool breeze at prom, but most of all, the way I felt on the weekend comes back. How safe I feel in his arms, and how justified I feel, to just be who I am. I have no idea what I was nervous about at school, or ten minutes ago, but now, all of that has melted away. Now it's just us. When I pull away from him, I notice the scar above his left eyebrow, where he had stitches after the car accident. I raise my hand to his face and gently press my fingers to it, running them along the pink skin. His hand comes up to mine at his face, and he twirls our fingers together, bringing my hand back to his shoulder.

"Sorry," I say quietly, and realize that I'm completely pressed into him, making him lean back against his car. I straighten up a little and he gives me a quick smile.

"For what?" he asks.

"I don't know, are you self-conscious about your scar?"

"Oh is that what you were touching? I thought you just had a thing for eyebrows." The corner of his mouth curls and he kisses me quickly on the lips before breaking away from me and walking around the car to the driver's seat.

"Come on," I say. "You knew what I was doing." I get in the car at the same time as him and do up my seat belt.

"Did I?" His smile doesn't falter as he drives us towards the movie theatre.

I'm much more comfortable with him now, but my legs still turn to Jell-O when he reaches for my hand in the parking lot of the movies. When he held my hand before, like when I was hurt after the car accident, I really just thought he was being my friend. Like he was holding my hand to comfort me because he was my friend and I was in pain. And maybe that wasn't what it was, but at the time, that's what it was to me. So now when he holds my hand, I know it's more than that, and I love that it's more than that. He stands close to me while we wait in line for our tickets and food, and whispers in my ear to talk to me, which sends goosebumps down my neck. We have to let go of each other's hands when it's our turn, and then our hands are full with giant cups of pop and giant bags of popcorn. I follow him into the cinema and up the stairs to an empty section near the back. There are a lot of other people here already, but it's still easy to find two seats together in a good spot.

"Are you ready for exams?" he asks me when we sit down.

"I guess. As ready as I can be."

"So you're taking a year off after you graduate?"

"Yeah," I say.

"To save for school? Or?"

"Um, no. I mean, yes. I'm going to work, and save for sure, but I mean… I have school money… Um, from my parents. When my parents died."

He nods. "But I thought you said you don't have a lot of money?"

"Because it's for school."

"Computers are for school."

"Okay, I mean it's for university or college."

"Okay," he says, "Fair enough. So if you have money for school, why are you taking a year off?"

"I don't know what I want to do. I don't know if I feel ready." I shrug. "I mean I don't have a *lot* of money for school, so I should wait until I know what I want to take, don't you think?"

"Yeah, that's a good idea. But you don't want to do a victory lap? Take some extra classes with me?"

"No," I laugh. "I definitely don't want to stay in high school for an extra year after I graduate."

He stretches in his chair and sticks his arms up. "Fine. Don't be cool like me."

"Fine, I won't."

"But we could be together," he says. "Because we'll both still be here."

"Yes, this is true," I agree. "We'll both still be here."

"So Sadie," he says, as the lights dim around us and the previews start to play.

"Teague," I reply with a smile, letting him get closer.

"Do you like what we're doing here?"

"Yes," I say.

"Do you want to keep doing it for the foreseeable future?"

"Yes."

He kisses me, gently, and slowly, and I want to run my hands through his hair, but I also don't want to drop my popcorn. We don't kiss for long though, just until the end of the first preview.

"Does that mean you're my boyfriend?" I ask.

"Why yes, it most certainly does. Does that make you nervous?"

"No," I say with a smile.

♥♥♥♡♡

"I came up with the best idea!" Uncle Adam says later in the week.

"What!?"

"And you can run it during your year off!"

"Okay, what is it?"

"Laser Tag Leagues!"

"Laser Tag Leagues?" I ask, sounding skeptical.

"Yeah! We only ever get people using the arcade during the week, and laser tag is usually only busy on the weekends, but we don't make a lot of money off the arcade."

"Right," I say slowly.

"So we make leagues! We could have, say, six teams, and have two teams play each night, on Tuesdays, Wednesdays, and Thursdays. And at the end of each league season, we could have a party for them, that they also have to pay for! And we could have two, like a Fall season and a Spring season!"

"That's actually a really good idea," I say. "Why didn't we think of this before?"

"I don't know! But we could spend the summer planning it, and setting up, and we could start it in September."

"Yes!" I say, getting excited. "I'll make Teague join! And Mat! Who else do we know?"

"Well we should get people we don't know to join."

"Right, yes, that's a good idea."

"Hey, so what time are you going to Mat's on Friday to watch the dog?" he asks.

"I'm going right after school, he's picking me up."

"Okay, do you need me to get you for work on Saturday?"

"No, Teague's driving me."

"But he's not staying there with you." I think it's funny that it's totally a statement and not a question.

"No," I say, rolling my eyes. "Emma might come over on Friday night, but Uncle Mat said Emma could."

♥♥♥♡♡

Emma and I clean out our lockers at the end of the day on Friday, and it's really weird taking the pictures down from my locker door knowing I'm not going to be putting new ones up in September. Emma gets a little tearful and I laugh at her, which makes her shove me.

"But we still have to come back next week for exams," I say as we head down the hall.

"I know but classes are over now! Everything's changing!"

"It's just the summer. We did the same thing the last three years," I try.

"Yeah but this time we're not coming back."

"I am," Teague says, coming up behind us and putting an arm around my shoulder.

"Yeah, but you're special," Emma says, glancing back at him.

"Of course I am!"

"Plus there's graduation," I add.

"Yeah, the day to remind us that we're all leaving each other."

"We'll come visit you at school," Teague says.

"Or maybe just I will," I say. "You can see her at Christmas."

"Fine, whatever, I see how it is." He winks at me and takes his arm back. "So you're going to Mat's tonight?"

"Yeah, he's picking me up. Are you still taking me to work tomorrow?"

The three of us stomp down the main staircase together, the glass ceiling flooding the hall with sunlight.

"Of course," he says. "Just text me later what time you need to be there at."

We get to the front doors and Emma takes a deep breath before walking through them. Once outside, she takes a few steps back and looks up at the school.

"You're ridiculous," I say. "We'll be back on Monday."

"Shut up." She shoves me in the shoulder. "Go watch your uncle's stupid dog."

"You're coming over later though, right?"

"Yes!"

The three of us go our separate ways, Emma to the bus, Teague to his car, and me to Mat's car at the edge of the parking lot.

"I read Uncle Adam's letter for your adoption thing," I say to break the silence in the car. I don't know why I can't just tell him about my day at school, or literally anything else, but there you have it. I just love to bring up awkward conversation topics, it seems.

"Oh," he says, glancing at me quickly. "Um, what did you think?"

"It made me cry."

"Me too," he says with a smile.

"Really?"

"Yeah." He lets out a deep breath and then looks at me after stopping at a red light. "It was really nice of him to write that for me. When he didn't want you writing one, I never thought he would do it instead."

"I'm sorry, what? He didn't want me to write one? Did *you* want me to write one?"

"Yeah," he answers easily. "We actually fought about it a few times. But you were going through a lot, and I'm sort of ashamed how much I pushed him to agree with me. I tried to ask you myself when he kept saying no, but we got interrupted."

"Oh my god," I say, thinking back to all the times Adam went in his room with the phone and shut his door, or when they were bickering in the kitchen and I could tell it was about me, but couldn't make out their words. "Why am I the centre of all your fights?" I lean my head back and knock it against the headrest behind me a few times.

"What? No, no, you're not. It's us, it's always us. You're just very important to both of us, and because we're not together anymore, that makes it hard. I mean I used to see you every day, Sadie, and now I see you twice a week at best. It's just hard. And even though you weren't a part of it, I'm sorry I tried to push him to make you do it. You had just been in a car accident, and you were still dealing with us breaking up, and I was just being selfish."

"It's okay," I say. "I would have done it. I would have loved to."

"I know. And Adam knew you would have too, that's why he didn't want me to ask you. He was definitely being the better parent."

"Neither of you are better than the other," I say carefully. "But…" I smile a little. "He would love to hear you say that, you know."

❤❤❤♡♡

Emma's parents drop her off after Mat leaves and we immediately take Pasta out for a walk. We walk all the way across town and down to the water, making our loop over two hours long. We stop for snacks at a little variety store on the way back, and they even let us take Pasta in with us. We're still quick, afraid that he'll knock something over or try to pee on the shelves, but he behaves well while we find our goodies. I get Teague some blue sharks from the candy bins because he mentioned his friends got him some after the accident. It made me remember our trips to the convenience store when were little, and he always got the same thing. I always got something with peanut butter, and he always got the blue sharks. We thank the cashier for letting us take the dog in and he smiles and tells us to have a good night. After we get back and change into our PJs, we order pizza and take pictures of Pasta sleeping on the couch.

Emma's parents pick her up in the morning and I hop in the shower and start to get ready for work. I play with Pasta as much as I can and make him pee about three times before I have to go wait for Teague. He goes into his crate without any trouble, and I grab my stuff and slip outside.

I walk around the house to the driveway at the front and wait at the edge of the road for him. He pulls up with a smile after a few minutes and I get into the passenger seat, holding out a bag of his blue and white gummies.

"What's this?" he asks, not taking them.

"A present."

"What for?"

"Just because," I say. "I saw them at the variety store last night and I thought of you."

He finally takes them and moves the candies around a little inside the bag. "Aw, gummy sharks! These are my favourite! How did you know I liked these?"

"I remembered you always liked them when we were kids," I say.

"Amazing! Thanks!" He eats one right away and then puts the bag in the cup holder between us. And then he leans over and kisses me. "You're officially the best girlfriend ever."

"Really? All I had to do was buy you candy?"

He checks his blind spot and then starts to drive towards Laser Tag. "No," he says with a laugh, "it's not because you bought me candy. It's because you remembered something from when we were kids! It was really thoughtful."

There are three birthday parties and the arcade is busy all day. People come in wearing towels from beach trips, and kids' faces are sticky with ice cream. It smells like sunscreen inside the building and every time the door opens, a wave of heat comes through. It wasn't this hot this morning, but I'm thankful to be in the air conditioning as it continues to warm up. During my downtime in the later afternoon, I sit behind the counter and try to plan for the league in September, scribbling in a notebook. Teague comes by at the end of my shift, but I try to finish helping Adam clean up for a group coming in later.

"You can go," Adam says with a bit of a laugh.

"But we're not done and the party's coming in soon."

"It's fine, Alex is coming in to close, so she'll help when she gets here."

"As long as it's fine."

Adam smiles and shakes his head. "Have a good night, Sadie."

I find Teague playing *Clown Fish* and he's on a level I haven't seen before.

"Whoa, how long have you been playing?"

"Not long, someone else was here and they said I could keep their game going 'cause they didn't want to spend any more money."

"This is so cool." I want to watch him play more. He's in a level where the water is crashing in huge waves and the fish is swimming near the top, so every time a wave comes, the fish goes back a bit.

"We should go though," I say. "So I can let the dog out."

"Yeah, of course." He smiles at me and we leave the game running behind us, the clown fish probably being swept backwards off the screen.

Teague drives me to Mat's and he pulls up in front of the house. We both get out of the car and he walks me around to the back door, squeezing my hand the whole way. He gives me a quick kiss on the lips, but as he starts to pull away, I grab his shoulders and bring him back.

"Wait," I whisper.

"Okay."

He stares at me and even though I'm looking in his eyes, I can tell that he's smiling. I close the gap between us and kiss him again, making it last longer this time. He wraps his arms around my waist and pulls me closer, and I run my fingers through his messy hair. I wish we could kiss forever. Our kiss slows down and trickles off into little pecks until Teague finally pulls away again. He kisses my nose and then steps back.

"See you later, Zed," he says.

"Yeah. See you later."

I watch him until he disappears around the brick, and then I let out a sigh, and go inside.

❤ ❤ ❤ ♡ ♡

Uncle Adam is at home when I get back from my exam on Monday afternoon, and he's just standing in the living room with a huge smile on his face.

"What?" I ask.

"We got the new air hockey table!" he shouts.

"What!? We did!?"

"Yes! It got set up this morning!"

"Why didn't you text me!?" I screech with excitement.

"Because you were writing an exam! I thought it would be more fun this way anyway."

"Well can we go see it!?"

"YES!"

Adam drives us over to Laser Tag and Alex looks at us with a twisted expression when we walk in.

"It's beautiful!" I say, running over to it. I'm sure Alex understands what we're doing here now. I run my hands along the chrome sides, and then grab onto one of the mallets. I slide it across the smooth surface, slowly and carefully.

"Let's play a game," Adam says, putting in some coins.

The air turns on and the score counter lights up, and it feels like more than just a new air hockey table to me. It's shiny and new, and exciting, because I thought we were just going to be the arcade without an air hockey table, but now we're us again. We have a new air hockey table, and it's got some upgrades, and the air coming out of it somehow sounds softer and smoother, and when Adam shoots the puck at me and I deflect it off my mallet, the sound of plastic pinging against plastic is like music to my ears. I'm going to miss the old table, but this new one is really nice.

I beat Uncle Adam by three points, and I throw my arms in the air in celebration.

"Do you need to study for another exam tomorrow?" he asks.

"No, I handed in my music project already, and I don't have my other exam until Thursday."

"Great," he says. "So let's go get something to eat. Maybe we can go somewhere nice, out of town."

"Yeah, okay."

We say goodbye to Alex and head out into the parking lot.

"I can drive," I say, as we approach the car.

"We'll have to go on the highway," Adam says carefully. "Are you sure?"

I smile at him, and slide into the driver's seat. "Yeah," I say. "I'm sure."

Acknowledgements

First of all, thank you to everyone who read this book. Thanks to everyone who bought it, checked it out at the library, borrowed it from a friend, or got it from a second-hand store. It means so much to me when someone reads my books, and especially when they review them or tell their friends about them.

Thanks to Lisa Belyk for letting me steal her school project idea for this book. She was the one who actually sent soccer balls to African countries for her Challenge and Change project in high school, and I remember having so much fun at the soccer shoot out she and her group organized for the fundraiser!

Thank you to Sandy Dunsford, and my dad, John Cuddington, who read early drafts of this book, and thank you to my mom, Francyne Dufault, Keri Bailey, and Sarah Jane Wetelainen for helping me make this book the best that it can be.

Laura! Laura Kulson once again has floored me with her incredible talents in creating the beautiful cover. I don't think it's possible to fully express just how much I love it. Thank you thank you thank you.

And last but not least, thanks to Lyndsay Beech for letting me read basically this entire book to you as I wrote it. It really means a lot.

Listen to the Spotify Playlist!

You can also search for it!
It looks like this: